D0312645

Skinny Bitch
in Love

Also by **Kim Barnouin**

Skinny Bitch

Skinny Bitch in the Kitch

Skinny Bastard

Skinny Bitch: Bun in the Oven

Skinny Bitchin'

Skinny Bitch: Ultimate Everyday Cookbook

Skinny Bitch: Home, Beauty & Style

Skinny Bitch Book of Vegan Swaps

Skinny Bitch
in Love

A NOVEL

KIM BARNOUIN

G

GALLERY BOOKS

New York   London   Toronto   Sydney   New Delhi

G

Gallery Books
A Division of Simon & Schuster, Inc.
1230 Avenue of the Americas
New York, NY 10020

First Gallery Books hardcover edition June 2013

GALLERY BOOKS and colophon are registered trademarks of Simon & Schuster, Inc.

For information about special discounts for bulk purchases, please contact Simon & Schuster Special Sales at 1-866-506-1949 or business@ simonandschuster.com.

The Simon & Schuster Speakers Bureau can bring authors to your live event. For more information or to book an event contact the Simon & Schuster Speakers Bureau at 1-866-248-3049 or visit our website at www .simonspeakers.com.

Designed by Jaime Putorti

Manufactured in the United States of America

10 9 8 7 6 5 4 3 2 1

Library of Congress Cataloging-in-Publication Data

Barnouin, Kim
    Skinny bitch in love / Kim Barnouin. — First Gallery Books hardcover edition
        p. cm
1. Women cooks—Fiction. 2. Cooking schools—Fiction. 3. Santa Monica (Calif.)—Fiction. I. Title.
    PS3602.A77714S55 2013
    813'.6—dc23

ISBN 978-1-4767-0886-7
ISBN 978-1-4767-0892-8 (ebook)

To my bookworm mom, Linda, thank you

for inspiring me with your love of books.

And to Jack, you assisted in the inspiration

of this book, thank you.

Skinny Bitch
in Love

Chapter 1

If anyone had told me five, even ten years ago, that one day my life would depend on a plate of nine butternut squash ravioli with garlic and sage sauce, I would have said, "Shit, yeah, it would!"

O. Ellery Rice, food critic for the *Los Angeles Times,* sat at Table Three, *the* table at Fresh, sipping a glass of organic white wine and tapping her blood-orange nails into her iPhone. O was also the "anonymous" Lady Chew of *Los Angeles* magazine. Obviously, she had a lot of juice.

I was born to be chef of Fresh, the hottest vegan restaurant in Santa Monica and maybe all of L.A. And because Emil Jones, our superstar chef, was down and out with an ailment unmentionable in a kitchen, sous chef—that would be me—had her chance.

"Blow it, Clementine—one mistake—and you're dead," Emil had called to scream into my ear a half hour earlier when he'd heard from probably twenty people that O's silver Mercedes had pulled up outside Fresh.

We had nothing to worry about. I stood at my station, working on the ravioli in the gleaming, stainless steel kitchen, oblivious to the clangs of pans around me, the hiss of sautéing oil, the chop, chop, chop of knives against cutting boards, the comings and goings of the waitstaff. I filled each delicate wonton wrapper with perfectly seasoned yellow-orange squash and whisked the sage sauce until it magically appeared both translucent and opaque at the same time. The ravioli would be perfect.

I'd spent years working toward this night, toward this moment, training under the best. And I wasn't talking about the famed Vegan Culinary Institute teachers or my executive chefs at Candle 22 or Desdemona's, restaurants where I'd chopped, sliced, and scalded my way from vegetables to line cook to assistant sous chef. I was talking about my father, organic farmer and amazing cook, who'd given me a chef's hat for my ninth birthday and taught me how to nudge flour and water into a pasta dough so sublime it melted on the tongue. How to take one vegetable from the ground—eggplant, for instance—and make a savory dinner that would satisfy a family of five. How to simmer a chipotle chile that had won me a sparkly blue ribbon at age eleven.

Even before that chile, I knew I wanted to be a vegan chef. Veganism was in my blood.

Let's get something straight right here, since I get this question all the time: what the hell do vegans eat? First let me tell you what vegans *don't* eat: anything that comes from an animal. Yeah, even if you don't have to slaughter the creature to get it. So no eggs, either. No milk. No brie on that cracker. And yes, fish are animals. Then what *do* vegans eat? Duh: everything else.

Nothing made me happier than being in the kitchen, learning, experimenting, perfecting. But like an idiot, I'd decided to forget all that the summer I graduated from high school and before I started cooking school in the fall. Away from home—in L.A.—for the first time, I ate whatever the hell I wanted. Having your first hamburger at eighteen? Enlightening. I lived at In-N-Out Burger that July. Stuffed my face with cupcakes. Drank every kind of sugary alcoholic beverage imaginable. Hit up diners after drinking till 2 a.m. and had fat omelets stuffed with bacon and Swiss cheese. I even thought about trying to switch from the Vegan Culinary Institute to Le Cordon Bleu or the Culinary Institute of America.

And guess what? Also for the first time ever, I started feeling like shit. And not like the hot shit I thought I was for "breaking free" from my parents' way of life, doing my thing. My once clear skin? Zits everywhere. My one pair of expensive, perfect jeans? Suddenly too tight. And was I allergic to something? Everything in me felt clogged, including what little brain I had left.

I gave up the meat. Bad kinds of booze. Dairy—all of it. I went back to eating the way I had growing up, and within weeks, right before I started at the Vegan Culinary Institute, I was back to my old self. I gave up the crap and stopped feeling like crap. *Quelle surprise*. It made me more committed than ever to becoming a vegan chef.

So last weekend, when the stricken Emil announced he was making me chef for O's scheduled visit, there was only one place to go to practice under the best eye: my parents' farm in Bluff Valley, three hours north. I'd made Fresh's entire Italian menu for my dad so that no matter what O chose, it would pass his test. Fresh's gimmick was that the menu changed every week. On Fridays, when the guarded secret was revealed via a one-word mosaic tile sign that Emil hung in the window, a line wrapped around the block. This coming Friday: Italian.

And so in my parents' big country kitchen, greens and root vegetables and apple trees as far as the eye could see when looking out the window over the sink, I made it all. From the intense minestrone soup to the melt-on-your-tongue butternut squash ravioli to an orgasmic tiramisu. My dad couldn't stand next to me at the center island the way he used to—not since his cancer went from stage two to three. Before the C word came into our lives, he'd tower beside me, shaking his head and dumping the entire tray of seitan I'd just over-seasoned or tasting the soup and pointing at the garlic cloves. But now he watched from his wheelchair, opinionated as ever, nodding, directing, and occasionally giving me the prized, "You make me so proud, Clem."

Twice I had to step outside and gulp in air. My mom, with her long graying braid and red Wellies, had come over while harvesting the cucumbers and assured me that every time I visited, my dad was happier and stronger. I drove up every month since his diagnosis more than a year ago, but sometimes, the sight of my formerly robust father—now so frail and weak, his cheeks gaunt and his eyebrows gone along with the blond hair I inherited—made me burst into tears. And trust me, I'm no crier.

I'd had to make the pizza primavera twice and the butternut squash ravioli three times to pass my dad's test. (The second time it only got a 9.5 out of 10.)

For O. Ellery Rice, no less than perfection.

I turned down the burner on my sage sauce, then gestured for my sous chef, the trusty Faye (thank *God* Emil hadn't forced me to work with Rain—definition of frenemy—even though Rain was sauté chef and technically should have been named my sous chef during Emil's absence), to man the pan while I dashed over to the peephole. James, the Shakespearean drama student/waiter chosen to serve O, stopped at her table with the one hundred seventy dollar bottle of biodynamic white wine to top off her glass. O shook her head so slightly that a waiter less dramatically trained than James might have missed it and bothered her by asking the unnecessary question.

You don't scare me, I silently told her as she slid a forkful of escarole and plum tomato into her mouth. In her early fifties, rail thin and tall, her dark hair in her signature bun, and her face almost obscured by the trademark huge black sunglasses, O sat regally, alone—as always. Her MO was to announce the day she'd visit a restaurant, but not the time. I'd been on red alert since five thirty. The moment that silver Mercedes pulled up, I went to work on the ravioli, working the dough the way my father taught me long ago, precisely cutting each square, filling each space extra lightly with the mixture of squash so it would layer on the tongue. The sage sauce was simmering, awaiting the final sauté of the boiled ravioli, the tiny crumbles of garlic at the ready.

I watched Service, as Emil called the waiters, in their blinding white uniforms, gliding past the rectangular steel tables. It was lateish, almost nine, and all but two of the fifteen tables were taken. O. Ellery Rice tapped at her phone. Took a sip of wine. Another bite of escarole. I gestured for my sous chef to turn the burner on for my garlic, then darted over and waited for the oil to ping exactly right before sliding in the crumbled bits.

"She's tapping on the phone now," Jane, a busgirl, reported at the peephole. "Eyeing the plate of fusilli that just passed. Tapping again. Fork going up. That's it, Clem, three bites of the salad." O never took a fourth bite of anything.

I added the ravioli to the sage sauce for a perfectly timed infusion, gently stirring the garlic one pan over. In two minutes, I plated the ravioli and scraped up the garlic, then shook the slotted spoon with such a practiced shake that each crumble landed perfectly atop the sauce.

The ravioli would go out in exactly five seconds.

Four. Three. Two . . . As James held the plate for my final inspection, his white T-shirt, white pants, and white shoes so pristine you'd never guess he'd been serving for three hours, I knew it was perfect. This ravioli would make my father proud. An eleven, maybe even a twelve.

The plate went out. The kitchen applauded. Ty, vegan pastry chef and one of my best friends, placed a cup of his sick tiramisu at my station, CHEF spelled out on top with chocolate shavings. I loved that guy. After closing tonight, Ty and his boyfriend were throwing me a little party at their amazing West Hollywood house to celebrate my big night. T-minus three hours.

I quickly went to work on the backup plate, just in case James tripped or someone crashed into him (happened to my least favorite waitress last week) and waited. My heart was beating in my ears.

Please let her love it. Please let her write that Clementine Cooper, just twenty-six, is a chef to watch, that the ravioli melted on her tongue, that the explosion of squash and garlic in her mouth was like "being made love to with exquisite rough tenderness by your fantasy lover," which is how she'd once bizarrely described a shepherd's pie.

In less than thirty seconds, James returned to the kitchen, the plate of ravioli shaking in his hand.

"Oh shit, she's leaving!" Jane whispered from the peephole.

"Who's leaving?" I said.

"O," she said.

What? I stared at the plate in James's hand. One third of one ravioli had been eaten. That was not three bites. It was only one third of one! I darted to the peephole. O. Ellery Rice's table was empty.

What just happened?

James, never at a loss for words, was practically choking. "She said—"

The kitchen went dead quiet.

James tried again. "She said—"

"What the fuck did she say?" I shouted.

"She said it's no wonder people rave about Fresh's pastas when there's real butter in the sauce."

I laughed. The way people did when something made absolutely no sense. "*Butter?*" Butter was almost a dirty word. There would no more be real butter in the kitchen of a vegan restaurant than there'd be a cow carcass hanging in the pantry and a bloody ax against the wall. I'd perfected my own vegan "butter" sticks from soy milk, vinegar, and coconut oil, and though they were good substitutes, no one, and certainly not O. Ellery Rice, would mistake it for churned milk.

I looked around the kitchen as though I'd suddenly spot a tub of Land O'Lakes. My gaze stopped on Rain Welch. Her long, dark hair was in a bun secured with two chopsticks, and she was stirring a pot of fusilli. Calmly. As though the ceiling hadn't just caved in.

Because it hadn't caved in on her. Just me.

Had my dear frenemy slipped a pat of butter in the sauce when I had been racing around the kitchen like a madwoman? Come on. No way. Even I wouldn't believe that. Anyone who worked at Fresh cared about the place, worshipped Emil. And Rain was madly in love with him; everyone knew that. A couple of months ago, I'd caught them in the secret room inside the pantry, Rain bent over the steel safe, Emil standing behind her. I'd assumed the reason I hadn't caught them since was because they were being more careful, but maybe Rain had cut him off when he promoted me over her to sous chef last month.

Maybe she hated both of us enough to ruin Fresh.

With gray eyes colder than the stainless steel counters, Rain glanced over at me with the almost-smile of the victorious.

Holy shit. "Rain, if you—" I started to say, but my cell phone interrupted me.

Emil.

"YOU ARE FIRED," Emil screamed into my ear. "Get out of my restaurant. Now."

Just like that, I was standing outside Fresh at the tail end of the dinner rush, unable to move or think, until three blondes in the same L.A. weekend uniform of tiny skirt and four-inch heels said "Excuse us" and made me realize I was standing in the middle of the sidewalk. My hands were shaking. My hands never shook.

"Let's get out of here," Ty said from behind me.

I turned around to find Ty shoving his apron in his messenger bag. "You've got two more hours to go," I said.

"Like I'd work for that ass?" he said, taking my hand. "I called Emil to make sure he knew you'd been set up. Gave him the 'If she goes, I go.'"

"He told you to go?" Ty was one of the top pastry chefs in L.A. Everyone wanted him.

"Actually he offered me a raise to stay."

"Ty—"

He held up his hand. "We'll both have new spots tomorrow. No one fires my best friend."

Did I mention Ty was great? He was also drop-dead hot. Six one and lanky, sweetly gorgeous, with a shock of jet-black hair and eyes so green that people often stopped in their tracks to stare at him. No one got "Are you a model?" more than Ty.

We wound our way down to the Third Street Promenade, even more crowded than usual for a Friday night in June. At our favorite juice truck, Ty got us frozen pomegranate smoothies, then we walked through the crowd.

"I can believe Rain would screw you like that," Ty said. "But she screwed Emil worse. I thought she was crazy in love with the guy."

"She hated my guts for getting promoted over her. And she must hate Emil's guts for all that wasted sex." I sipped my smoothie. "Now I'm the one who's screwed."

"Hey." Ty slung an arm around me. "It'll blow over. Emil will call you tomorrow morning when he's calmed down, and he'll tell you you're not fired, that he knows 'someone' wanted to screw you *both* over. We'll be back at work and it'll be Rain who's gone."

"Nice try, but I'll never work in this town again."

He stopped and tipped up my chin. "Yes, you will. The

whole thing is stupid and conniving; anyone will know some-one sabotaged you."

"Who wants to hire a chef that people want to sabotage?"

"All chefs are both revered and despised. And anyway, Clem, you're one of the best vegan chefs in L.A. Seriously. You've proven yourself at three of the hottest restaurants. If Emil doesn't hire you back, you'll get a job anywhere you want. Don't worry."

I was a lot of things, but naïve wasn't one of them. Within twenty minutes, Ty would be named pastry chef at another top restaurant, but I wasn't kidding about my not being able to "work in this town again." A vegan chef who cheated to make the food more irresistible to a non-vegan critic? Through. Done. Over.

Ty spent the next half hour not answering the ten or so calls he got—clearly executive chefs who'd already heard he'd quit Fresh—and coming up with all the delicious ways that karma would take care of Rain Welch and assuring me no one would *really* believe I used butter in the ravioli. But then he had to leave. The only call he'd answered had been from his boyfriend, Seamus, who said that Pippa, their enormously pregnant Siamese cat, was about to have her kittens and could we postpone my party till tomorrow. Yeah. No problem.

Instead of going home to my own hot boyfriend who'd dumped me six months ago when he "accidentally" fell in love with a barista/model (such a cliché I'd almost laughed, but hadn't because my heart felt like it was being stabbed by a thousand sharp stilettos), I called Sara, roommate and best friend, told her today's whole shitty story, and headed to our apartment.

Of course, because it was a Friday night, Third Street Promenade was full of couples holding hands. Kissing. Laughing. Happy people with jobs.

As I walked up toward Montana Avenue, I felt like all those happy people with jobs were staring at me. The dumped, fired cheat who put real butter in the ravioli at Fresh for O. Ellery Rice.

I was about to call Faye, my sous chef for two seconds, and ask what was going on, who'd taken over the kitchen, and what everyone was saying, but a text came in from Claudia, vegetable chef, who was usually hilarious.

Little container containing remnants of real butter found under asparagus in the pail at your station. WTF?

I texted back one word. Well, one name. *Rain.* And waited.

Oh. And then a minute later. *Shit.*

Oh shit was right. Because the next ten minutes were a flurry of texts.

From Faye: *Rain swears up and down she didn't do it, that yeah, she was pissed she wasn't promoted, but she'd never . . . Not sure what to think, Clem.*

Not sure what to think? *What?*

From Jane: *OMG—Emil just fired the whole staff except the waiters, not including James, of course, dishwashers, and buspeople.*

Oh shit. Shit, shit, *shit!*

Then this gem, from the new guy on vegetables. *Fuck you, Clementine.*

From the juice bar: *Thanks a lot, C.*

And then, from Rain herself: *Bitch.*

Did these people I'd worked with for more than a year think I'd really use butter in a recipe? Me? The one raised on the organic farm by the vegan hippie parents?

As I finally slogged onto 15th Street, the sight of the empty storefront on the corner made me stop, as it always did. I didn't exactly forget about Fresh, about pats of butter, about being hated by everyone I worked with—*used* to work with. But the storefront *was* beautiful. The curved red oak door looked like it was from an enchanted cottage; the arched window caught the sun in the mornings and the moonlight at night, illuminating the glass brick and stained glass back wall. This was the place, my dream space. Where I would open Clementine's Café. (I was still deciding about adding "No Crap" between "Clementine's" and "Café.") Ten or so tables, a combination of round and square, polished wood. I'd repaint the pale yellow a Mediterranean blue and whitewash the floor. Add an amazing juice bar. I'd be chef, of course, and hire a small but brilliant team.

Clementine's No Crap Café.

Of course, if I opened it now, half the people I know would come and spray paint out the "No" and add in "Full of."

Chapter 2

Because I was still in bed at eleven the next morning, Sara barged in, opened the curtains, and flooded the tiny space (it wasn't a real bedroom) with sunshine. She whipped the covers off me and told me to shove over and sit up against the wall. She then placed a tray on my lap and sat down next to me. Green tea. Blueberries. Whole grain toast with crunchy natural peanut butter.

Incredibly thoughtful. Especially because Sara was a greasy-fried-eggs-and-bacon-and-coffee-with-four-fake-sugars type chick. She'd made me my kind of breakfast.

"Thanks, Sara. But I can't eat."

She twisted her wildly curly auburn hair into a bun and stuck a pencil in to secure it. "You have to eat because you need your energy. You're going to every vegan restaurant in L.A. today and introducing yourself and explaining what happened."

"Waste of time. Emil knows everyone. No one will hire me. I called him five times last night. Left four messages swearing on anything he wanted that I didn't use butter in the ravioli, that someone—and he knew who—screwed me. He answered the fifth call, and before I could say a word, he barked, 'I don't give a shit how the butter got in the ravioli. You were chef. It's your fault.' *Click*."

I had been chef. I put the breakfast tray on the floor, slid down the wall, and pulled the covers up. The normal me would have been calling everyone I knew last night, ripping on the story—"Guess what that twatzilla pulled on me . . ."—and totally confident I'd have a better job—full chef—at another hot restaurant by midnight. But the double whammy of O. Ellery Rice *and* not realizing I'd been burned by BUTTER in the first place? Sudden death.

"Clem, what do you tell me every time I don't get a callback for a role I don't even want? That it's all in the trying, in the putting myself out there."

Sara was an actress specializing in the overweight best friend or bullied outcast. She was beautiful, with Pre-Raphaelite long curls and huge, driftwood brown doe eyes, but she was at least forty pounds overweight and only occasionally got cast—as a "fat extra."

Let's get something straight right now. Anyone who has a problem with the fact that Sara doesn't look like a model can go fuck himself. She's been my best friend since we were both sweating pretzels in the hot-yoga studio we now live above. We'd both needed a roommate, and the crappy apartment on the fifth floor with a sloping floor became available. That was four years ago. Have something to say about Sara's weight or that "Maybe you shouldn't be eating those fries?" like that asshole at her favorite food truck at the Pier? I'll hunt you down. Seriously, I stink-eyed that loser very close to the water's edge.

"I know what'll perk you up," Sara singsonged. "Thanks to that very good advice of yours, guess who got up the guts to ask out Hot Pete, and guess what he said?"

I whipped the covers off me. Sara supported herself by temping as an office drone. For the past month, she'd been filling in for a clerk typist on maternity leave at an ad agency that specialized in the wine industry. She'd been crushing on Hot Pete since day one—and figured she had no chance. "I know what he said," I told her. "He said 'Hell, yeah!'"

She grinned. "We were both in the elevator together, and I was like, *Do it! Do it!* So I blurted out, 'Want to grab a coffee or a drink or something?' And he looked at me and said, 'Yeah, sure. How about tomorrow after work because I have a gig?' He plays bass in an alt rock band—well, they're just getting started. And so we talked about that for like ten minutes in the lobby and now we have a date tomorrow after work!"

I squeezed her again. "That's amazing, Sara. You should have told me last night—we could have celebrated instead of you being forced to mope around with me."

"You needed to mope," she said, taking a sip of my green tea and grimacing. "Anyway, Clem, you really have nothing to worry about. It's so obvious that Rain screwed you—she had

nothing to lose since she was probably planning to quit anyway. And what happened at Fresh is *legendary*. Everyone will
want you after this."

Legendary. The chef someone took down with a pat of butter. Right.

"Everyone will want the chef who didn't even realize there
was butter in one of her signature dishes?" I asked. "I've made
that exact ravioli two thousand times. I should have smelled
the butter. I should have seen the difference in the glistening
of the sauce."

Sara took a bite of my peanut butter toast. "Trust me, Clem,
this time tomorrow, you'll be chef anywhere you want. You're
a legend now."

The Legend of the Land O'Lakes. Ha.

I didn't believe it for a minute. But at least it got me out
of bed.

I spent the next hour with my laptop and a pot of very strong
tea, making a list of every vegan restaurant—big, small, and
truck, that last one just in case—in L.A. I starred my top six
choices, where I'd stop in this afternoon and ask to meet with
the manager or chef. That's how it worked: chefs wanted to see
you, size you up, and most were able to tell in two seconds if
you could handle getting screamed at and humiliated and were
therefore worth interviewing.

Next there were five second choices.

Three third choices.

Four trucks.

"Not that it'll come to the trucks," Sara assured me in our tiny bathroom as she stood surveying me in the mirror.

My green-hazel eyes showed no signs of the previous night's tossing and turning. I stood tall at five-foot-seven in my three-inch sandals. Still, managers and chefs tended to underestimate me because I was a) blond and b) skinny—until they saw me wield a fifty-pound cast-iron pan like it was a tomato.

Sara handed me a tissue to blot my berry lip-stain. "You look great. Now go. We'll celebrate your new job—and my new boyfriend—tonight. Oh, wait, you have to help me pick out what to wear. Then you're out the door."

She was right. I was being ridiculous. Of course, I'd get a new job. I'd been sous chef at Fresh for God's sake. Fresh! That alone would open doors. A backstabber's pat of butter would not slam doors in my face.

Six hours later I had eleven flat-out No's the moment I walked in the door. Six "We can't risk it, sorry"s. And from the cute guy in the Vegan Express truck at a choice spot on the beach: "You're lucky Emil didn't put cement shoes on you and dump you off the pier like I woulda."

That night, Sara and I sat on the living room floor of Ty and Seamus's small but gorgeously decorated Spanish bungalow. It was light-years from the pre-Seamus hovel Ty had lived in across the hall from me, which is how we met. Just as I'd figured, Ty had a new job as pastry chef at Chill, with a huge raise since he'd had his pick of offers. But even that bit of good news and the weirdly cute kittens, which looked like bald hamsters huddled up asleep next to their mama in a big padded box, were unable to console Sara or me. I was blackballed in all of L.A. And Sara had had a hellish date with Hot Pete, now known as Dickhead Pete.

"You know," she said, "I wish he'd told me yesterday in the elevator that 'by coffee you mean a blow job, right?' At least I wouldn't feel like such an idiot."

Dickhead Pete and Sara had met, as arranged, in the lobby of their office building after work. Since he lived right around the corner, he suggested going to his place for a drink because he "really wanted to play her a song on his bass," which slayed her, of course. But when they got there, he "suddenly" remembered he'd left the bass at his bandmate's studio. He didn't even have a coffeemaker, let alone a bottle of wine. All he had was a six-pack of cheap beer. He sat down and unzipped his jeans and said she should probably just start because it took him awhile. When she asked him what he meant, he reached in and pulled out a very small limp penis.

"You should have said, 'Well, where is it?' and looked all confused," Ty said. "Then added, 'Oh,' and walked out."

What she *had* said was that she had no intention of putting her mouth anywhere on him—"not yet, anyway," she'd added with a coy smile. His response was, "Come on, what did you think? We were on a *date*?" That's when she picked up his beer, poured it over his head, and booked out of there

"I love that part," I told her.

"Me, too," Ty said. "And it's probably better he showed what a total prick he is now instead of you getting all involved with him and then finding out."

"Why did I think for one stupid second that a hot guy in a band would actually go for me?" She let out a long sigh. "It's like my mother always said and, in fact, said yesterday on the phone—no guy likes a fat girl."

"Is that supposed to inspire you or something?" Seamus asked. "Jesus." Seamus was cute and as blond as Ty was dark.

"She calls it tough love," Sara explained. "It's been her way since I was six. You can see how well it's worked."

"You're amazing, Sara," I told her. "Just as you are."

"Well, *we* know that," she said with a grin. "But I can't win. This afternoon, I actually got a callback for Overweight Woman on Bus for some prescription allergy commercial, and get this—the director tells me I'm not fat enough. Then he adds that he doubts I ever get work because I'm too in between. Not thin enough for a regular spot, not fat enough for a fat spot."

"Douche bag," I said.

"Yeah, but he's right. I can either get really fat, and probably work like crazy. Or lose weight and *maybe* get work. My almost-agent once told me I'd have better luck fat than skinny because there are a million skinny wannabes. She told me I should hire a particular plus size talent coach so I could gain more weight 'as attractively as possible.' Of course, the coach turned out to be her sister. Anyway, if I went the skinny route, I might actually get a date."

"You know what?" I said. "I hate that. I know we're best friends, but if I just met you I'd think you were incredibly awesome. Like every guy should."

"Kind of like if every vegan restaurant owner just met you and didn't know about the stupid butter, you would have a job like this." She snapped her fingers.

"I should just open up shop in my own kitchen," I said. "Hang up a shingle somehow. After the last door got slammed in my face, I started thinking about what else I could do—to shove it in everyone's faces, too. Maybe I could become a personal chef and build up clientele and my reputation again. Am I crazy?"

Sara's eyes lit up. "Not crazy! That's a great idea, Clem. What I just said, about the fat coach, that reminded me how at the callback today, one of the other naïve candidates had her acting coach with her, and she was telling me how she got ten clients in a month just by posting signs and ads saying she was an acting coach with tons of experience. You could also do that—be a vegan coach! Teach people how to be vegan—what to eat, how to cook, whatever."

"It really is a great idea, Clem," Seamus said. "We got a gift certificate for a personal chef as a housewarming present. The guy came over, cooked an amazing dinner, then made a week's worth of incredible meals that he froze with instructions on how to reheat. I heard it cost our friends a fortune. You'd make good money, Clementine."

"And you'd be your own boss," Ty added. "You know how you hate bosses."

"In like a year, you could have enough money to open your own place," Sara continued. "Clementine's No Crap Café will be a reality. You should totally do this."

"Personal vegan chef," I said, letting the words really sit this time instead of *yeah, right*ing them like I did earlier today. Wasn't that the whole reason I became a vegan chef, especially after my summer of eating crap and feeling like crap? To show people you could cut the crap out of your diet and not only ooh and aah over every delicious bite, but feel and look amazing instead of sluggish and zitty every day. And L.A. *was* full of vegans. Wannabe vegans. Committed vegans who were crappy cooks. Rich people obsessed with their bodies. And probably a bunch who just thought veganism would be a cool thing to do for a few weeks.

There might be something to this.

I had next month's rent in my bank account—well, minus two hundred something—at the moment. Emil's manager, who'd always been very friendly to me, would probably mail me my pay for the last week and a half. Or not. All I had to my name was nine hundred and twelve dollars. Almost my share of the two thousand four hundred dollar rent on our ridiculously tiny one-bedroom apartment. (Sara paid three hundred more than I did because she got the bedroom.) Even though the building was cute and right on Montana,

it was the top floor of a fifth-floor walk-up, the floors really did slope, and the hot water took eons to turn hot. My one-hundred-square-foot "bedroom" included a tall window, and Ty had managed to make the space look and feel like a real separate room. He did amazing things with bookshelves and white muslin and glass brick he'd found at a flea market.

I was not getting a job at Whole Foods behind the cheese counter. I was not slinking anonymously into a restaurant with vegetarian offerings and ending up touching dead fish. And I was not bailing on Sara and moving back in with my parents to harvest corn, though I did love doing that. I was twenty-six years old and I wanted to make something amazing happen.

"You know what, Clementine?" Sara said, standing up and putting her hands on her hips. "You start your own vegan personal chef business, and I'll be your walking billboard of how not eating crap can totally change your life. I'll give up Doritos and Diet Coke. I'll switch from bacon double cheeseburgers to garden burgers with those weird sprouts on them. I'll do it, Clem."

"Seriously?" Sara loved her Doritos. And bacon double cheeseburgers, extra mayo. She also had a special fondness for Hostess Devil Dogs. Not to mention her all-time favorite food that she grew up on in Louisiana: chicken fried steak, smothered in some kind of thick white sauce.

"Seriously," she said. "I'm sick of this. I'm sick of looking like shit and being treated like shit."

"I was treated like shit and I'm skinny," I pointed out.

"Fair enough," she conceded. "For now. But if I'm skinny and get treated like shit, at least I'll look good."

"I could teach you how to bake some sweet potato fries that will blow your mind," I told Sara, giving her a hug. "Skinny Bitch," I said. "That's what I'm calling the business. It's about living a crap-free life. Skinny bitches don't eat—or take—crap."

"To Skinny Bitch," Ty said, heading into the kitchen and coming back with four insane-looking cupcakes on a plate, one with red velvet icing with CHEF CC spelled out with tiny multi-colored bits of sugar. "I baked these for your party last night. Now we have something to celebrate, so eat up."

I was a decent baker—and made amazing cakes anytime someone had an occasion—but no one baked vegan treats like Ty. This piece of perfection would melt in my mouth.

Sara clinked her cupcake to mine. "I'll start the Skinny Bitch diet tomorrow," she said, laughing, and then taking a huge bite.

"Oh, this is totally on the diet," I said and practically ate the whole thing in one bite.

I realized I wasn't all clenched and miserable the way I'd been for the past twenty-four hours. I might be blackballed in L.A. with barely any money, but I had a plan.

Chapter 3

Skinny Bitch at Your Service

Don't feel like cooking? Want to look and feel amazing? Stop eating crap and start becoming the person you always knew you could be.

Veteran vegan chef (Candle 22, Desdemona's, Fresh) Clementine Cooper, graduate of the famed Vegan Culinary Institute, will create delicious vegan dishes—from appetizers and main dishes to desserts—and deliver them to your door. Or she'll come to your house and teach you how to make orgasmic soups, salads, entrees, and desserts.

Call (310) 555-7214 or friend me on Facebook (Skinny Bitch) for more information.

Despite my swanky new website, in the two days since the ad was posted all over L.A.—on Craigslist, Facebook, Twitter, and anywhere else my friends and I could think of—I had exactly two phone calls: 1) from a teenager in an argument with her mother over whether you really could get enough protein from a vegan diet (yes, I assured Mom) and 2) from a man who had the wrong number.

When my phone rang on day three while I was writing a check for the electric bill and watching my rent money for next month slowly disappear, I lunged for it. *Please, universe. Let it be a client. A rich client.*

"Skinny Bitch, Clementine Cooper speaking." According to my sister, Elizabeth, a corporate lawyer four years older who wore severe business suits and drove a Beemer (and whose real name was Apple; she'd insisted on being called by her non-fruit middle name the minute she hit middle school), this was how you answered the phone.

"Hey, Clementine, it's Ben."

Ben.

Know that feeling where every bit of you goes completely still, except for a tight squeezing of your heart? That's how I felt.

"I know it's been a while," he said, "but I saw one of your flyers for vegan cooking lessons, and I'm slowly easing from vegetarian to vegan, so . . ."

I could picture him so clearly. He was probably out walking his yellow Lab, barely noticing that every woman—and man— was checking him out. Ben was insanely cute. Slightly longish wavy-curly sunlit brown hair. Deep blue eyes. Dimple in his left cheek. And his body. Whoa.

"So you want me to teach you how to cook vegan."

"Yeah. And we could catch up."

For the first time in six months, I was talking to Ben Frasier, the guy who loved me "more than anything on this green earth" until he dumped me right before Christmas at the Santa Monica Pier because—

He'd fallen in love with someone else.

I could still hear him saying "I'm sorry, Clem," over and over. Watching him walk away, then run, as though he was crying, which he might have been, since he was so annoyingly nice and it probably did break his heart to break mine. Not enough to stay, though.

The thing about Ben was that he wasn't just some boyfriend. He was the guy I'd thought I'd end up with. Forever.

"Ben, I don't know. I—"

"You're the best cook, Clem. And you're the only vegan chef I know. I saw the flyers, and . . . maybe I was looking for an excuse to call you, too. You know?"

Yeah, I knew.

"I was thinking that in addition to the cooking lesson, you could bring over a bunch of meals to freeze—maybe two weeks' worth? Just dinner entrees, you know, like the risotto and the pad thai. A couple of those interesting pizzas you used to make all the time."

I forced myself not to go there, remembering those interesting pizzas and a thousand other shared meals, eating together on his tiny deck overlooking the ocean.

I focused instead on the numbers. Two weeks' worth of dinner? Fourteen dinners. Between the three-hour cooking lesson, fourteen entrees, and my Very Important Time, I ca-chinged in my head more than two thousand dollars.

Holy shit.

Maybe he didn't realize how much money he was about to spend.

"The photos of the Mediterranean pizza and the falafel on your website look amazing," he said, which meant he must have checked out the fees page. "Definitely make those. He rattled off a list of the fourteen dishes, which I copied down in the little notebook I carried everywhere. "Are you free the weekend of the 18th?"

"Let me check my calendar," I said, counting to fifteen. "I'm sorry, but I'm double-booked—oh wait, I see here that my assistant noted a cancellation for the afternoon session on the 18th." Elizabeth would be proud.

As he was going on about the falafel kick he was on lately, I tallied up a price of two thousand four hundred bucks.

Ben had money, but still.

And after rattling off a tony address in the Hollywood Hills (he'd clearly moved), he said good-bye and I hung up. Half of me wanted to call every person I knew, everyone who was still speaking to me, anyway, to scream from the rooftops that I'd gotten my first client. Leaving out the part that it was Ben, I called my sister, who *still* did her usual parade-drizzle by reminding me it was *one* client. A good client, but one client. And to put the two thousand in the bank and not blow it on sandals or a trip to Brazil.

"As a freelancer, Clem, you need to—" Elizabeth started, but I told her the smoke alarm was going off and I had to go, then I called Ty, who appropriately whoo-hooed, until I told him who said client was.

"Clem. That's dangerous territory. Obviously he wants you back. Or some afternoon delight. He wants something."

"I know. And if he wants me back, why is that so bad?"

"Because I scraped you off the floor for a month," he reminded me. "You didn't eat for a week. He crushed you, Clem. Don't go back there, okay?"

But.

"Fine, whatever," he said. "Just be careful."

I'd try.

That night, Sara, who totally got it, told me we were going out to celebrate the gig—but we were banned from what-ifing about Ben. And so we went dancing at Olios—not a single what-if coming out of my mouth, despite the many swirling through my mind. But after one idiot told Sara she would be "so hot" if she lost some weight, we left and went home. Sara made a mental note of the asshole so that when she did get "so hot" and he asked her out, she could tell him to suck it. I sprawled out on the sofa, writing up lists of ingredients I needed to buy at the grocery store and the farmers' market, drifting off to thoughts of artichokes, deep red tomatoes, and two thousand four hundred necessary dollars. Oh yeah, and Ben Frasier.

On the way to 5202 Violet Drive in Hollywood Hills on Saturday, I swore I saw Scarlett Johansson jogging with a German shepherd trotting beside her perfect body. I drove slowly, not only because, yeah, I was actually kind of nervous, but because I had fourteen expensive dinners packed very carefully in coolers on the backseat.

House after beautiful house reminded me so much of Ben, how we'd spend Sunday afternoons driving in the Hills and West Hollywood, gaping at the homes. I passed my favorite, the English country stone cottage with the blue door and fruit trees. Every time Ben and I would drive past it, I'd sigh, and he'd say he'd buy it for me as my cooking studio when he made his first million. We'd picked out "our house" on the next street, a gorgeous Spanish hacienda that was practically all windows, and Ben had pulled up in front of it and told me all the delicious things he'd do to me under the Jacarandas and orange trees at night in the backyard. That was more than six months ago, and I could still remember how he'd looked at me, the way he'd kissed me in the car, how we'd freaked and then laughed when a gigantic Rhodesian Ridgeback suddenly jumped at the passenger side window.

Did I want him back? On a scale of one to ten, a nine. One point taken off for the scraping Ty did have to do that first month. So, yeah, Ty was right. But maybe Ben had had to work something out of his system, and now he was ready for the real thing. Me.

Ben's place was a stunning limestone mini castle. Clearly Ben had gotten some big-money clients himself. I parked my ten-year-old Toyota in the driveway behind a black BMW. I got out, put my chef jacket on, and loaded up the pull cart I'd borrowed from Sara, who used it for lugging props to auditions. I put my case of pans and utensils down first, then carefully arranged the flat coolers of entrees, which I'd loved every minute of preparing. I'd made the Mediterranean Pizza and Pizza Rustique, two pastas, two tofu-based dishes, including my pad thai, two amazing rices, the risotto, an Indian-style seitan-vegetable biryani that Sara and I ate half of, my kick-ass African chile, my sick falafel, and two noodle dishes, yuba and soba. I used only the best, freshest ingredients.

I sucked in a quick breath and rang the chimy doorbell.

A woman opened the door. Model gorgeous, with the kind of long, slightly wavy light brown hair shot with gold so perfectly it looked naturally sun-kissed. She was almost six feet tall and rail thin, but still managed to look lush. She wore low-slung jeans and a tiny white tank top. Bare feet, red polish, silver toe ring.

"So *you're* Clementine," she said, smiling.

And who the hell are you?

"You're just darling," she added, a big honking diamond twinkling on her left hand.

Darling? I forced a smile.

"Come on in. Ben's really looking forward to seeing you."

Okay. What the hell was going on? Was she his maid? Personal assistant?

The chick he dumped me for?

If Ben had gotten engaged—after only six months—I would have heard about it somewhere, wouldn't I? I mean, I *had* told everyone I knew not to mention his name to me again because when I finally found myself able to breathe, to eat, to get up and function, one person mentioned they'd seen him walking his yellow Lab, and I went back to bed for two days. But still.

"Baby, Clementine's here," she called out.

Oh, hell.

I held my breath and followed her into the huge cook's kitchen, and there he was. Ben Fucking Frasier. In jeans. Navy blue T-shirt. Chucks.

The yellow Lab, Gus, was gnawing on a bone under the round table by the window.

Fuck. Are they fucking kidding me?

"Clem, it's so good to see you again," Ben said, coming toward me with that gorgeous face, those dark blue eyes, those goddamned pecs. He gave me a quick kiss on the cheek. "This is Laurel, my, um, fiancée."

I stared at him, then at her.

I watched her eye me up and down, then slide her pale brown eyes to Ben. She smiled at him. A sweet smile, then giggled. Giggled. What the—

"Okay, sweetie, I'm going," Laurel announced, slinging a huge red handbag over her shoulder. She walked up to him, planted a hand on either cheek, and kissed him as though they were having sex. I heard him murmur something. Saw his hand graze her perfect ass before it sashayed out the door.

"What the hell is this?" I said.

Ben leaned against the counter. "It's everything I said on the phone. I didn't mention I was engaged because Laurel has nothing to do with the cooking lessons. And it would have been weird to bring it up." He ran a hand through his hair.

"So you just thought you'd hire your ex-girlfriend to teach you to cook and make you two weeks' worth of meals—in the home you share with your fiancée. Right, Ben."

"Look, I heard from a few mutual friends that you got fired and that you're kind of blackballed now. At least five people called to tell me. And then I saw your flyer on a lamppost when I was walking Gus and . . ."

"And you felt bad for me." Jerk.

"Okay, yeah, I felt bad. I've been looking around for a vegan cooking class and couldn't find anything. Then I saw the flyer. So it all just worked out."

Because I knew him so well, I knew that he was just trying to do me a favor. Nothing malicious. Nothing salacious. He broke my heart, felt bad about it, had a moment of "oh, that's too bad" when he heard about me getting fired, and saw his opportunity to feel better.

"So let me guess," I said. "You told your fiancée you wanted to hire me, that you felt bad—about everything—and she said something all faux-concerned like, 'I don't have anything to worry about, do I?' and you said, 'Come on, *of course* not. Be here when she arrives and you'll see I don't feel anything for Clementine anymore.'"

He sighed and ran a hand through his hair again.

"Something like that, maybe," he said. "I'll always care about you, Clem. And you are the best vegan chef I know, and I want to learn from the best."

I looked at him and forced myself to see two thousand four hundred bucks instead of the guy I thought I'd spend the rest of my life with. I needed money. And I wasn't going to be stupid and walk out.

"I'll help you unload," he said, reaching for the cart, and that was that.

As we put each container away in the freezer, I went over the taped-on instructions for reheating as though he were just anyone. He was standing so close to me—not "I still want you" close, but close enough that I could smell that clean, fresh marine-based soap he used, the one I turned him on to. He was so tall, with such broad shoulders, and for a second I was back in bed with him, my eyes closed as he trailed wet kisses down my neck and—

"So what are we making?" he asked, snapping me out of my memory and back to this ridiculous kitchen.

"One of your favorites, actually—falafel, topped with cilantro, onions, tomatoes, and tahini, with garlic hummus and pita bread."

"My mouth is watering already," he said. "Set me to work."

So I did. I handed him a clove of garlic. He forgot how to remove the skin from the clove, and I had to take his hand and press down, my heart shifting in my chest. There was now an actual ache there. Not like six months ago, of course, but a lingering longing. Maybe it would never go away.

"So how's your dad?" he asked, adding the coriander to the bowl of mashed chickpeas.

That was nice of him. At least he still remembered my life, even if he was probably just making conversation. "Good and bad," I said. "Holding on. Fighting."

He looked at me with compassion in those dark blue eyes. "He's a great guy."

"Yeah, he is," I said, remembering the first time Ben met my parents. It was their twenty-ninth wedding anniversary. We stayed for the weekend, my sister good-naturedly arguing with my father over the whys of corporate greed; my younger brother, Kale (whose food-of-the-earth name suited him fine as a perpetual student working on his masters in marine biology), talking about his deep-sea expedition to study the mating habits of orcas. My dad had been bringing in a basket of carrots and was humming. The next second he was on the floor, his face ashen, the carrots rolling in every direction.

Ben had stayed with me an entire week at my parents' farm while my father was in the hospital undergoing tests. He'd been there when I'd first heard the word *cancer*.

And now, he was someone else's fiancé.

"Oh, not that much pressure forming the balls," I said when I realized he was compressing the chickpea mixture in his palms. "Gently, like this," I added, showing him how to use a lighter touch.

I wondered if he'd make some sort of sex joke, some reference to how I used to like the rough way he touched me in bed. If he'd grab me up against the zillion-dollar stainless steel refrigerator and go at me.

Of course, he didn't. He just gave me that sweet smile and asked if he was doing it right now, and he was.

We fried, we plated, we ate. Ben declared the falafel the best he'd ever had. As he licked tahini sauce off his lips, he occasionally brought up something from our past as though it was just a fond memory that didn't matter a whit anymore, because, of course, to him, it didn't.

"Uh, Clem, did we forget to put something in the hummus? It's kind of . . . boring," Ben said, handing me the fork.

Shit. Shit, shit, shit. I could make orgasmic hummus in my sleep. Did I screw it up?

"Oh, no, her hummus isn't great?" Laurel said, coming into the kitchen with two boutique bags in each hand. Of course, she had to come in at that exact moment. Not when Ben had been "Oh my God"ing over the tahini-drizzled falafel. "Baby, I thought you said she was an amazing cook." She eyed the two-thousand-plus check stuck to the fridge with a little barbell magnet, narrowed her eyes at me, then dipped a spoon into the hummus. "Huh. Yeah. Bland." She glared at me, then cut a tiny piece of falafel. "Oh my God, *this* is incredible."

Saved by a teaspoon of cumin.

"I forgot to add the garlic to the hummus when she told me," Ben said. And it was true; he wasn't covering for me. "Don't worry—my money was very well spent."

As I started cleaning up, Laurel told me not to bother, that their housekeeper came every afternoon to do a basic tidy-up. She handed me my check. Instead of feeling like the teacher, the businesswoman, the brilliant chef who'd just earned two thousand four hundred dollars, I felt like a loser.

I had barely left the kitchen with my pull cart before Laurel launched herself into Ben's arms for another sex kiss.

"Thanks again, Clem," Ben said as he and Laurel headed

out the opposite end of the kitchen through the French doors toward the grand staircase, probably to rip off each other's clothes.

"Just close the door on your way out," he added.

I wanted to spread that dull hummus all over their bed and let them roll around in *that*. But you bet your ass I closed that door—permanently—and walked out with my big fat check, all I really needed.

———

"That's insane, Clem," Sara said as she stripped down to her bra and underwear to step on the scale in our bathroom. "I ran into Dickhead Pete, but that's nothing compared to that. Seriously, that is messed up."

"Let's not mention either of their names in our little sanctuary again," I said. "They don't exist." I blinked my eyes like a genie. "Poof. Gone."

She blinked and added a genie arm cross for good measure. "Now let's hope I made even a little bit of my ass disappear, too."

"Don't worry about the stupid scale," I reminded her. "Being a Skinny Bitch is about feeling good, not what some digital numbers say." She stepped on the scale and I crossed my fingers for her. If she hadn't lost any weight, she might get discouraged. That date from hell usually would have sent her into a sugar binge, but she'd been working really hard on the eating plan, not a Dorito in sight. Going from eating whatever you wanted to being a Skinny Bitch wasn't easy—I knew that firsthand. But Sara was really into it and sticking to it. I wanted the scale to show a loss to give her that extra *hell, yeah*.

Three and a half pounds.

"Sara! That's awesome!"

Her face lit up and she put her tank top and yoga pants back on. "I can't believe I'm losing weight while I'm stuffing my face. That breakfast sandwich you made me this morning? I can't believe that's on the plan. Scrambled 'egg' tofu, soy bacon, vegan cheese."

"Breakfast of champions."

"Fettucini alfredo last night that almost tasted like the four-thousand-fat-gram version I ate last week. And I even get my dessert. I can do this, Clem. I thought I'd have to starve to get skinny."

"Nope. And wait till you taste the almost-cheesecake I'm making you today. One small slice a day."

We headed into the kitchen for Sara's lesson on how to make very low-fat, low glycemic-index sort-of cheesecake. I got out the flour and the Stevia. "Hey, maybe we should film this for my website."

"Good idea," she said and set up her phone to videotape it, but we moved around so much that all we got was some decent footage of a big silver mixing bowl. And the finished product, which was pronounced "fucking amazing" by Sara.

"Clem, you should be teaching everyone how to cook."

"I've been thinking about that, actually, ever since I got back from Ben's. Some people might just want me as a personal chef—making the meals and delivering them in reheat-able cookware. But others might just want cooking lessons."

"I totally want both."

"I'd do it, but where? I can't afford to rent a kitchen some-where, and it's not like I can teach in this tiny kitchen with the electric stove and half-dead refrigerator. I can't stop thinking about it, though. Planning the menus for the classes, maybe taking field trips to farmers' markets."

"Tons of people would sign up, Clem. I would. And who cares if the kitchen is small? It's actually the biggest room in the apartment, and"—she glanced around—"I'll bet eight people could fit in here without it being killer claustrophobic. Remember the party we had when I got the orthotics com-mercial? At one point, everyone was in the kitchen to see that shoe-shaped cake you made me, and that was, like, twelve people."

Sara had gotten cast as Real Woman on Sidewalk Rubbing Foot for an insole commercial. I made her a cake in the shape of a strappy sandal to celebrate. "You really think I could get students? It's not like anyone beat down my door for the per-sonal chef thing."

"People are totally into cooking classes. Learning some-thing, meeting new people, the whole thing. And the vegan angle makes it new and different for people. Everyone's heard of veganism, but no one really knows what it is. I mean, my mom always says, 'But she still eats fish, right?'"

If I had a student like Sara's mother, I might jump out a window. No, Sara's mother, I do not eat fish. Yes, bacon counts as meat. No, I don't eat eggs. No, I can't (and don't want to) have even one tiny taste of cheddar. Yes—and add megaphone here—I do get plenty of protein. But teaching vegan cooking was a great idea. People *did* love cooking classes. And between the personal chef business—if it ever picked up—and the cooking classes, I could probably eke out a living.

Thanks especially to the happy couple's big fat starter check.

I took a bite of almost-cheesecake and sat down with my trusty notebook.

Skinny Bitch Cooking School!

What: Learn to make crap-free favorites, from lasagna to pad thai, from almost-cheesecake to not-your-grandma's apple pie. Only $400 for a six-week class from famed vegan chef Clementine Cooper.

When: Tuesdays, 7/2 – 8/5. 7 p.m.–9:30 p.m.

Where: Montana & 14th, Santa Monica

How: (310) 555-7124 or email ClemCoop@umail.com

After posting ads for Skinny Bitch Cooking School everywhere, from light posts to coffeehouse bulletin boards to Twitter, Sara and I waited for my phone to ring and my email to ping.

Day one. Nothing.

Day two. Nothing.

Day three. Sara signed up, leaving the four hundred dollar fee (and it wasn't like she had it to spare) in cash on my dresser.

Day four. Nothing.

Day five. A stranger signed up! Eva Ackerman. That made two students.

Day six. Another stranger signed up. Duncan Ridley.

By day eight, Sara and I stopped straining to listen for the phone and pings of email. But I had three students. Enough for a real class. A cozy, hands-on cooking class.

Three students at four hundred bucks a six-week session. Suck it, Emil.

I was on my way. To not being evicted, for a start. It was something.

Chapter 4

My three students were due to arrive in five minutes for the first class. Well, two of the three, since Sara was already there. I'd spent the day shopping at the grocery store and the farmers' market for the menu—lasagna, sundried tomato and eggplant bruschetta, and a simple salad—and scrubbing the kitchen with white vinegar and baking soda until it sparkled.

My cell rang. *Please don't be one of the two calling to cancel*, I prayed.

It was just my mom and dad calling to wish me luck. Then Ty. Then Sara from the bedroom, asking if her Target Missoni skirt would be too short if she were sitting on one of the kitchen bar stools. It wasn't.

The buzzer rang, and I pressed TALK. "Skinny Bitch Cooking School," I said.

"We're at the right place then," a guy said. "It's me, Duncan, and—I'm sorry, what's your name?" Silence. "And Eva right behind me." I buzzed them up.

"He sounds cute," Sara said.

The doorbell rang. I took a deep breath and opened it.

He *was* kind of cute. A bit uptight looking, maybe. Twenty-something with short, sandy blond hair and blue eyes behind wire-rimmed glasses. He had a messenger bag slung over his torso. "Hi, I'm Duncan. Ridley."

Behind him, a scowling thirty-something redhead with a chin-length bob and dark circles under her eyes said, "I'm Eva Ackerman. Eva. Not Eve. Not Eves. Not Evie. Eva. Just Eva. For some reason, people have trouble with this."

"Hi, Eves!" Sara said, sticking out her hand. "Just kidding."

"I have no sense of humor," Eva said, marching in with a great eye roll at Sara. "In fact, my soon-to-be ex-husband screamed that into my ear about five minutes ago before he hung up on me. Tell me, is this funny? 'Maybe you wouldn't need to request so much alimony if you stopped eating like a cow.'"

"I don't think that's funny," Duncan said. Quite earnestly, too, which meant he'd already won Sara's heart.

"Yeah. Not funny," I said. "But come in. I'm Clementine Cooper, your teacher."

"And I'm Sara, the teacher's roommate, but also a fellow student. No discount, either. I'm not a vegan. Or a vegetarian. But I'm following Clementine's Skinny Bitch diet, and I've already lost almost five pounds in a week."

"Really?" Eva asked, eyeing her up and down, then down and up.

"Well, you can't totally tell yet," Sara said.

"Since we're a small group," I said, thinking I'd better separate Sara and Just Eva, "why don't we sit down for a minute and do that dopey introduction thing—why you want to take the class, what you eat now, what you hope to learn, all that jazz." I got that break-the-ice idea from my sister, naturally. "I'm Clementine Cooper, and I grew up on an organic farm in northern California. I could peel and chop an onion without crying by age five. The summer after high school I went nuts and ate everything my parents wouldn't put on their table—burgers, lobster rolls, fried everything, eggs galore, sugar—and fake sugar—up the wazoo. After a month I felt and looked like total shit and went back to how I grew up eating. I have a certificate in vegan cooking from the Vegan Culinary Institute and have worked at a slew of restaurants. What I'm really into is helping people cut the crap out of their life."

I glanced at Eva, and she cleared her throat.

"I'm Eva Ackerman, just Eva, as I've said, which is something my boss's moronic assistant can't seem to remember. 'Hey, Eves,' every fucking morning. 'Night, Eves,' every fucking night. And she's twenty-two and has an amazing body and I hate her guts and—"

"I hate twenty-two-year-olds with perfect bodies, too," Sara chimed in.

Eva gave a wobbly smile and went on. "My husband left

me two weeks ago for some absolute child in his Pilates class. I didn't even know he was taking Pilates. I'm dealing with the separation agreement now, and it is a nightmare. My therapist says I need something positive in my life to focus on, something just for me, and suggested I take a class, writing or healthy cooking or something. I've been shoving McDonald's super-size French fries in my mouth lately." She glanced around, seeming like a human being for the first time. "I probably wasn't supposed to give you guys my life story in the first five seconds, was I?"

"I like people who lay it on the table," I reassured her. She shot me another wobbly smile.

Sara introduced herself as an office drone/aspiring actress on a self-appointed mission to go from fat extra to ingénue. "Your turn, Duncan," she said, turning to him, rather rapt.

He cleared his throat. "Duncan Ridley, twenty-eight. Vegetarian interested in going all the way. Oh, and librarian. Anyone laughs or says 'Really?' gets shot."

Sara laughed. "Really? I mean, you'd really shoot us?"

He didn't smile. "Male librarians and nurses freak people out. I can't love books?"

"My husband takes Pilates, so, yeah, I'd say you can love books," Eva muttered.

Before we explored that little gem again, I stood up and said, "Okay, so everyone up, and let's hit the kitchen. We're making a vegan lasagna, but you won't be able to tell you're not eating ricotta cheese or ground beef. That's how amazing it'll be. We're also going to make one of my favorite things—

sun-dried tomato and eggplant bruschetta. And a simple green salad with a miso-ginger dressing."

They crowded around me at the long stretch of counter, which wasn't hideous formica but a nice white tile that I was suddenly really grateful for. "We'll start with the lasagna, since it takes the longest to prepare and assemble. Tonight we'll use prepared strips of pasta, but in another class I'll teach you how to make your own dough."

Everything was laid out on the counter, including the recipe, which I adapted from Candle 22, the restaurant that gave me my start as vegetable chef. No one's lasagna was better—except for mine. Big pot of water on the stove, baking dish prepped, I was showing them how to properly peel and chop garlic when the intercom buzzed.

Another student off the street? I grabbed a dish towel, wiped the gunk from my hands, and pressed TALK on the intercom. "Skinny Bitch Cooking School, Clementine speaking."

"Um, yes," said an English accent. "Clementine, my name is Alexander Orr. I'm the new sous chef at Fresh."

Never heard of him. I pressed TALK again. "And?" Had he come to rub his job in my face?

"Um, well, I was sorry about what transpired at Fresh and all, and was passing by and saw your sign for the cooking class, and realized I was right in front of your building, and—"

Jesus. I pressed UNLOCK and let the poor English sap up.

"'Transpired' is a nice word," Sara said, whipping her knife around so fast that she almost maimed Duncan.

"I like that you appreciate words," Duncan said. Sara smiled.

Interesting. He wasn't her type at all. But Sara had an open mind. When it came to eating *and* dating. This was a good thing.

I held open the door and could hear him clomping up the steps. Finally, there appeared a very cute guy, thirty tops, with sandy-brown almost-curly hair and dark brown eyes. He had a dimple in both cheeks. He was tall and lanky and wearing a long-sleeved button-down white shirt and army-green cargo pants. Converse sneakers.

"Ah, the famous Clementine in the flesh," he said, and his cheeks actually reddened. "It's been a long time since I last saw you."

"We've met?"

"At Desdemona's. I was waiting for my interview with the chef. You were a line cook, working on artichokes, I recall. You told me if I wanted the job I'd better talk extra fast during the interview because the chef was in a shitty mood. I didn't get the job, but he said he could tell I was an okay bloke and recommended me to Organic X, where I worked for the past year as an assistant sous chef until Fresh recruited me."

"Oh, yeah! I do remember you." He'd tripped over the sack of potatoes and his glasses went flying off his face and almost landed in a sauté pan full of onions. He must have gotten contacts.

He glanced through the archway into the kitchen. "I can see you're in the middle of your class. I guess I just, well, wanted to say I'm sorry I got a great job at your expense. Though I see you're doing quite well."

The compliment, accent, and dimples conspired against me. "You can hang out if you want, be co-teacher tonight."

He looked at me intently for a moment as if trying to decide if I was just being friendly. I wasn't sure myself. "I would love to, Clementine, I really would, but I promised my ill grand-mum I'd stop by with some soup." He pointed at the bag he'd put down by the door. "Maybe I could, um, give you a call sometime? Or you could call me." He pulled a card out of his wallet, scribbled his number on the back, and handed it to me.

Wow, picked up in my own apartment. That was new. "Um, sure," I said.

"Cute!" Sara said when the door shut behind him. "And bringing his ill grand*mum* soup!"

He *was* cute. Not totally my type, which was a lot more jerkish from the get-go, unfortunately. But cute. And a chef. And, like Sara said, bringing his grandmum soup.

"Watch out," Eva said, knife pointed at me. "British guys trap you with their accents and use all these terms that make you think they care much more than they actually do. I dated a Brit once, and two seconds after dumping me he said he 'fancied a shag.' It sounded so polite I couldn't resist."

"My college roommate was from Wales and he was a great guy. Chap," Duncan said, sliding the garlic bits off his knife with his finger.

I helped Eva chop her garlic more finely. "For all I know, he was sent by Emil—the executive chef at this restaurant that unfairly fired me—to spy on me or get back at me in some way." I'd never been much of a cynic until a pat of butter entered my life. "I mean, who could think that sweet face and Englishness could be up to no good?"

"Well, at least go out with him," Sara said. "You can get him to convince everyone that you were set up. Clear your name."

Smart thinking. "We'll see. Okay, now on to the mushrooms."

There was chopping, talking, laughing, instruction, and there were sips of wine. And a few minutes later, everyone crowded around me to learn about tofu—how to buy, how to handle, and how braising it first before sautéing it with the vegetables would give it flavor and texture. "Okay, so you take the block of tofu and—"

A booming drill sounded right outside the window.

"What the hell is that?" Sara asked, going over to the living room to peer out the window as another mind-blowing whir of drill blasted us. "Oh, shit."

"What?" I asked, following her. The noise was deafening, like someone was drilling into my head. By the time I got to the window, it stopped. Because the guy on a ladder across the street was done hanging a huge sign that was covered in bubble wrap.

Above the beautiful arched windowpane of my space for Clementine's No Crap Café. Oh, shit was right.

Sara rubbed my shoulder. "Sorry, Clem. I know you had your eye on that space. But just think, by the time whatever's going in goes out of business in three months like the last place, you might have enough money to lease it."

That actually made me feel better.

A man came out the door, put on dark sunglasses, and stared up at the sign. He seemed to be okaying how it had been mounted. The man on the ladder started unwrapping the bubble wrap. After two solid minutes of unwrapping, facing right at me was a 3D silver steer's head. A steer's head. Fucking horns and everything. As he unwrapped the entire sign, I could clearly read the etched name from here.

THE SILVER STEER.

"Why not just call the place 'Meat'?" I muttered. Fuck. Shit. Fuck shit! No way was I doing my sunrise yoga while looking out the window at a dead steer head. "Sara, can you hold the fort while I confront this carcass-eating moron about his stupid sign? I'll be back in five."

"You're gonna tell him to move it?" Eva asked, and I could tell I went up a few notches in her estimation.

"Shit, yeah, I am. Or at least to take off the dead deer head. It's totally offensive."

I marched downstairs and crossed the street and pulled open The Silver Steer's door. A group of people was crowded around the one table in the place, a roll of blueprints spread out. An officious-looking woman with a clipboard and safety goggles around her neck came storming up to me. "No one can enter without authorization," she said. "For safety purposes."

"I have a problem with the sign outside. For *my* safety." And yours, lady.

"The sign meets city regulations, Miss. Now if you'll—"

"Who owns this place?" I asked, looking around for the guy in the dark sunglasses.

"Miss, Mr. Jeffries is very busy. If you'll—"

"Is there a problem?" a man asked, leaning back from the table to eye me. "I'm Zach Jeffries." It was the guy in the dark sunglasses, except now he wasn't wearing sunglasses. And he was so unbelievably good-looking that I couldn't speak for a moment. Tall. Thick dark brown hair. Intense dark blue eyes. Okay, yes, a teeny bit like Ben's. White shirt, sleeves rolled up. The slightest cleft in his chin.

Because I'd gone mute, he'd leaned back in, and the meeting resumed.

"The sign," I said, raising my voice. "It has to go."

He leaned back again and stared at me. "What about it bothers you?"

"I live across the street," I said, pointing up at my window, not that he'd know which one it was. "I'm a vegan chef and I am conducting cooking classes out of my home. I was about to teach my students how to properly handle a block of tofu when your dead animal sign went up and is now staring with its dead eyes directly into my living room."

There was a hint of smile. "And?" he prompted.

I thought I had covered the *and*. "And it's bad enough that you stole this space out from under me before I even had a chance—" I took a deep breath. Stick to the subject. "*And* this is not good for business! The smell of rotting animal carcass will make my students—and me—want to hurl." Although I was the only vegan in my apartment at the moment. Not that this asshole needed to know that. "My students are very upset. They might not even be willing to return next week. And it's only the first night of class."

"I sympathize," he replied, his dark blue eyes looking straight into mine. "My sister Avery is a vegan. Drinks all sorts of raw vegetables for breakfast, carries around her own not-cheese in some sort of purse cooler."

"So you'll take down the dead cow?" I asked, hopeful.

"Steer," he corrected. "And no, sorry. You're cute, though."

Someone laughed. Trust that it wasn't me.

Could he *be* more condescending?

"Zach, I've only got ten minutes," someone at the table said.

"Excuse us, please," Zach said to me. "And again, my apologies."

"This way, Miss," Clipboard said.

"You'll be hearing from my lawyer," I shot toward Zach Jeffries like an idiot. My carnivore lawyer sister would probably ask if I could get her into The Silver Steer on opening night.

As I left, I saw him watching me go.

I forced myself to take deep cleansing breaths on the way back to my apartment. These people weren't paying four hundred bucks to listen to me snarl curses at an aluminum sign. So when I opened the front door, I calmly announced that the owner was an ass and we had bruschetta to make and a lasagna to assemble.

Eva was a little aggressive with her chopping, but she seemed to need this class more than I needed perfectly sliced zucchini. Duncan and Sara were becoming very chummy as they parboiled the tomatoes for the bruschetta and sliced the Italian bread, rubbing the rounds with olive oil and garlic.

Once the lasagna and bruschetta were in the oven, we sat around my laptop and Googled The Silver Steer, Santa Monica. Up came more than twenty articles about how Zach Jeffries, thirty-two-year-old millionaire restaurateur, was opening a new steakhouse on Montana Avenue in a prime corner location.

As Duncan and Sara worked on the salad, and Eva and I started the miso-ginger dressing, the buzzer buzzed. I pressed TALK. "Skinny Bitch Cooking School, Clementine speaking." Honestly, I didn't know how much longer I could go around spitting out that mouthful.

"It's Zach Jeffries. From across the street. I assume you're the woman who doesn't care for my sign?"

It took a lot to shock me, but Zach Jeffries just pulled it off. I turned toward the table. They were as shocked as I was. I mean, two seconds ago, we were staring daggers at the guy's picture in the L.A. Times, reading about his new blood-dripping restaurant, and here he was, using the tinny intercom downstairs.

"Can I speak with you?" he asked. "I mean, face-to-face. I really don't like the idea of offending a neighbor and potentially hurting a fellow business across the street."

A fellow business. That was nice. I pressed UNLOCK.

"Maybe he's not a jerk," Duncan said. "He seems to actually care that the sign bothers you."

"Please. Look at her," Eva snapped, upping her chin at me. "He wants to get in Clementine's pants, and he sees his opportunity. A few dinners, a good lay or two, and you'll back off the sign. By then, he'll have all his permits in order."

"God, you're cynical," Sara said to Eva. "I love that."

Eva stared at her and then belly laughed.

Normally I would open the door and await him, the way I had for Alexander, nice British vegan chef, but Zach Jeffries, of the dead animal signage, could knock.

I could hear him jogging up the five flights.

Finally, the knock. A firm rap of the knuckles.

I opened the door.

Damn. He held a motorcycle helmet, and a black leather jacket was draped over his arm. In his other hand was a bottle of wine. Red and expensive.

"So it's just you four?" he asked. "That must mean you have room for one more student."

I stared at him. "Lady with the clipboard?"

He smiled. "Me."

I laughed. "You? Right."

"I'm interested in all kinds of food, neighbor."

"So you want to take my class."

He put down his stuff and pulled out his wallet and a Skinny Bitch Cooking School flyer that he must have ripped off the light post on the corner. "Four hundred, right?" He took bills from the black wallet and handed me two hundreds and four fifties. Then he walked right in and sat down at the table. "I'd introduce myself," he added, glancing at the laptop, open to his photo in the *L.A. Times*, "but I see you've met me."

Sara studied him, head to toe. "I'm Sara, teacher's roommate, so, also a neighbor."

"Duncan Ridley, librarian," Duncan said and we *all* waited. But Zach's expression didn't budge.

Eva shook his hand. "Eva Ackerman. Single?"

"I'm not married," Zach said, his eyes on me. "So, by the amazing smell coming from the oven and this dressed salad, I assume I've missed most of class."

Sara started setting the table. "We get to eat our work. You're just in time for the first course."

Definition of surreal: sitting at your thrift-store kitchen table, eating student-made leafy greens with miso ginger dressing while Zach Jeffries poured the wine he brought, listening to him talk about the thousand-acre cattle ranch his family had owned for generations in northern California, where he grew up, not too far from Bluff Valley.

"We seem to have more in common than not," he said to me as he popped an olive into his mouth.

"Really? Because I don't drink wine made with red dye from crushed beetles."

Everyone pushed their glass away from them. Except Zach.

"My motto is everything in moderation," he said, taking a sip. "Mmm, that's good."

Sara, Eva, and Duncan looked from Zach to me like we were at Wimbledon.

My turn. "We have northern California in common, but you're a leather-jacket-wearing carnivore and I'm a faux-suede-wearing vegan," I said, extending one silver sandal for emphasis—and so he could get a glimpse of my yoga-toned leg.

His eyes went up my leg, to my skirt, and finally landed on my face.

Oh shit. My toes tingled. My *toes*.

He'd taken one bite of the bruschetta and declared it "damned good" when his cell phone rang. He listened for a moment, then said, "On my way, Baby."

Oh. Deflated back to earth. I glanced at Sara. She looked disappointed, too.

Of course, there was a *Baby* in his life. A supermodel, no doubt, that would blow even Laurel soon-to-be Frasier off the runway.

But who cared? Zach Jeffries grew up slaughtering animals and thought nothing of selling twenty-seven-dollar burgers and spewing fuel emissions into the atmosphere. Being attracted to him was ridiculous.

But I was. *Very* traitorously attracted.

Chapter 5

The moment I opened my eyes the next morning, Zach Jeffries was the first thing on my mind. I *was* a traitor to my own self. Last night, as I'd peeled off my cotton tank top because it was so hot and the stupid fan was useless, I lay in my bed, staring outside at the sliver of moon and the twinkling stars, imagining Zach lying right next to me. On top of me. Under me.

I did not have such thoughts about the cute vegan chef, whose name I kept forgetting.

"Earth to Clementine," my sister was saying, a forkful of pad thai on the way to her mouth.

Once a month, Elizabeth and I took turns having a "your world/my world" lunch to keep in touch, since those two worlds didn't often collide except for family functions. Last month was her world, which meant having an uninspired fruit salad in her stodgy law firm's cafeteria while listening to her and a colleague talk shop. This month was my world, so Elizabeth, in her severe suit and dull pumps, sat beside me on a bench in Palisades Park, having vegan pad thai from my favorite Asian-Fusion truck.

"God, this is good," she said, fork in mouth.

Elizabeth might be uptight, but she appreciated good food, even if it was vegan, which she gave up a zillion years ago. When she was thirteen, Elizabeth had her first hamburger with an incredulous "I can't believe you've never had a hamburger" friend at In-N-Out Burger. She came home and informed our parents she was now a carnivore. She took it for granted that they'd respect her choice to be who she was (which, of course, they did), and that was that. At the time, I was annoyingly militant about being a vegan and tried my best to make her feel as gross as I thought she was for going to the dark side. She'd ignored me and often brought home burgers and lobster rolls to eat in front of me while smacking her lips. When I went off the rails that one summer, she'd said "Ha, told you!" ten times a day. I *Ha*'d right back at her, pointing out zits on my once-clear forehead and how I'd had to drop out of training for a 10K because I was such a slug, but she'd claimed she felt perfectly fine and always had. Elizabeth *did* have amazing skin. And worked twelve-hour days and then hit the gym for an hour every other night. She got lucky, that's all.

From the looks of us, you'd never know we were sisters, unless you noticed we had the same color green-hazel eyes. I looked like our dad, blond and tall. Elizabeth was a dead ringer for our mother, except my sister's chestnut-brown hair was cut in a very clean bob, whereas our mom's hair was down to her waist and graying. And I don't think our mother ever wore a suit. Our differences aside, Elizabeth and I had always been close, even though she was four years older and lived to be conventional. In our house, that made her a rebel.

As we'd waited in line at the truck, I hit her up for information about ordinances and regulations about huge signs on commercial buildings, and she knew all about websites to check for size regulations and other arcane details about petitions and offending neighbors and potentially hurting small businesses. Of course, the minute she heard I was talking about The Silver Steer, she said she and Doug, her fiancé, were already on a waiting list for opening night.

"You're a million miles away, Clem," she said, taking a sip of her iced tea. "Are you worried about your new initiatives? I can help you with a business plan. Did you—"

"Business is great, actually," I said as a guy on a skateboard almost ran over my foot. "The cooking class is going better than I expected, and I'm sure the students will be word-of-mouth spreaders. And I got two calls this morning about the personal chef and private lessons side, so right now, it's all good."

"Right now," she repeated. "You probably have, what, a thousand bucks left in the bank?"

Ha. Mucho more, actually, thanks to my ex-boyfriend and my new frugality, ever since I no longer had a steady paycheck. Between that and the money that would come in here and there from the personal chef stuff and the next session of cooking classes, I could make a real go of being my own boss.

"Elizabeth, I'm fine. Trust me. Okay?"

She raised one eyebrow and peered at me. "Okay, fine. But if you need money, ask. Got it?"

"Got it." We stood up, took last sips of our iced tea, and threw our boxes and bags away. "And thanks." She might be bossy, but she rocked as a sister.

We headed over to the farmers' market, where Elizabeth oohed and ahhed at the rosemary artisan breads while I bought ingredients for tomorrow's personal chef clients—two college students who were thinking of going vegan and hired me to teach them how to make some easy, freezable meals, like pizzas and burritos.

With three loafs of bread sticking out of her tote bag, Elizabeth joined me at a big basket of gorgeous red bell peppers. I took six and moved on to the green and yellow.

"Bringing a date to Mom and Dad's party this weekend?" she asked, her two-carat diamond ring glinting in the brilliant July sunshine. Elizabeth was engaged to a fellow lawyer who didn't believe she really came from organic hippie farmers until he met our parents last summer. No matter what any of us said, his response was a half-good-natured, half-appalled, "That's so interesting."

Our parents were celebrating thirty years of marriage and having a huge party at the farm. A weekend among my kind and I'd be better armed against the face and charisma of Zach Jeffries.

"Nope," I said, paper-bagging some mushrooms and moving to the garlic bushels. "Not seeing anyone." Shit. Shouldn't have said that. Elizabeth was constantly trying to set me up on blind dates with any lawyer at her firm who had remotely cool hair or carried a messenger bag instead of a briefcase. Once she tricked me into being anecdotal data for a case involving an employee demanding vegan options at her workplace cafeteria. The guy and I got into a huge fight, and I ended up dipping the end of his tie into his coffee. But the fix-up offers kept coming.

"Glad to hear that," said someone with a British accent.

I turned around to find the cute vegan chef—Alexander, I now remembered, with his nice-chap smile and dimples— standing with two reusable shopping bags full of produce and wrapped goods. He looked so fresh-scrubbed, like he'd just washed his face a second ago. Two days had passed since we'd re-met in my apartment during the cooking class, and he hadn't called. There'd been something so puppy-dog about him, I had almost expected a call that night.

He lifted the bags. "One of today's three specials at Fresh. Cherry Barbeque Seitan Napoleon. Eight layers."

"Barbeque week was my idea," I said. And ha. Emil probably hated that he'd been unable to resist trying it.

"And a good one. Crazy reservations for the weekend."

"Sounds like dinner at our house growing up," Elizabeth said. "Not just vegan, but weird vegan."

Alexander smiled and stuck out his hand, which Elizabeth shook. As I introduced them, I could tell Elizabeth approved.

We made the usual small talk and I could also tell that Elizabeth was aware of how Alexander was looking at me, as though he couldn't bear to drag his eyes away from my face (which I appreciated, even if he didn't quite inspire the same can't-take-my-eyes-off-you lust in me), so she moved on to the gingerbread table three booths away to give him a chance to ask me out.

Except he didn't. He told me a funny story about one of the new waiters at Fresh. Asked how the cooking class had gone. Told me I had to try the baba ghanoush from Mediterranean, a former favorite restaurant that had scorned me on my job hunt, so no. And said he liked my shirt. But he didn't ask me out. Which, of course, made me slightly more interested in him. He wasn't even looking for an in, like asking if I'd seen a certain movie, if I'd been to a certain restaurant.

He glanced at his watch, said he had to go, called "Nice to meet you, Elizabeth" at my sister, flashed us a wide smile, and took off.

Huh.

"He's so cute," Elizabeth said, biting into a gingerbread man's head as we watched him disappear into the crowd.

"Yeah, he's cute, but not my type."

"Too nice?"

"Ben was nice," I reminded her as she stopped at a table full of chocolates.

"Yeah, I guess he was."

"Alexander's just lacking . . . something." Like not being Zach Jeffries. What the hell was wrong with me?

She bought a pound of almond bark. "Well, I guess you can't help who does it for you. Though, I'll tell you, the first time I saw Doug—even the second time? I was a little meh on him. Third date? He made my knees weak."

Doug looked a little bit like Elmer Fudd. So maybe there was hope for Alexander.

"See, I told you that vegans don't look like shriveled-up vampire ghosts," said a short redhead to an even shorter blonde when she opened the door to her apartment the next morning.

My newest clients—sisters, roommates, and Santa Monica College students Morgan and Dana. Their apartment—right around the corner—was even smaller than mine.

"You're, like, skinny, but healthy-looking," the blonde said, eyeing me up and down. "We want to be skinny bitches," she added, holding up one of my flyers, which Morgan, the redhead, said they'd seen on the community billboard at the hot yoga place I lived above.

"I'm not really that bitchy, though," Morgan said.

"Being a skinny bitch is about cutting the crap out of your life," I said, putting down my bag of ingredients on the little round kitchen table. "Eating good stuff. Speaking up. Out. Treating yourself right."

"Sign us up," Dana said.

We got to cooking, sautéing veggies and shredding vegan cheese and creating six different pizzas, including my barbeque seitan, which I had no doubt would be the most ordered item at Fresh. I showed them how to fill fajitas, roll enchiladas, and make an insane chile.

Their fridge and freezer full, I started packing up. I liked this personal chef thing a lot more than I thought I would. Especially when it didn't involve former boyfriends and their fiancées.

Dana handed me a check. "Our mom said to tell her if you were good. She has this whole group of friends who do book clubs and Zumba and whatever, and they want to do cleanses and learn about veganism. I'll give her your flyer."

"Do that," I said. Middle-aged moms had money. This was good.

Much richer, I headed out into brilliant California sunshine. My phone rang, killing the Zen of the moment. Unfamiliar number, too.

Maybe another potential client. Or the cute vegan chef.

"Clementine Cooper," I said.

"Clementine, it's Zach. Jeffries. I have a business proposition for you," he said, his deep voice sending the tiniest jolts up my spine.

"I think you're forgetting I don't do animal innards," I reminded him.

I could see him smiling. This was bad.

"Well aware," he said. "I want you to come up with two vegan offerings for The Silver Steer. The menu should have something for everyone. I'd like to arrange for you to do a cooking demonstration and tasting for me."

I rolled my eyes, which I was sure *he* could see. "I charge two hundred per hour, two-hour minimum," I told him, making up numbers. "And the cost of ingredients is extra, of course."

"Email me a shopping list and I'll have my assistant pick everything up," he said, as if that was perfectly normal. "How's Monday night at my place? Seven o'clock."

Monday night. Not Monday morning. Not Monday afternoon. Not the ole nine to five regular business hours. Night. Interesting. Maybe *Baby* wasn't his girlfriend, after all.

And *his place*. No doubt something amazing right on the beach. "Let me check my calendar," I said, silently counting to ten. "I have a cancellation, so sure. I have you booked for Monday night at seven."

He gave me an address on Ocean Avenue, as expected.

Zach Jeffries. And me. Alone in his house.

———

Sara and I spent the weekend coming up with the two vegan entrees. Something that would complement the regular menu and specials, which were all dead-cow related, unfortunately. If I came up with something too out there, like the cherry barbeque napoleon that was presently being served to many a table at Fresh, Sara would bring me back to reality. We were talking about a menu of meat. Steak fries. Twelve dollars for a side of steak fries, but fries.

By Sunday afternoon, I'd narrowed a long list of possibilities down to two. I sat at the kitchen table with a notebook and my laptop while Sara made us lunch—hummus and home-made whole wheat garlic pita chips. From the delicious smell wafting over to the table, I had taught her well. "Sar, what do you think: a portobello mushroom burger and some kind of tofu stir-fry."

She handed me a plate. "Yes and yes. The wannabe models who come in with their steak-eating dates will all order your stuff even if they're not vegan."

Good point.

Sara turned on a *Downton Abbey* rerun, and I worked up some original recipes. An hour later, I had an incredible-sounding portobello burger with avocado slices and roasted red peppers and a basic but kick-ass tofu stir-fry. For added inspiration, I checked over different recipes from the school I attended, the restaurants I'd worked in, and I called my dad to get his three cents. The man never disappointed. He suggested blackened Cajun tofu for the stir-fry—brilliant as always.

"So is it just gonna be the two of you?" Sara called from her bedroom. "Or will his chef be there?"

"I don't know. I'm kind of hoping we aren't alone. Zach is too . . . something."

"Yeah, too unbelievably gorgeous," she shouted back. "So what are you gonna wear? I say make him crawl."

"What does that even mean, you goof?" I couldn't imagine Zach Jeffries crawling for anyone, really. "Anyway, I've already decided to dress like a chef. I want him to take me seriously. I'm wearing my white skinny jeans and chef's jacket."

"Sorry, Clem, but you actually look hot in that."

I smiled. "I didn't say I didn't want him to think so."

"Smart girl," she said. "Holy crap, I just stepped on the scale and I lost two and a half more pounds!"

"Awesome!" I called back.

She walked over with the scale, put it down by my feet, and stepped on it. "Two and a half pounds! Gone! And a pound and a half last week. And I'm not even starving."

I looked down at the digital readout. "I'm really proud of you, Sara."

She smiled. "You know what? I'm going for the Attractive Friend spot in the yogurt commercial—the go-see is Monday. I didn't think I had a chance—and I know I've only lost seven and a half pounds, but whatever, I'm going."

"Yogurt. Blech. But that's so great, Sara. You absolutely should go for it. And you're gonna get it, too."

She grabbed me into a hug, then swiped a hummus-laden chip and skipped into her bedroom with the scale.

Zach's place *was* on the beach. On. The. Beach. A narrow three-story white and windows mini palace with balconies on the second and third floors. I wouldn't have been surprised if a butler opened the door.

I was a few minutes early, and there was no way I was ringing that bell before exactly seven. I turned to look at the beach, the Santa Monica Pier just a block away, stretching out under the still blue sky.

At exactly seven o'clock, I rang the bell. My palms were sweating.

No butler. Just him. He stood in the doorway in a dark blue T-shirt, jeans—low-slung, slightly worn—and bare feet. A beagle that was standing behind him eyed me, then waddled back to a red floor pillow by the fireplace and curled up.

"Hey, Chef," Zach said, holding open the door for me to enter.

I dragged my eyes from him to the incredible house. There was lots of glass and leather and serious pieces of art. One wall was entirely windows.

"This kitchen is bigger than my entire apartment," I marveled as I followed him in. Stainless steel and soapstone counters. And no one else. Like a girlfriend. Or the chef from The Silver Steer. We were alone.

He leaned against the counter. He had to be six foot two. Maybe three. I hadn't noticed last week how incredibly broad his shoulders were. "I liked your place," he said. "What I saw of it, anyway."

Yeah, right. "I'll bet you never lived in a place like mine."

He went to the refrigerator and took out two bottles of beer. I shook my head, and he put one back. "Okay, that's true. I made a lot of money while still in college. I started a company at my dorm room desk and got lucky."

"Lucky? You believe in luck?"

"Actually, no. I believe in smart. And action."

"Me, too."

"I can tell, Clementine. That's why I specifically wanted

you to design the vegan offerings for The Silver Steer. What are you, twenty-four? Twenty-five? And you've already worked at some major restaurants and have your own business."

"I'm twenty-six. But thank you."

He smiled. "I admire people with strong convictions, and passions. I always have. I liked that you barged into the restaurant that day and stood up to—what did you call her? Lady Clipboard."

I laughed. "So the admiration still holds even if it's against everything you're about."

He opened the beer and took a swig. "I'm more than what I eat, Clementine."

"But you live very differently than I do."

"How do you know? I wasn't aware we'd spent that much time together."

"Ha. But still. You own a steakhouse. You spew fuel emissions into the air with your motorcycle. You use that crappy dishwashing liquid with tons of chemicals," I added, jerking a thumb to the sink.

"Huh. Definitely never thought about the dish soap." He opened the refrigerator and pointed to two shelves. "Those are the perishables." He opened a cabinet. "And the rest of the ingredients. My chef approved your entrees. Get past me and I'll hand him your recipes and pay you well for them."

"You talk money a lot," I said, taking out ingredients for the stir-fry.

"I own a restaurant. It's all *about* money."

"My place is going to be about the *food*," I said.

He laughed and lifted his beer in salute. "I have no doubt that place will be a hit. So talk to me about tofu," he said as I placed the block of firm tofu on a cutting board. "What the hell is it?"

I told him all about tofu, that it was made from soybeans and water, was high in protein and beautifully absorbed the flavors of spices and marinades. How it had less than a hundred calories, ten grams of protein, and five grams of fat per half cup serving. Good stuff.

And he listened to every word. His eyes on my face. On my lips, I noticed. Then back up at my eyes. Then surreptitiously glancing lower, checking me out.

As I stood next to him by the sink, draining the tofu, he was so close that I could smell his soap.

He seemed to notice he was staring at me and took a slug of his beer. "Did you start cooking after culinary school or did you always cook?"

Man. I had to actually force myself to look away from him, too. "I learned the basics from my father. My earliest memory is being in the kitchen with him, learning how to snap peas and tear the husks off corn." I thought of my dad, in his wheelchair, so weak now, and I got that awful clenching feeling in my chest. "So, your dad took you out hunting the minute you could walk?"

There. Good, Clem. You have to remind yourself that this guy is a total carnivore. He's the anti-you. Do not get suckered by that face. Or body.

He smiled. The kind of smile that said he liked being challenged. "I'm not a hunter. Ours is a breeding ranch. But I did grow up with cattle and chickens and rabbits walking in my path all the time. There was a time—I was thirteen—when I was really awkward and skinny and my hair stuck up in all directions, and I transferred to a new school and had no friends. A goose and a rooster were the only creatures I talked to for months. I told them everything."

Huh. Unexpected. "They say anything back?" I asked as I sliced the tofu, added the spices to the food processor, and then got busy slicing scallions and then shallots. I found myself moving a bit closer to him. My right arm brushed against his left one, and a freak tingle shot up my spine. From his *arm*.

"They were good listeners."

He looked right at me, and we just oogled each other for a very long moment. Dammit.

I nodded, trying to break whatever this crazy thing was that was happening between us. "Yeah, animals are amazing listeners. I grew up telling our chickens and dogs and cats my life story and my sob stories."

"I can't imagine you had an awkward period," he said, peering into the pan, where the spice-dredged tofu sizzled on low heat.

"Actually, I did. Before braces and filling out some I looked like a bucktoothed pole." He didn't need to know that until I discovered Frizz-Ease as a fourteen-year-old, I also had Bellatrix Lestrange's hair, only blond.

"Well, it seems to have worked out okay," he said, looking right into my eyes again. "You can't tell me you're not seeing anyone."

A little jolt spiked up the back of my neck. "Nope."

"Well, that must mean you're getting over someone, then."

I turned to face him. "How do you know that?"

"Because you're beautiful. And passionate about what you do. Like I said, you're doing your own thing, Clementine. It's very attractive. So if you were interested in a relationship, I'm sure you'd have one."

I turned back to the pan and added the veggies. "Something ended six months ago. Badly—for me, anyway. So I put blinders on and focused on getting promoted to sous chef and chef, and I thought it worked. But then—"

I stopped talking. He didn't need to know every detail of my life.

"But then what?" he asked, stepping closer until he was right next to me, his back to the counter, our shoulders touching.

He didn't move. And neither did I.

"Someone blindsided me again and I got fired from a top restaurant. That's why I'm trying to get the Skinny Bitch biz off the ground—being a personal chef, offering cooking classes so that one day I can open Clementine's No Crap Café."

"So do you think The Silver Steer and your Skinny Bitch world can coexist on Montana and 14th?"

I smiled. "I wouldn't have thought so, but maybe."

He lifted up my chin with his hand and leaned down and kissed me.

"You just kissed me," I said like an idiot. Duh.

"Yeah, I did. Couldn't help myself. I guess that means we're not enemies anymore."

"I never said *that*."

He laughed. "I've always liked a challenge."

Yeah, no kidding. *And remember that, Clem. A zillionaire who gets everything he wants? Of course, he's interested in the vegan who doesn't worship at his feet like every other woman probably does. Remember that. Live it. Don't be lured.* "You know what I find challenging? Making sure blackened tofu doesn't get so black that it's burned to a crisp," I said, turning off the burner and plating the stir-fry. The tofu was fine, but I wasn't.

"I'll let you focus on your work," he said, staring at me for a moment. "I'll get out the stuff for the portobello burger. I admit I like the sound of that better than the tofu stir-fry, but my chef—Walker—says both will definitely move."

As he opened the refrigerator, I could still feel the imprint of his lips on mine.

And then he was standing in front of me, kissing me again. Instead of taking my own advice, instead of not being lured, I kissed him back. Hard.

The doorbell rang, and Zach went on kissing me as though someone wasn't obsessively pressing the bell over and over.

Like a girlfriend.

"It's like someone knows you're here and isn't giving up," I said, heart unexpectedly plummeting. I shouldn't care.

The bell would not stop ringing.

"Excuse me," he said, looking pissed.

He stepped outside and closed the door behind him, so, of course, I went right to the peephole to get a look.

She was stunning, of course. Very tall. Long blond hair and huge boobs.

And in seconds, she was in his arms. I couldn't tell if they were kissing, but he was holding her. Very close.

Dick. He was just all over me!

You're here to cook for a job, I reminded myself. Do not walk out. Do not tell him he sucks. Just do what you're here for. Make your four hundred bucks. More money will come for the recipes themselves.

Just grab the portobello mushrooms and pull off the fucking stems.

The door opened, and in walked Zach and this woman who I still thought of as *Baby*.

"See," he said to her, his arm extended toward me. "Chef jacket. The smell of an amazing meal cooking. This is Clementine, and she is here making some vegan options for The Silver Steer."

Baby glanced at me, her big blue eyes on my jacket. "I'll wait for you upstairs," she said to Zach. "In your bedroom," she added, eyes, suddenly cold, back on me.

Before he could say anything, she was marching up the stairs.

"Sorry about the interruption," he said. He looked as though he was going to say something else, then slightly shook his head. "I'll leave you to the burger. Call up when it's ready for the tasting."

He started for the stairs.

My blood started to boil. "You've got to be kidding me. You

just kissed me," I whispered—unnecessarily generous. "And now you're dismissing me to go fuck your girlfriend while I audition my cooking for you?" I threw the knife I'd been using to slice avocado in the sink. "Have a nice life."

I grabbed my bag and stalked toward the door.

"Clementine, wait."

"For what?" I pulled open the door.

"At least let me pay you," he called.

Bastard.

Chapter 6

"Call Alexander right now and ask him out," Sara ordered the next morning when I dragged myself into the kitchen, the smell of pancakes in the air.

When I got home last night, furious, she'd called Ty, who'd come over with potato-leek soup; more insanely good cupcakes, which I stuffed my face with; and my favorite wine, which I drank too much of. We watched the Food Network for hours, and by the time Ty left and Sara turned out the lights, I felt slightly better. Zach was a jerk, but was that ever really in question? And, as always, my friends had my back.

Sara flipped a buckwheat pancake at the stove. "You guys will go on some perfect vegany date and you'll be madly in love with each other and you'll be like, 'Zach who?'"

Except that Alexander, with his fresh-scrubbed cuteness,

couldn't compare to the utter hotness of Zach Jeffries. Still, I did like Alexander. He was my kind. And obviously too shy to ask me out. I would put him out of his misery.

"But wouldn't that be using him to get over someone else?" I asked. "I ran into him the other day when I was having lunch with my sister. He's too nice to use."

She added the pancake to the stack of four already on a plate. "Who says you're using him? Alexander could be the perfect guy for you. How are you supposed to know either way if you don't give him a chance?"

"You spun that well," I said, going into my bedroom for my phone. I found his card in my wallet. Alexander Orr. Sous chef, Fresh. Good thing he'd scrawled his cell number on the back, because there was no way I'd call Fresh.

"And hurry up because breakfast is ready. Spiced buckwheat banana pancakes from your recipe," she called from the kitchen. "Please tell me I can use maple syrup."

"Yup. The real stuff is in the fridge. But not too much," I added, heading into the living room and peering out at the dead cow head sign for fortification. I dialed.

"Clementine," Alexander said, sounding truly happy to hear from me. "I'd love to see you. I'm attending a special concert at two. Want to join me?"

A concert at two in the afternoon? Maybe some outdoor lunchtime thing.

"Sounds great," I told him.

"Terrific. Meet me in front of Taft Middle School at 1:50."

Middle school? What?

I tried to do the math fast in my head. Alexander couldn't be more than thirty. How old were middle-school kids? Eleven? Twelve? Could he have a twelve-year-old kid? He could.

Crap. Not that I didn't like kids and all, but . . . did I want to watch that twelve-year-old kid blow into a clarinet or whatever for an hour? Not really.

Before I could come up with a good excuse, he said, "Looking forward," in that cute British accent and hung up.

What did you wear to a middle-school concert at two in the afternoon, anyway?

My own middle-school years sucked, just as I'd told Zach. My parents had switched me from a crunchy private school, where you took electives in African drumming, to the public school, which had four times the number of students. It took me a while to find my people.

And it took me a while to spot Alexander among the throngs of people walking and milling around the school. Everyone's parents and grandparents and bored-looking little siblings were heading toward the main entrance. No one else was wearing incredibly cool four-inch over-the-knee ecru faux-suede boots, though.

Sara, who'd once substituted as an aide in a middle school, told me I could wear my skinny jeans and sheer, flowy shirt and amazing boots.

Alexander was sitting on a stone bench and stood up and

smiled when I approached. Damn, he was cute. He took off his sunglasses and squinted his sweet dark brown eyes at me.

"So, you were a teen dad or what?" I asked as we headed in.

"More like a teen mentor," he said with that irresistible British accent. "It's a Big Brothers–type program. I mentor a great young bloke called Jesse. He's in sixth grade. Crazy good tuba player."

He was a Big Brother. Brought his grandmum soup. The guy might be too good for me.

"What kind of stuff do you do together?"

He led the way into the auditorium. "Everything from basketball to helping with science fair projects. My father took off on my mum when I was young and I had a few different mentors in a similar program. One taught me how to cook, and here I am."

Huh. "That's really great," I said, noticing that he smelled great, too. Like the ocean and clean. He also had a handsome profile. Strong, straight nose. Excellent chin.

"So Jesse knows you're here?" I asked as we sat down close to the stage. Under the dark blue curtain across the stage, I could see lots of little feet moving around.

He nodded. "His mum can't take off from work, especially since she works so far from here, so I go to all the school events she can't attend. Make sure he's represented, you know?"

Man, that was nice.

"You might make me want to become a better person," I whispered, because the audience was quieting down.

He smiled, his eyes on mine. He took my hand and held it for a second, then began clapping as a woman in a really long skirt walked onto the stage.

The principal. She made her introductions, there was more clapping, and then the curtain parted to reveal a bunch of kids of wildly varying heights, some looking like munchkins and others like teenagers, sitting with their instruments.

"Which one is Jesse?"

"See the kid in the second row with the floppy blond hair and tuba next to the redheaded girl?"

"Aww, the tuba is bigger than he is."

They weren't half bad, which I expounded on to Alexander, who smiled and squeezed my hand again.

I liked this guy. Thank you, universe. I wouldn't even remember Zach Jeffries's last name in a couple of hours. Or the way that kiss of his shot straight from my toes to every part of my body. One little kiss did all that. But by four, maybe five o'clock when Alexander would have to head to Fresh for work, I should be completely over that kiss.

Forty-five minutes later, after a standing ovation, we headed backstage. I could see Jesse in a crowd of kids being hugged by proud, beaming parents, craning his neck in all directions to look for Alexander. When Jesse spied him, he broke out into a smile that melted even my cynical heart.

"You came!" Jesse said, pushing past the crowd to get to Alexander.

The two did some fist-bump hug combination, and then

Alexander pulled a small wrapped gift out of his back pocket and handed it to the kid.

"What's this?" Jesse asked excitedly.

"Open it," Zach said.

Jessie ripped off the wrapping paper to reveal an iTunes gift card. "Awesome!"

"It's for classical music with tubas," Alexander said. "Not Ne-Yo."

"Gotcha," Jesse said with a sly smile. He waved Alexander close and whispered something in his ear, then shouted, "Thanks again," before disappearing into the sea of kids lining up to head back to their classes.

"What did he whisper?" I asked.

"Hot babe," Alexander said, then laughed. "He has crushes on two girls at the moment. And, apparently, now you."

I smiled. "I had a great time. You're one nice guy."

"So everyone says." He mock-rolled his eyes. "White Blossom for late lunch?"

"I can't show my face in there," I said as we made our way back outside. "I asked about a job at White Blossom after I got fired and they told me they don't take Emil's sloppy seconds."

"Finch said that?"

I nodded. Finch was one of the best vegan chefs in L.A. And clearly a big dickhead.

"I'll never eat there again," he said. "Wanker."

I laughed. "You curse, too? You might just be perfect for me."

He flashed me a dimpled smile and took my hand. And

held it all the way to the Pier, where we decided on Indian from his favorite truck.

We sat on a bench and ate and talked and people watched. He told me about growing up in a rural town an hour from London, with three brothers and one sister. How all the brothers looked so alike that even his mother sometimes called them by the wrong name. He'd been accepted to cooking school in New York, then got into veganism, and ended up in L.A. to train with Peter Farkoff, one of the best vegan chefs in the country. Alexander had figured at least one of his siblings would follow him to America, but only his cool grandmother did after she was widowed and needed to shake up her life. She lived in a retirement condo and did yoga on the beach every morning.

"Fresh is one of her favorite restaurants and she's not even vegan," he said. "Do you hate that I work there?"

"Eh, I'll get over it." I ripped off a piece of garlic naan. "So Emil didn't keep anyone at Fresh? Everyone's new?"

"He only kept the support—waitstaff and dishwashers. He fired James, the one who waited on the critic, but then hired him back."

"Where's Rain these days?"

"Looking, I hear," he said. "Word got around she sabotaged you."

"That's good."

As we finished up our samosas and chana saag and naan, he told me about his two dogs, a German shepherd named Brit and a crazy Jack Russell named Lizzie. He asked if I wanted to take the dogs for a walk, which I did, so we headed to his place, which turned out to be a tiny house with a surprisingly big backyard (a must for the dogs, he said). I got the German shepherd, who was better behaved than the Jack Russell, and we went to a dog run in a park nearby. The minute the dogs were off leash, I was reminded of early mornings just like this with Ben and his yellow Lab, but the memory popped out of my head in seconds instead of slow-burning with the usual sensation of someone sticking a fork in my chest.

Because you like this guy.

We traded funny—and not funny—stories about the kitchen, about tyrannical executive chefs and bosses who made us better cooks. About our signature dishes and favorite foods. (Alexander was crazy about portobello mushrooms, which luckily weren't ruined for me for all time.) Then it was time to get back to his house so he could let the dogs in and grab his chef whites. I was surprised by how much I didn't want to say good-bye.

On his tiny front porch, he took both my hands and smiled at me, then leaned down and kissed me.

I expected a mini parade. Tubas clanging, even.

But damn. Nothing.

Nothing.

It was as if my brother, Kale, were pecking me on the cheek, and Alexander was going full-out on the lips. He pulled back and looked at me, his smile so sweet and full of "I'm so into you" that I felt really bad.

I forced myself to put my sister's voice in my head, telling me to give him a chance, that despite her fiancé looking like Elmer Fudd, she now thought he was incredibly hot, but it took until the third date for her to see it. Feel it.

And Alexander Orr was no Elmer Fudd.

Hadn't I learned that lesson with my first boyfriend from way back in high school? Dylan Frick, who I never noticed until we were paired as partners on Dissect the Murdered Frog Day in freshman science, refused, as I had, to touch the little knife. Fade-into-the-woodwork, quiet Dylan stood up and gave a short speech that had me jumping up to clap. We were both sent to the principal's office and we became a couple during the march down the long gray hall to Mrs. Perlmutter's office. That romance lasted two years until Dylan's family moved across the country. After that, though, I fell for guys who were both gorgeous (to me, at least) and incredibly cool. The last love of my life broke my heart. I wouldn't mind not going there again.

If Elmer Fudd could win over my no-one-is-good-enough sister on the third date, I could at least give the very cute, very sweet Alexander Orr till the second.

———

In my kitchen that night, my Skinny Bitch Cooking School students and I stood at the counter working on ratatouille. I was showing them how to blanch tomatoes when Eva asked if the "cute Brit" ever called.

Which got me thinking that Zach Jeffries sure hadn't. Not even a fake apology. All day I had expected at least a text—something, anything. At least I hadn't blown money on ingredients.

"They went out yesterday," Sara said, chopping a tomato. "And—"

"Chop more coarsely," I said, hip bumping her with a look that said "Shut it." "Like this." I took her knife and demonstrated for everyone.

Sara totally ignored me. "He took her to his teen mentee's band concert at his middle school. Can you see Clementine making small talk with the moms?"

"I can, actually," Duncan said. "Clementine is a teacher, after all."

"Thank you, Duncan," I said, shooting Sara another "shut it" look. It was okay if the three of them talked about their personal business, but mine was off-limits.

"But then he kissed her," Sara went on, "and she said it was like kissing Kale. As in, her brother, not the vegetable."

"And moving along to the eggplant," I said, slapping it down on the counter. "We need to cut it into cubes."

Eva set down her knife and took a sip of her wine. "A blah kiss makes him a keeper, Clem. When you're in love, they rip your heart right out of your chest. From now on, I'm only interested in men who do nothing for me. Someone to see a movie with. Dinner. A decent shag, as your British chef would say. But all the bullshit and heartache that goes along with falling in love? No, thank you."

"Talk about giving up," Sara said.

"Not giving up," Eva said. *"Growing* up. A real relationship ain't gonna be about lust anyway."

Sara went back to cubing. "Well I think you can have both. Who's with me?" She was forever trying to find out if Duncan had a girlfriend. Or boyfriend.

He started slicing the onion on his cutting board a little too forcefully. "I thought I had both with—I can't even say her name."

Past tense. "Oh, we have those, too. The Exes Who Won't Be Named. We know all about those."

"I just call my ex *Fucker,*" Eva said. "That solves the problem."

Sara burst out laughing, then put her hand over her mouth at the sight of Duncan's miserable expression.

"I don't think of my ex-girlfriend that way," he said. "She was perfect. Is perfect."

"So what happened?" Sara asked.

He put down his knife and took a gulp of the wine I'd poured everyone at the start of class. "She just dumped me out of nowhere. One minute we're talking about moving in together, and the next day, she says it's over, and her toothbrush is gone and she won't answer my calls or texts or explain why."

"Let me guess," Eva said with a kind of snort. "You cheated on her."

"I didn't. I've never cheated on anyone."

I believed him, actually.

"You must have done something," Eva said. "Told her a dress made her look fat? Called her a bitch? Forgot her birthday?"

He shook his head. "None of the above."

"What's so amazing about her, anyway?" Sara asked.

"To be honest, I didn't realize she *was* so amazing until she broke up with me. She was a bit rough around the edges, so I tried to introduce her to a more cultured life. Such as reading better books. You should have seen the trash she spent good money on. I reminded her she could get great free books from the library, and she acted like I was judging her."

"Duncan, you kind of were," Sara said.

Not kind of, even.

"And I might have suggested she go back to school instead of 'figuring herself out,'" he added. "She's going to figure herself out from tending bar? Come on."

"Yet because she left you, you suddenly don't care about any of that?" Eva asked with another snort.

He sighed and took another sip of his wine. "Sometimes you just don't realize what you had until it's gone. Clichéd, but oh, so true."

"Let me guess," Eva said. "She's hot."

"Well, she is beautiful." He pulled his phone out of his pocket and showed us a photo.

She was beautiful. A little edgier looking than I'd expect from Duncan Ridley, librarian. She had very straight brown hair and there was a little tattoo peeking out from the bottom of her cropped T-shirt.

"So she dumped you because you were trying to change her?" Sara asked.

He shook his head. "She always told me she appreciated all the stuff I was introducing her to. But then she just up and dumped me. No reason given. She just kept saying it was her, not me."

Something told me it *was* him.

"How do you get someone back when you don't know what you did wrong?" he asked. "I keep calling and texting, asking what I did, if she met someone else, and she just won't respond. She sent one text that said *It's over, sorry.* That's it."

"She sounds cold," Eva said. "No offense. Cold *and* dumb."

Duncan glanced at the photo on his phone, his expression truly sad. He put the phone back in his pocket. "She's not, though—either. That's why it doesn't make sense."

"You could go see her," Sara said. "Insist she talk to you. You can't just disappear on someone. Not allowed. She owes you an explanation."

"I've tried that. She doesn't open the door. Pretends she's not there."

"You could write her a letter," Sara said. "On paper."

I glanced at the time. We had to get back to cooking if everything was going to be ready in time to give us a chance to scarf it down.

"That's not a bad idea," Duncan said.

Sara beamed at him. "Just call me the relationship guru. No experience required."

This time Eva snorted extra loud.

"You don't need experience at relationships to be compassionate and smart," Duncan said.

There was no arguing with that, so we got back to the ratatouille, slicing peppers, onions, and zucchini, ripping parsley and basil. Despite the endless talking and over-sharing, if you asked me, we managed to create an amazing sauce that was simmering on the stove while we began sautéing the vegetables. While the ratatouille cooked, we worked on a salad.

As Sara set the table, I drifted over to the living room window and stared at the dead steer sign. Zach was probably in bed with the blonde or kissing some other idiot who'd fallen for his "tell me your life story" crap. Had the girlfriend not practically broken his doorbell, Zach and I just might have ended our little cooking lesson in his bed. I'd think we were starting something, and he'd just be screwing another woman, no big whoop.

"You know, the more I think about this relationship BS," Eva mused, stirring the vinaigrette, "the more I realize I'm totally right. Now I know what I've been doing wrong on Love dot com. I'm clicking on profiles of men whom I'm attracted to. I should click on the ones I'm not attracted to."

"That *is* giving up," Sara said. "You can't do that."

"I'm thirty-four and about to be divorced," Eva said. "I want a family. Two kids. Maybe four. I don't have time to get my heart smashed. I need to find a good guy."

"Wait—four kids?" Sara repeated. "You're kidding, right?"

"Okay, one," Eva said. "But I want the whole fucking thing. A husband. A kid. Family game night. PTA. I thought

I was heading there, and it all came crashing down on my head."

"You know what I think?" I asked, coming back to the kitchen and placing the salad bowl on the table. "You can only do what feels right at the time. Anything else is bullshit."

"To no bullshit," Duncan said, holding up his glass.

We clinked and sat down to warm ratatouille. I was about to take a bite when the buzzer on the intercom rang.

"Yeah?" I gave up the business-name mouthful.

"Flowers. Delivery for Clementine Cooper."

"Oooh, one kiss and flowers," Sara said. "Score one for the cute vegan chef. The guy has class."

I opened the door and a man jogged up with a huge, wrapped bouquet and a small package wrapped in white paper with a red bow. "Sign here."

I signed and took the bouquet and package inside.

Sara and Eva crowded around me. "Open the flowers first," Sara said.

I unwrapped two dozen red roses in a vase, baby's breath all around. Beautiful.

"Whoa. You definitely have to give the dude a second chance, Clem," Duncan said.

"Looks like I do," I said, pulling the little envelope from its clip and tearing it open to read the card.

Clementine, my life is complicated right now, but
I'm not sorry about the kiss. Sometimes

being confused is what makes you figure out
what you really want. Truce? Better yet—
another chance?

—*Zach*

Crap. That was unexpected.

"It's from Zach, not Alexander," I told them.

Sara grabbed the card and read it aloud. So much for privacy. "Holy shit, Clem."

"Now she has two hot guys after her?" Eva asked with a frown.

"What's in the package?" Sara asked, poking at the bow.

I tore it open. A block of extra-firm tofu.

"That's romantic," Eva said with her now-trademark snort. "Not."

"For a guy like Zach Jeffries, it probably is," Duncan pointed out.

"Totally," Sara agreed.

It was for me, too, but I wasn't going to tell them that.

"So who's the better kisser?" Eva asked. "The meat-eating millionaire or the do-good, plant-based Brit?"

"One of the best pieces of advice I ever got was never to kiss and tell," I evaded, taking the card back from Sara and reading it again.

Okay, Jeffries. Fine. Truce.

I wasn't sure about "another chance" though.

After midnight, when I was finally in bed, I texted Zach a thank-you for the flowers and tofu—and a *Truce accepted, conditionally.*

In minutes he texted back. *Can we schedule a do-over? I owe you an explanation. Please? P.S. The blackened stir-fry was so good I ate it all, so you'll just need to make the mushroom burger. Thursday evening?*

I waited an hour. Then texted *See you at seven.*

Immediately, he texted back *Good.*

Chapter 7

Once again, in my chef's jacket and white skinny jeans, I rang Zach's doorbell at exactly seven o'clock. And once again, the sight of him when he opened the door had me speechless. The combination of his tanned face; those intense blue eyes; strong, straight nose; the high cheekbones, that damned cleft, and his thick, silky dark hair that looked like he'd just run a hand through it was male perfection. Throw in the dark gray T-shirt, jeans, and the adorable beagle at his knee, and, yeah, he had his truce. With conditions.

"I wasn't sure you'd agree to a second go," he said, shutting the door behind me. I followed him back into the kitchen where ingredients, pans, and utensils for the portobello mushroom burger were set up on the counter.

"Your assistant does everything for you?" I asked.

"Everything I don't need to do myself, yeah."

"Must be nice," I said, getting busy with onions and garlic.

"It *is*."

Entitled rich jerk.

"Can I help?" he asked. "I do help, even when I don't have to," he added, shooting me a smile.

I shot him back an I'll-be-the-judge-of-that look and put him on slicing onions and the avocado. When he slid them into the sauté pan that was crackling with oil, his shoulder and hip brushed lightly against mine. I didn't move, and neither did he.

"Stir gently, right?" he asked, glancing at the recipe.

"Right."

As I was making a thick paste of avocado and garlic as a condiment, I was aware of him cleaning up around me. Aware of him, period.

Forget the explanation, I told myself, slathering the warm brioche buns—which I'd made myself a few hours ago—with the avocado paste. It doesn't matter. You can't go there with him.

Especially since anything he said the other day was canceled out by the way he'd dismissed me.

"So I'd really like to explain about the other night," he said.

I turned to face him. "Zach, no need, okay? You've clearly got a girlfriend. I clearly am a vegan. Two good reasons why there shouldn't be a second kiss. So let me just audition the best not-meat burger you will ever eat, and we'll exist in harmony on Montana and 14th."

He poured us glasses of one of my favorite organic white wines. He'd clearly done a bit of homework. "To harmony."

I took the glass and clinked his.

"But I'd still like to explain. Tabitha—the woman you met Monday night. She's actually an ex-girlfriend. We were dating for a few months, and it wasn't working out, so I ended it, but she took it hard." He sipped the wine. "She's been kind of . . . fragile about it, so I didn't just want to show her the door or make her feel like I'm already seeing someone new. I'm sorry for how I handled things. So the kiss stands."

"Except you said 'an' ex. Which makes me think there are lots of women in your life."

"Can I get nothing past you?" he asked with his slickest smile yet.

"Just be straight with me. You've got a few girlfriends, I assume."

"I date," he said. "If I meet someone who makes me want to commit, I'll commit."

I went back to the brioche buns. I was not getting involved with this guy. He was probably sleeping with half the models and wannabe actresses in Santa Monica. *Cook and leave, Clem.*

"I made you something." He opened the refrigerator and pulled out a covered dish, then got a bag of tortilla chips from the cabinet. "My homemade guacamole. When I was a kid, I ate guacamole like it was chocolate."

"Me, too. I made my own guac when I was five. It sounds

crazy, but I knew even that young I wanted to be a chef."
While my sister was having her dolls interrogate each other
as a sign of her future profession, I was in the kitchen with
my dad, kneading pasta dough, learning about herbs, soaking
beans.

"You're lucky you figured that out so young. I never really
knew what I wanted to be."

"Rich?"

He laughed. "Maybe, actually. My grandparents started
with nothing and were self-made. They took acres of land in
the middle of nowhere, started with maybe ten heads of cattle,
some pigs. They turned the Silver Creek Ranch into a major
operation. How they did it, what it took—that's what interested me. Not necessarily the getting rich part, but how you go
from nothing to something."

I realized I was staring at him and turned around to top the
burgers with the buns. He walked over to me, a guacamole-
laden chip in his hand, which he held up to my mouth. He
kept his eyes on me as I parted my lips for the chip.

Damn. It was delicious.

Ruin this, I sent to him telepathically. *There's no way I'm
falling for you. I can't fall for you.*

He would definitely ruin it. He had both times we'd gotten together. In my apartment when *Baby* called in the first
place. And here, last time, when she shook her ass up the
stairs. *Where are you when I need you, Tabitha? Barge in now.
Save me.*

"What do you think?" he asked.

I think I want you to kiss me again. Everywhere.

"It's really good. Really, really good, Zach."

He smiled and touched his finger to my lip. "Crumb." As he was about to kiss me, my phone started ringing. No. Not ringing—chiming.

"Oh, shit," I said, lunging for my bag on the windowsill.

"What?"

Six months ago, I'd been at a club with Sara and Ty and had ignored my ringing phone, especially when I saw it was just Elizabeth, who'd been calling the past few days to make sure I'd bought renter's insurance like I said I would. I'd thought she was just calling to nag. So I hadn't answered. And my father had been lying in a hospital bed, fighting for his life from a cancer-related complication. She'd had to leave Santa Monica without me and race up to Coastal General. I hadn't called back till the morning.

I never wanted to feel that bad again. Never wanted to make Elizabeth feel that alone again. And so when she insisted on setting up a special ringtone to indicate an emergency, I let her.

If my phone was playing that chime, it was Elizabeth calling with bad news about my dad.

I grabbed my phone. "Elizabeth, what's wrong?" I tried to hear what she was saying, but she was crying. "Just tell me where you are, and I'll come right now."

"I'm at Coastal General," she said. "Oh God, I drove up to Mom and Dad's to help set up for the party, and we were just in the living room having tea and cake and laughing about something one of the inept interns did, and then Dad just slumped over. Clem, just get here as soon as you can."

My heart stopped. "Elizabeth, tell me now. Is he *okay*?"

I heard her suck in a breath. "They don't know."

I closed my eyes. "Okay, I'm coming. I'm leaving right now." I shoved the phone in my bag and turned to Zach, who was staring at me. "It's my dad. I have to go. Oh my God. My dad's back in the hospital. I have to go."

"I'll drive you," he said, shutting off the burner and taking my hand and heading toward the door.

"He's at Coastal General in Grovesburg. That's three hours from here."

He nodded. "So we'll take the car instead of the Harley."

I stared at him. "You're going to drive me *three* hours to the hospital?"

"Yeah, I am. So get moving."

Half numb and half scared I followed him, barely remembering to buckle the seat belt in the soft leather seat of his black Mercedes. I stared out the window and didn't say a word until we got to Route 5 and set on a long stretch of the trip.

"Please let him be okay," I said, my eyes closed.

He put his hand on my shoulder for a moment. "Clementine, if it helps, my father had a massive heart attack last year. When I got the call, no one knew if he'd make it. But he pulled through. He's fine now. You can't focus on the what-ifs."

"But he has cancer. He's so weak. He can't withstand whatever happened—last time, some infection almost killed him."

"You can't think worst-case for these three hours, Clem, or it'll tear you apart. Right now, tell me about Dad. Tell me what makes him strong."

"He is strong. If it wasn't for the fucking cancer eating away at his organs, he'd be in the fields at the farm with his dogs beside him, checking on the crops or harvesting or giving an elementary school class a field-trip tour. He loves kids."

"He sounds like a great person."

"He is," I said, my stomach churning. I turned to look out the window, and Zach seemed to sense that I needed some quiet time and privacy. He put on some bluesy jazz. I listened to the music and focused on the passing scenery.

Just after ten thirty Zach pulled up to the hospital's emergency room and told me to go, that he'd find me. I took his hand, said a fast "Thank you," and then ran.

Pneumonia. My dad would be fine. For now, anyway. The thousand-pound weights lifted off each shoulder as my mom said he might have to stay for a few days but would be all right. I kissed my dad's cheek, hugged my mother, who sat down at his bedside, then I quietly left the room to see if Zach had come up yet.

Down the hall, Elizabeth was waiting for the elevator for a Starbucks herbal tea run when the doors pinged open. Zach stepped out; Elizabeth went in. I'd make the introductions later.

"Any word?" he asked.

"He's going to be all right—for now."

He squeezed my hand. "Glad to hear that."

"My sister went on a tea run to Starbucks. My mom's expecting the docs back with my father's test results in the next half hour or so. Looks like a waiting area over there," I said, gesturing across the hall.

Zach sat beside me in the otherwise empty waiting room. He didn't touch the stack of magazines scattered on the table. He didn't pull out his iPhone and check his messages. He just sat there, next to me. "Zach, thanks for being here. For bringing me. I couldn't even think straight when my sister first called me. I owe you."

"You don't owe me anything."

"Except maybe to admit I might have been a *little* wrong about you," I said.

He smiled and slung an arm around my shoulder. "Oh, wait, you do owe me that mushroom burger. Someone clearly doesn't want me to ever try it, though."

I laughed—and I didn't think I was capable. "Who knows what'll happen the next time I attempt to audition it for you?"

He smiled and took my hand, holding it between us on the armrest of his chair.

———

At midnight, Zach and I were in the bar of the Mayfair Hotel, which was right across the street from the hospital. When he'd heard that my dad would need to stay the weekend, Zach had booked three hotel rooms for my mother, sister, and me through Sunday—and paid for them in advance, which we were stunned to discover when we'd checked in.

"You two must be serious," my mother had said with a prompting smile at the registration desk.

"He's sort of a client, actually. Maybe the tiniest bit more. We'll see. He's dating all of L.A."

"Well, all I know is that he's incredibly generous. He drove you here and he took care of your family's hotel arrangements with your dad in the hospital?"

"He seems like a nice guy, but don't have expectations," Elizabeth said as she'd pocketed her room key.

"He eats meat anyway," I mumbled.

"So do I. And we get along fine."

"Yeah, but I have to get along with you."

Elizabeth yanked the ends of my hair, then she and Mom headed to the elevator, both looking as exhausted as I'm sure I did. I went to find Zach; he was waiting for me at a little round table by the window in the hotel bar. He looked so damned gorgeous under the low lights, a half-moon in the high window above his head. We had a glass of wine and made small talk, mostly, about hospitals, about this part of California, about how you just never knew what life would throw at you.

"So now I owe you even more," I said. His generosity had almost knocked me on my ass. There was a lot more to Zach

Jeffries than I ever expected. Which, to be honest, made me a little nervous. It meant I couldn't pigeonhole him. Couldn't know what to expect.

"Nope, not a thing."

"I wouldn't have pegged you for such a nice guy, Jeffries."

"Always keep 'em guessing. That's my motto." He glanced at his watch. "It's almost one. You'd better get some rest. Your sister will drive you back to Santa Monica on Sunday?"

I nodded.

"I'll walk you up to your room."

"You don't have to."

He put some bills on the bar and led the way to the elevators anyway. In that tiny space he was so close, and I was so surprised by him, confused by him, that I wanted to turn and grab him, just feel his arms around me. But then the elevator pinged open.

He slid the room key in the slot and opened the door, but didn't step inside. "Get a good night's rest."

Don't invite him in. Don't invite him in. Don't invite him in.

"You could come in for a bit, if you want," I said.

"I want, Clementine. But for a few reasons, I'd better get back."

Oh. What were those reasons?

"I'm headed to New York tomorrow afternoon for business," he said. "I won't be back till next Thursday, maybe Friday. I'll give you a call."

Why did I feel so dismissed all of a sudden? Like I made

too much of all this and now he'd morphed back into Zach Jeffries, zillionaire meat eater with multiple girlfriends.

But then he very slowly, gently, backed me against the wall and kissed me so hard that my knees buckled. Then he looked at me, touched my face with the palm of his hand, and left.

Chapter 8

"Wait, Zach Jeffries drove you three hours to the hospital?" Eva asked as she sliced the seitan on her cutting board on Tuesday night. For our third class, we were making black bean tortilla soup and seitan fajitas.

Duncan stood at the stove, stirring the black beans that I'd rinsed this afternoon. "And stayed with you in the waiting room?"

"Pleeeeease let me tell them the rest?" Sara asked, taking a sip of her wine.

When my sister dropped me off on Sunday night, I told Sara everything—but made her promise to keep the kiss against the wall of the Mayfair Hotel to herself. Not that it was the equivalent of hot wild sex on the carpet or anything, but still, it was private and I didn't want it blabbed to the class.

Eva gaped at me. "Omigod, you slept together all weekend and now you're pregnant."

"Not even close," I said. *We had just one kick-ass kiss.*

One kiss that I couldn't get out of my mind. On Monday, Zach texted me with *How's your dad? Hope you got home ok. Z.*

I texted back *He's doing fine and so am I. Thanks again for all you did.* I wanted to add something else, a little sappy X for a kiss or something, but I didn't want to be a total moron. I didn't know what he was thinking.

But I did know I was sunk. Because when very nice, everything-in-common cute vegan chef Alexander Orr had called on Monday morning to ask if I'd like to have dinner Saturday night, at his house, I made up an excuse. For Sunday brunch, too.

"Are we just friends, then?" Alexander had asked, kind of wistfully.

I thought of our meh kiss. Then of the way I turned to liquid when Zach just looked at me.

"Is that okay?" I'd asked. "We do have a lot in common, and you're a really cool guy."

"I guess it'll have to be. Plus, you never know, do you?"

"That is so true," I'd said. So true.

I stirred the soup, which smelled amazing.

"Clem said he kissed her so hot and hard that her knees almost buckled," Sara announced.

I rolled my eyes. "Sara, is nothing private?"

"One kiss? Kind of a letdown from my version," Eva said, giving her shoulders a little shimmy. "And what, you're sud-

denly a priss?" Eva asked, turning the peppers over in the
sauté pan. "At least tell us if you're officially seeing each
other now."

I took a sip of wine. "Well, he had to go to New York on
business. He's not coming back till Thursday or Friday. But I'll
give you this piece of information: I kind of miss him."

"Well, I think it's all great," Duncan said. "I mean, you
hated him last week. It gives me hope."

"About your ex?" Sara asked, slicing a red bell pepper.

Duncan sat down with a heavy sigh. "I can't stand how
much I miss her. I just wish she'd talk to me. But she won't.
I tried going to the club where she bartends, and she had the
bouncer make me leave."

I turned off the burner for the soup. "Maybe you need to let
her go, Duncan. She sounds pretty sure."

He looked miserable. "The day before she dumped me she
told me she loved me. Then I come home and all her stuff is
gone and she won't talk to me. I even tried calling her best
friend, and she hung up on me."

"I wonder what went wrong for her," Sara said.

"Me, too. I can't sleep. I can't eat. I can't do anything. And
I'm learning to be a vegan for a woman who won't even talk to
me."

"Maybe we can find out what's up," Sara said. "Clem and
I could go hang out at the bar and start talking about our jerk
exes. She'll chime in. Maybe. Worth a try."

"No way I'm missing this," Eva said. "I mean, who slams
an ex better than me? Let's go tomorrow night. Early enough

so it won't be crowded and we can set up the convo for her to overhear."

Duncan raised an eyebrow and gnawed his lower lip for a second. "Don't let her know you're my friends. She'll have that giant dude throw you out."

"Clem, I think we forgot the tortillas," Eva said, sniffing the air. Something was burning.

"Oh, shit," I said, grabbing my oven mitts to pull out the cracker-like tortillas. "We can warm up some more."

"We're busy saving a man's life here," Sara said. "That's worth a burned tortilla."

The woman who wouldn't be named was named Gwendolyn Paul, hated to be called Gwen, and worked at Ocean 88, a hot little nightclub with a tiny dance floor and a famous square-shaped bar that those semi-lucky to be chosen could shake their stuff on for a minute and get a free fourteen-dollar drink. Sara and I went there once, and the very hot male bartender nodded his chin at Sara and said, "Show your stuff, babe," and she said, "Really?" totally game to get up there and shimmy for her free frozen margarita, and the jerk said, "No, not really." He looked at me and said, "But you can." I told him he was a pig and we left and never went back. My scathing email to the owner went unanswered, too.

That Gwendolyn a) didn't like to be called Gwen and b) worked at Ocean 88 didn't bode well. The woman had to be a total bitch. And not in a good way.

"If that jerkoff is there, I'm leaving," Sara said. "I like Duncan, but I can only take so much."

"If he's there, I'll get him back for you," Eva said, pulling out her compact and lipstick and making her lips even redder. She fluffed her bangs, gave her lips a press, then snapped the compact shut.

"How?" we both asked in unison.

"Oh, trust me. I'm the master at making people pay."

Sara laughed. "You scare me. Make sure I don't get on your bad side."

"Oh, you'll know if you do," she said.

Sara stood to the side of Ocean 88's big window. "Clem, look in and see if he's there. Do you remember what he looks like? Beefy with blond ponytail."

I peered in. At seven o'clock on a Wednesday, the bar wasn't crowded; Ocean 88 didn't serve food, and the dance floor didn't get going till at least nine. One very hot bartender with longish brown hair and a huge wooden cross necklace was filling steins at the tap. Another male bartender who looked like a grown-up Harry Potter, down to the round glasses, was pouring martinis for four middle-aged women. Across the bar, a couple had their tongues all over each other, and luckily, where Gwendolyn was unloading bottles of beer, there were three empty stools.

She looked just like her photo, but sexier. She wore a tiny black tank top and skinny jeans with high-heeled boots. Excellent cleavage, the kind that made you stare and order more drinks, male or female. I wouldn't have thought she'd go for

Duncan. He was somewhat cute, but this chick looked like she only went out with heavy-metal dudes.

"Jerk bartender's not there," I assured Sara, and we headed in, sitting in front of Gwendolyn.

She took our orders, and the second she was back with the drinks, I got the plan rolling.

"I just wish I knew why he broke up with me," I said kind of loudish, tilting my stool to face Sara and Eva. "He just stopped calling. We were together for over a year and he just stops calling?"

"He owes you an explanation, something," Sara agreed. "How will you ever move on if he keeps you in this weird limbo of no closure?"

That was diabolically good.

Eva took a sip of her drink. "You should be kissing the floor with gratitude that he did dump you. Anyone who'd just disappear on a relationship the way he did, no explanation, no nothing, has mental problems. He's probably bipolar."

"Or maybe he's just confused," Gwendolyn said as she placed Sara's appletini in front of her.

Score.

"Confused?" I repeated. "Why would he be confused? I'm the one who doesn't know what I did wrong or where we went wrong."

Gwendolyn put a bowl of taro chips and salsa in front of us, which Eva immediately hit up. "Well, maybe an old girlfriend came back into his life and he fell in love with that person all over again."

Oh. Sorry, Duncan. That was hard to compete with.

"Sounds like you've been there," Sara said to Gwendolyn.

Gwendolyn took a swig of Pellegrino. "I was madly in love with this guy named John. Wanted to marry him—the works. But he dumped me for someone else. So I met this guy named Duncan, and though he wasn't exactly right for me, I just fell into it, you know? And stayed for almost a year. But then John came back a couple of week ago, begging for forgiveness and wanting a second chance, and I couldn't resist."

"What wasn't right with you and Duncan?" I asked. "Maybe it'll help me understand."

"Well, he'd have to change practically half of everything he is for me to be happy with him," she said. "And that's not fair. I'm a vegan. He's not. I like to go out. He doesn't. I can't stand his conservative family. He can—and wanted to hang out with them a little too often. He thinks I should go back to school. I don't. He was always trying to change me. He's who he is, right? And he's fine. But so am I, you know?"

"Yeah, you are," Eva said, stuffing her mouth with another chip. "What an ass this Duncan sounds like. Wanting you to change for him?"

Sara and I shot Eva a "remember whose side we're on" glare.

"Well, to be fair," Gwendolyn said, "I wanted him to change just as much. Go vegan. Blow off his annoying family. Lose the plaid bowling shirts. Lay off me."

"It's too bad neither of you accepted the other," Sara said. "But I guess that's how you figure out who's right for you and who's wrong for you. When it gets to the point where it just doesn't work, you know it."

Gwendolyn raised her glass at Sara. "Exactly."

"But it took you a year to figure that out," I said, now shooting Sara a "Stop agreeing with her!" look. "So you must have been really into Duncan, right?"

"Look, I know you want your boyfriend to come back," Gwendolyn said. "But sometimes, two people are just too different. And whatever makes them click just isn't enough."

Who could argue with that?

I wanted to, though. I wanted that *whatever* that made Zach and me click to be enough to make a relationship possible. I was incredibly hot for him, but it was much more than that. There was real chemistry between us. There was growing up on farms—even if his family "farm" was a zillion-dollar ranch empire. There was talking to goats and chickens when we were kids. There was ambition. Determination. The world of cooking, albeit different ends of the spectrum. There was a three-hour drive to get to my dad in the hospital. Generosity and kindness.

So yeah, we were different. But there was something very real between us.

"Just sounds to me like this Duncan really loves you," I said.

"I know, but it was hard enough for me to tell him it was over. Then he wouldn't stop calling and texting and showing up here, and so I started getting pissed and ignored him."

"Pathetic," Eva said. "Kinda like I was when I kept calling and texting my soon-to-be-ex-husband when he dumped me for some bimbo."

"Any chance of you two getting back together?" Sara asked Gwendolyn. "I'm just asking because it might give her"—she patted me on the shoulder—"some hope."

Gwendolyn shrugged. "I don't know. I doubt it. I'm seeing where things are going with John. Duncan and I are just too different."

"But what if it's not over for *him*?" Sara asked. "What if he's ready to stand outside your window like that old movie with John Cusack and the boom box over his head? Can't you at least put him out of his misery? Tell him the truth about your ex."

"I guess I should," Gwendolyn said.

At least we accomplished that much. "Maybe when you see Duncan again, you'll realize you do love him," I said.

Gwendolyn took a sip of her water. "I haven't really missed him, though."

Oh.

"Gwen, take over for me for ten?" another bartender said.

"Gwen*dolyn*" she shot at him. She turned back to us. "Oh, and that first round's on me. Talking to you guys helped me clear up some stuff I wasn't even too sure about. I think it's pretty clear that Duncan and I are wrong for each other." She headed to the other side of the bar.

"Oh shit, now we have to tell Duncan we helped her realize she doesn't want to be with him," Sara whispered.

Damn. We didn't bother finishing our drinks. Eva wanted to flirt with the too-young-for-her guy doing shots on the other side of the bar, but I reminded her that he was good-looking, which went against her new plan.

"Good point," she said as we headed around the bar.

I was about to pull open the door when I froze.

Zach. Walking outside, his arm around a very attractive red-haired woman in thigh-high boots.

Out of town till Thursday or Friday. Right.

Well, shit.

———————

I flung open Ocean 88's door to confront Zach, but three tipsy blondes in identical outfits (minidresses and stilettos) walked in, the last one checking her phone in the doorway. I took a step back, mentally and physically. "I think these chicks just saved me from making a total ass of myself."

"No, I would have grabbed you before you made it out the door," Sara said as we headed in the opposite direction Zach and the redhead had gone. "What were you going to say to him? 'Oh, so you're *away* on business, are you? And who's this?'"

"Shit, shit, shit," I said. "He *told* me he was seeing other people. And he just made it crystal clear. I have to forget he exists."

Sara looked at me like I was nuts. "Or you could just go with the flow, Clem. You're seeing Alexander. Sort of."

"Not really. I must have been insane," I said. "Me and a guy who's opening a steakhouse. Who puts dead deer on his signs. Who *lives* for steak. I can't believe I thought something was actually happening between us."

"Maybe because he took a six-hour drive round-trip to a hospital so you could get to your dad right away?" Sara said.

"And then paid for your family's hotel rooms? And then texted to ask if your dad was okay?"

Yeah, no kidding. "Don't remind me."

"He's been acting like your boyfriend, Clem," Sara said. "I totally get why you're upset. But you can't confront him for doing what he *said* he's doing."

"I think she should chase the fucker down and karate chop him in the balls," Eva said, turning around to peer down Ocean Avenue. "If you run, you can probably find him, Clem. Even in those crazy sandals. Wail him good for me."

"Wow, remind me that I really don't ever want to piss you off," Sara said to Eva. "Also, Clem, how many times have you been out walking with Ty and he puts his arm around you because you just said something funny. Or because you got fired. Maybe Zach is madly in love with you and that chick is just a bud. You never know."

Eva rolled her eyes. "Sara, you're sweet. Really. So sweet I might puke. But give me a fucking break."

"I'm just saying that chasing the guy down and confronting him over nothing isn't a good idea," Sara said. "And trust me, when *I'm* the voice of reason, you know you should listen. It doesn't happen often."

"But—" I started to say.

But shit. Sara was right. In the space of a minute, I'd gone from kind of stupidly crushed to being pissed at myself for being stupid again. The guy was a player. Period. A player with some redeeming qualities, but a player.

We walked down Ocean Avenue for a while, but when the

zillionth hand-in-hand couple passed us, annoying us with their coupledom, Sara upped her chin at Freddy's, a favorite little jazz bar. I shrugged and we went inside. The place was half-crowded. We sat at a round table, and Sara ordered us three dirty martinis.

I stared at the edamame in the silver bowl on the table. Dammit. What was this? How could I be so disappointed over a guy I was an idiot for liking in the first place?

"I'm gonna give it to you straight, Clem," Eva said, sipping her drink. She nabbed the waitress and ordered tapas. "Zach Jeffries is a zillionaire who makes *L.A. Magazine*'s most eligible bachelors list every year. He can have any woman he wants. You're a challenge, so he's interested. But if you're expecting him to be your boyfriend—an exclusive boyfriend—you're a dumbass."

"Comforting, Eva," Sara said.

"No, honest," I said. "Necessary honesty. I need to hear this." And I need to back the hell off of expecting anything from Zach.

"Damn," Sara said. "I like Zach."

Yeah, me, too.

Chapter 9

The next morning, while I was making banana/chocolate-chip waffles and thinking of ways to exorcise Zach Jeffries from my mind, like imagining him gnawing on bloody steak, my phone pinged with a text from him.

Back in SM. Dinner Saturday night? I'll cook. (Something you'll actually eat, too.) Z

Damn. I put down the phone and stirred the batter so hard a glob landed on the wall. Now he wasn't gnawing anything. Beagle at his knee, he was standing in his kitchen, handing me his homemade guacamole. Looking like Zach, absolutely gorgeous.

Yeah. Hold up. *Back in Santa Monica:* no kidding.

My phone pinged with another text. Don't look, I told myself, popping a chocolate chip into my mouth. Do not look.

I looked.

I have news, too. Z

Let's see. You have a new love interest? A redhead. You're getting married after a whirlwind weekend love affair. Or maybe this: I'm as bad for you as you thought I was. Like corn syrup.

"Mmm," Sara said as she came into the kitchen with her hair in some crazy bun on top of her head. "The smell of those waffles woke me up. Hope you made me some."

I slid two on a plate and handed it to her, and we sat down at the table. I wrapped my hands around my mug of spiced green tea and told her about Zach's texts. "He has news, he says."

"He's really an alien?"

"That's not news," I said, smiling for the first time since last night.

"Fuck. Fuckety fuckety fuck. Okay. Moving on. He's who I thought, nothing more, nothing less. Moving. On."

Sara made her "Yeah, I see that" face at me. "Sorry, Clem."

She got my mind off Zach by telling me she was damned sure she'd get another callback for the Attractive Friend commercial today. Hell, yeah, she would. Sara was always incredibly awesome, but ever since she became a Skinny Bitch, she'd begun developing a kind of confidence that went beyond talk—it was *real*. She ate her last bite of waffles then went into her room to practice making "friend smiles" in the mirror for the callback. And the more I sat there, looking through the living room window at that dead deer sign, I kept thinking about Zach, walking past Ocean 88 with that woman. Over and over and over. The happy expression on his face. The way his arm was around her shoulder.

I needed to get the hell out of the apartment, go breathe some air, take a long stomp, and maybe do some hot yoga on the way back. I grabbed my bag and clomped downstairs, and because I couldn't think straight, I walked left instead of right, the huge dead deer sign staring me in the face.

The more I stared up at that gross sign, the more I imagined Zach eating that bloody steak. Stealing my perfect dream location for Clementine's No Crap Café. Messing with my up-until-then very well-guarded piece of crap heart. Ben had managed to crush me, and I wasn't walking eyes wide open into another episode of "Clementine Gets Smashed."

He took my perfect location—so it was time to find another. Another place to keep the dream going, anyway. I walked up Montana, looking in the storefronts. A bakery. A coffee lounge. More yoga. Used books. The dancing Laundromat that blasted music and had a dance floor, seriously, between the washers' and dryers' sections. Every kind of restaurant—Indian, bar and grill, Mexican, Italian, Thai. Frozen yogurt. Between Flo's Fro Yo and a tae kwon do dojo was an empty spot with a sign—FOR LEASE. Former fifteen-table restaurant. Small outdoor dining area in back. I pressed my face against the glass and peered in. Fugly now, but with paint, Ty's interior design skills, Sara's elbow grease, and my ideas, this would be perfect for Clementine's No Crap Café.

I want this more than I'll ever want you, Jeffries, I said to myself.

Although if I were really honest, they had been kind of neck and neck for a while there.

I peered in again, mentally decorating the place. The walls, the floor, the rugs, the kind of tables. The waitstaff's uniforms. The flowers for the garden dining area.

Clementine's No-Crap Café, you are mine.

The sound of drills and banging woke me up at the crack of hell the next morning. Barely eight o'clock. I trudged to the window and shoved aside the gauzy curtains. Two huge guys in hard hats came out of The Silver Steer and lit up cancer sticks and started jabbering. I would have yelled down at them to shut it, but the drilling started up again from inside the restaurant. Assholes. I closed the window and crawled back under the covers, but my phone rang a second later.

My sister. She was on her way to her second meeting of the day, which sounded horrid, but wanted me to know she'd just spoken to our parents and that my dad was getting stronger every day. Also, my brother, Kale, and his longtime girlfriend, also a marine biologist, were "taking a break" and he was miserable, and I should give him a call and send him my family-famed peanut butter chocolate chip cookies to cheer him up. She asked way too many questions about how my Skinny Bitch business was going, and I was barely awake, so I said Sara was calling me and tried to fall back asleep. But the phone rang two minutes later. No one wanted me to sleep.

Not my sister again. This time: the sexy British accent of Alexander Orr.

"Hey," I said. "You didn't even wake me up."

"Good, because I have a huge favor to ask and wouldn't want you already pissed enough at me to tell me to sod off."

I turned over onto my stomach, trying to imagine Alexander Orr naked and eating strawberries. Or red grapes. I could imagine that. I wondered what he was like in bed. Which made me wonder what Zach would be like in bed. Shit. "What kind of favor?"

"As I said, huge and a pain in the arse. My awesome cousin Sabine is getting married tonight—she's eloping here, getting married at the pier, and I'm hosting the party at my place. The wedding cupcakes are my gift, but I have no time to make them myself without serious help, and I need forty-five *Dr. Who* cupcakes—you know that sci-fi TV show about the time-traveling alien bloke? The cupcakes have to be dairy-free and gluten-free. And I need them by six o'clock. Tell me you bake."

"Dr. Who cupcakes. And high-maintenance Dr. Who cupcakes at that. Seriously?"

"Seriously. Five different designs. I'd do it myself, but I have a staff meeting at Fresh this morning, and then I'm attending a science fair thing at Jesse's school, and then we're doing wedding party pictures before the ceremony at 4:30. I'm bloody screwed. And the Dr. Who designs are pretty elaborate."

"Well, you're in luck. Because not only am I a kick-ass baker, but I'm free today. I'm all yours."

He was quiet for a moment, and I thought he might say,

Well, not really or *I wish,* but he said, "Uh, the thing is, I kind of can't pay you. In money, anyway."

"What time?"

"Seriously? Clem, you're brilliant. My only time to work on them is between one and three, so could we make it at one?"

"I'll be there," I told him. Dr. Who cupcakes. I'd have to make an extra one for Sara who loved that show. And Seamus, too. And Kale. Dr. Who cupcakes would definitely cheer him up.

Wedding cupcakes. Theme wedding cupcakes, no less. Even though the idea of love and happily ever after made me want to punch something at the moment.

———————

On my way to Alexander's, Zach called and I let it go to voice mail. That was willpower. Part of me wanted to answer and tell him I saw him with that woman on Wednesday night—when he was supposedly still out of town. When he'd kissed the hell out of me in a hotel hallway and made me think there was something between us. Again.

But how could I without sounding like an idiot? So what if he came back early? So what if he was walking down the street with his arm around some model? Avoidance was the answer.

By the time I arrived at Alexander's house, Zach had left another text message.

Okay, now I'm worried. Is your dad ok? Let me know. Z

Shit. Shit, shit, shit. He had to go there.

I heard Alexander's dogs, Lizzie and Brit, barking as I started up the walk. I texted back *Everything's fine. Just busy. C*

I was busy. And good thing, too. Alexander came out, the dogs jumping at my legs, and I kneeled down to pet them both. Alexander looked great, as always, fresh-scrubbed and kind of hot at the same time. Maybe that blah kiss didn't mean that much. Maybe there was a much hotter kiss just waiting for us to get to know each other better or something. Elmer Fudd and all that. I'd keep an open mind like my sister was always telling me to.

I loved his little house. And the kitchen was the biggest room. It was a chef's kitchen: six-burner Viking stove, counter space galore. Racks hanging with great cookware. Score even more points for Alexander. My dream kitchen.

"So, I've got everything set out and have printouts of what Sabine wants." He pointed at a stack of paper. I took a look— lots of blue icing and hard, flat embossed faces and numbers. As Alexander started pulling things out of the fridge, including a beer for each of us, and cupboards, he told me all about the bride, his thirty-year-old cousin Sabine who'd finally said yes to her constantly proposing on-again/off-again boyfriend of three years, the long-suffering Wills.

"Hmm, maybe it took her so long for a reason," I said. "Does she really want to marry this guy?"

"Cynical, Miss C," Alexander said, handing me a large silver mixing bowl. "Sometimes shit happens. Or people need time to know. Or a lot of other stuff."

"Maybe," I said. "But I always thought you just know. Pretty much right away."

"You can hardly know someone right away, though," he said, adding the Earth Balance shortening sticks and sugar to his own bowl and creaming them together. "You can know if you fancy them; if there's something there. But you can't know you want to marry them."

I knew I wanted to marry Ben Frasier the second I met him. Where was he now? Marrying someone else. So maybe Alexander was on to something. Like an actual mature outlook.

"So you think your cousin's marriage is safe from the fifty percent divorce rate?" I asked, combining the vanilla and oil and adding it to the mixture.

"I hope so. She took her time and made sure he's the one. He let her take that time. So I think it's gonna work. They love each other; they're great together. They have everything in common. Like these Dr. Who cupcakes, for one. And they're both in love with America and California, much to my aunt's dismay. They're planning to move here."

I raised my beer. "To good love, then."

He raised his back. "So I guess you're seeing someone?" he asked as he lined five muffin pans with cupcake liners.

"Why do you say that?"

"Because you didn't give me much of a chance. One great sort-of date and that was that."

The that-was-that part was more about the uninspiring kiss, but I couldn't tell him that. "Actually, I have been sort of seeing someone. Someone completely wrong for me. I suck at dating."

"More like dating sucks. Well, sometimes. The part where you don't get the girl."

I smiled. "I'd drive you nuts."

He laughed. "Maybe."

As he spooned the batter—which a fingertip swipe of my spoon indicated was delicious—into the liners, I found myself checking him out. Tall, lanky, but muscular. Nice shoulders. Cool T-shirt. Very clear, very kind, dark brown eyes. He brought ill grandmothers soup. Baked for cousins' weddings. Mentored tweens. Had this amazing chef's kitchen.

Maybe I *should* give Alexander Orr that second chance. Give the tubas a chance to clank. Maybe a real relationship wasn't about instant lust and hot sex and an inability to stop thinking about the person. Maybe it was about slow and steady and all that boring stuff. Really knowing someone. A wedding with Dr. Who cupcakes as your wedding cake.

"So who was your last girlfriend?" I asked, wanting to know his history.

He mock shot himself in the heart and staggered backward. "A lunatic called Maeve. You know that crap Rain pulled with the butter in your ravioli? Well, the night Maeve and I broke up, she pureed a slice of ham into the vodka smoothie she talked me into having while we were having a three-hour break-up talk."

"You tasted it or she told you?"

"She told me as I was leaving with my sack of the stuff I gathered from her place—toothbrush, jacket, couple of books. She was like, 'You suck, and by the way, I pureed a slice of day-old ham into your fucking drink. Have a nice life.' Then she slammed the door in my face."

"Mature," I said.

"I threw up all over her welcome mat—unintentionally—so I sort of got her back."

"Ha. So no date for your cousin's wedding, huh?"

"Actually, I'm taking a new friend."

A new friend. Was that Britspeak for Woman I've Just Started Dating? The tiniest wham of jealousy hit me in the stomach, which made no sense. Maybe I just liked that he liked me since I needed the ego boost these days.

Before I could ask about her, voices came from the hall. In seconds, there were lots of people in the kitchen commenting on the delicious smells. I figured the woman in the many-tiered floaty white strapless dress was the bride-to-be. She looked like an angel, seriously. Big blue eyes. Tiny nose. Pink bow lips. Heart-shaped face. And perfect, light, frothy blond hair down her back.

"Oh my fucking God," she shrieked, eyeing the Dr. Who cupcake photos. "The cupcakes are going to look amazing!"

She jumped into Alexander's arms, completely not caring that his apron wasn't exactly pristine. I liked this chick. Alexander made the introductions, and she squeezed me into a hug, too, and announced that I saved her reception.

While the wedding party—there were at least twenty of them—had beers in the living room and wrestled with the dogs, again despite their fancy duds, Alexander said he had to go get changed. And I . . . kind of missed him.

I had nothing to do for the next twenty minutes, either. Which made thinking about Alexander a little too easy. Upstairs changing. Leaving. Coming back home after the ceremony.

Jesus. So now I wanted Alexander? What the hell?

You're screwed in the head, I told myself. Upset about Zach. And Alexander's a very cool guy. Once the cupcakes were finally done, I'd be forced to painstakingly focus on perfect number 7s and telephone booths and rectangular faces for forty-five cupcakes, and I wouldn't be able to think of anything else.

Alexander appeared five minutes later in something of a tux, but with a white T-shirt instead of a button-down and Chucks instead of shiny black shoes. He looked like all the other guys in the wedding party. California-weekday-wedding-at-the-pier style.

He smiled at me, and I told him he cleaned up well, and then after sheepishly asking if I'd mind letting his dogs out in the yard in about a half hour, he was gone. The house went from wildly noisy with happily barking dogs to dead quiet.

I peered in the oven. Ten minutes left to bake and another thirty minutes to cool before I could even get started on my Dr. Who skills.

I let the dogs out in the yard, then took myself on a tour of his house. I wanted to see his bedroom. I found it upstairs: smallish, with a bed dominating the room, made but mussed, and a bedside table with an oversized hardcover of *The Heirloom Tomato*. This made me laugh, because I actually had a book called *The History of Garlic,* which was a gift from my dad on my last birthday. Alexander also had a J. D. Salinger novel, a crazy-looking lamp, and a few photos in frames—one of him with five other people, four guys and one woman who looked remarkably like him. Another of him in a kayak, and one of him and Jesse, the kid he was Little Brothering. They were both on skateboards, and Jesse's helmet was covered in different stickers.

I picked up the picture of Alexander smiling in the kayak. He was damned cute.

I put it back on the table and sat down on his bed and tried to imagine sex with Alexander Orr.

I sort of could. He was good-looking, had that great, lanky body. Good guy hair. And that accent kind of swirled up on you, especially when you realized he was as great a guy as you thought, that some people didn't go from very cool to asshole in a split second. Like other people.

Which brought me back to Zach. Who I had feelings for in a way that I just didn't for Alexander, no matter how hard I tried.

The oven dinged. I went downstairs and took out the cupcakes to cool, then went out into the yard to hang out with the dogs; Lizzie was after me to throw her rubber bone for fetch.

Back inside, I spent the next hour and a half decorating the cupcakes. I screwed up one face and had to use a reserve cupcake—every baker always makes extras for just these fuck-up moments—but my designs looked damned close to the photos in the printout. I had the cupcakes all set on the heart-shaped triple-tiered cupcake holder when the door burst open with loud, laughing voices.

Perfect timing. I totally admit I wanted a glimpse of Alexander's New Friend but not long enough to have to hang around finishing up the cupcakes.

He came into the kitchen with a very thin girl with light brown hair and dark brown eyes. She was insanely pretty and didn't have a shred of makeup on her face. They were holding hands.

"Clementine, Shelby. Shelby, Clementine."

We sized each other up. She shot me a warm smile.

What, now I was jealous of her? Just a little territorial about Alexander, maybe.

He gave me a quick hug, thanked me profusely, and so I was done here. I boxed up the five extra cupcakes I made for my *Dr. Who*–loving friends, congratulated the happy couple who were making out on the couch in between telling stories about the wedding. "Oh my GOD, remember when that seagull shit on that guy's head?" Sabine was saying as I left.

I needed hot yoga and a long soak in a bath.

―――――――――

On the way home I passed by my new dream space for Clementine's No Crap Café. I wanted this place. Bad. Once again, nose to the glass, I peered inside. This time I could vividly see how I'd arrange the tables, the color I'd paint the walls. Me, executive chefing in the kitchen with a trusty staff around me. James, the Shakespearean student/waiter my first hire.

I reached into my bag for my cell phone and called Ty.

"I just baked a zillion Dr. Who cupcakes for a wedding as a favor to a friend. My hand is numb. *I'm* numb."

"Seamus loves Dr. Who!"

"I remember. I made one for him, too."

"You're totally even now for the work he did on your website," Ty said, then shouted at someone in the background that he was over-mixing.

"So, Ty, I'm standing in front of a perfect location for my restaurant. It'll be available in six months, right before Christmas. How can I make a shitload of money in under six months?"

"You could always waitress at a top place. Or bartend. Or make a thousand more of those Dr. Who cupcakes and sell them around town. I know pastry chefs who make sick money freelancing on specialty stuff like that."

"Really?" I loved to bake. But I always thought of baking as something I did for myself. My whole family—uptight lawyer sister included—baked. My dad taught my brother and sister and me to stir batter the minute we were strong enough, like at eighteen-months old. But being a chef—making it to sous chef at a top restaurant, then chef, then executive chef, and ultimately owning my own place—had always been my goal, so I never thought about baking for profit.

Ty was shouting at the same person again in the background that he was still over-mixing. "Lightly, like this," he said. "Sorry. I'm back," he said to me. "My friend Jen did a rush Dora the Explorer cake and got paid almost five hundred dollars. L.A. moms pay big bucks for amazing birthday cakes."

"Who's Dora the Explorer?"

He shouted again at someone to use two hands on the tray. "I don't know, some kiddie TV show. And I know someone who freelances in wedding cakes. He makes a fortune. You're an amazing baker, Clem. You could get into that. Thousand bucks a cake, two a week. Add that up for six months. Between that and your Skinny Bitch clients, there's your start-up costs."

"But I hate weddings. It's bad enough I have to go to my sister's wedding next year."

"Okay, forget wedding cakes. Skinny Bitch cakes, Clem. You could do all kinds of specialized baked goods. Vegan. Gluten-free. You could be the allergy free–cake chick. You'll have moms calling you every minute. And I could get you appointments to show samples in coffee bars and cafés. Word-of-mouth, baby. Make me some cupcakes, cookies, scones, a cake, a pie for Sunday morning, and I'll get you in all over L.A. You'll rake it in."

Skinny Bitch Bakes. Or something like that. Yeah. "I'm in." And now I knew what I was doing this weekend instead of thinking about Zach.

Or Alexander.

Chapter 10

Ty came over on Saturday morning with a shitload of parchment paper, two bags full of ingredients from his own kitchen, and suggestions for what to make— everything from the incredible Chocolate Espresso Raspberry cake I'd once made for him when Seamus dumped him for ten minutes, to vanilla chai cupcakes and cherry pies and tropical fruit scones and lemon-glazed cookies. Everything I made would be vegan, which really just meant no eggs or real butter, but half the samples would be unbleached flour and evaporated cane juice crystals and the other half brown rice flour or spelt or garbanzo fava bean flour, sweetened with agave. The ole something for everyone. Ty told me I could see which stuff sold better, then decide to specialize if I became known for being the crap-free baker.

He gave me lessons on making kick-ass whipped cream from coconut milk and on properly storing everything. A master class in thirty minutes. And the samples wouldn't cost me a penny. He'd brought over enough brown rice flour and agave and coconut milk for a hundred cakes, but I already had most of the ingredients in my cupboards and fridge for everything I wanted to make.

"And just because I love you, look what I had my boyfriend make for you," he said, opening up his messenger bag and handing me a manila envelope.

"What's this?"

"Duh, open it and see," he said.

I pulled out five sheets of different labels: Skinny Bitch Bakes. Different colors, fonts, shapes. I liked them all. One, black and white, had kind of a Japanese quality to it; I think that was my favorite. How incredibly amazing were these guys?

He reached into another bag and pulled out many flat white bakery boxes of different sizes. "And this is from me. Once you choose your labels you can get the right-color boxes."

"You're both the best," I said, hugging him.

"We know."

Then he left me to do my thing, and I cranked up the Red Hot Chili Peppers and mixed and stirred and poured and opened and closed the oven door a thousand times. By Saturday early evening, my kitchen was a glorious disaster, but it smelled amazing, and I had my samples packed and ready to take around Sunday morning to the seven cafés where Ty had gotten me appointments.

A knock at the door came just as I was about to drop on the couch.

It was the woman and her four-year-old from two doors down.

"Eli keeps asking me if he could have a bite of whatever is filling the halls with that amazing smell. He wore me down. I swear, I wouldn't have bothered you otherwise."

I smiled at her. "Hold on a sec." I went into the kitchen and came back with a tropical fruit scone for her and a peanut butter chocolate chip cookie for the kid.

He took a bite and shouted, "Mmm!" then practically shoved the entire thing in his mouth. "Can I have ten more?" he asked around a mouthful of cookie, crumbs all over his chin and shirt.

"He means thank you," the mother said, winking at me and leading the kid downstairs.

I knew kids liked anything sweet, but I still took it as a good sign that Skinny Bitch Bakes was going to be a huge success.

At 6 p.m. I left to meet a personal chef client and explained about tofu and seitan and all the good frozen not-meats. Four delicious dishes and three hundred bucks later, I again detoured past my spot for Clementine's No Crap Café.

Almost there.

Sunday morning Ty and I hit up the cafés on his list. First stop: Babe's, one of my favorite coffee lounges on the Third Street Promenade. On the counter were samples of blondies, and the display case was full of every imaginable baked dessert from scones to pies to cakes to brownies.

Bree, the owner, kissed Ty on both cheeks, shook my hand, then invited us behind the cashier's table, where Ty helped me unpack my samples and place them on the counter along the brick wall.

"Mmm, that chocolate cake looks amazing," she said, sniffing the air above it. "Agave nectar and coconut milk," she added appreciatively.

This was looking promising. I glanced around—the place was crowded with people with huge coffee mugs. Two women held up a scone and were taking simultaneous bites at either end. Later today that would be *my* scone that a couple's tongues would eventually meet over.

Bree tasted a sample of a peanut butter chocolate chip cookie and oohed and ahhed over that, too, then she tasted my tropical fruit scone.

"Fantastic," she said. "Amazing. And I love your labels. But to be honest, I really can't take on new vendors right now. I'm barely moving half the baked goods as it is. I really just took the appointment as a favor to Ty."

Well, shit.

"But, really, your stuff is great," Bree said. "You'll get in all over, no worries."

I forced out a "thanks," packed up, and got out of there. What the hell? All that buildup for . . . nothing.

"It's just one of seven stops," Ty said before I could say anything. He pulled out his iPhone and checked something, then pointed diagonally across the street. "Julia's is next. She'll love you."

"Bree supposedly loved me."

"Yeah, but Julia *will* love you *and* take your stuff. Trust me."

"Bree would have taken me on if my stuff was that good, Ty."

"Not necessarily. Did you see the whole cakes and pies in her display? If she can't move them, she really can't take on new vendors. She probably didn't want to admit that business is slow right now or something."

Okay. Maybe. But all the time I spent on the samples had better have been worth it.

Julia's was less crowded than Babe's. Another bad sign.

Ty introduced me to owner Julia, a very tall woman with long red hair. I realized I was kind of holding my breath as she tried the cherry pie. Then the scone. Then the vanilla chai cupcake. Then the peanut butter chocolate chip cookie.

"Mmm," she said around a bite of cookie. "This is orgasmic. Compliments to the baker."

I broke out into a full-watt beam. Orgasmic was better than good. "Thanks!"

She took another bite of a coconut shortbread cookie. "Just amazing. So light and fresh. It's almost hard to believe this is gluten-free."

"Yeah, because it's probably not," shouted a familiar voice. "That's the vegan chef who put butter in a dish to impress O. Ellery Rice, the food critic. If Clementine Cooper"—she enunciated loudly—"says a cookie is gluten-free and it's really good, I'd be wary if I were you. Your customers will demand their money back and sue you for their kids' doctors bills."

That raving bitch. I strained my neck past a huge guy to see Rain Welch sitting in a leather club chair, a teapot and bagel on the table in front of her. She had two friends with her. And she was staring right at me.

So was everyone standing around the counter.

"Clementine Cooper has been my best friend for years," Ty said to Julia. "A jealous freak, who happens to be sitting right there," he added, pointing at Rain, "was pissed that Clem got the promotion she thought she was owed because she was fucking the owner. Rain is the one who sabotaged Clem by putting butter in that dish. I know because I was there. Everyone knows."

The owner of the café seemed unsure. "Um, Ty, are you vouching? I totally trust you, so if you're telling me this is a non-issue, I'll believe you."

"It's a non-issue," he said, sending Rain a death stare. "O. Ellery Rice didn't even write up a review of Fresh that night because she'd heard the chef—Clem—was sabotaged. It's really pathetic when people have to try to tear down others because their lives aren't going well."

"It smells in here," Rain said to her friends. "Let's get out of here."

"Loser," Ty said as Rain and her entourage passed us.

"Will you excuse me for just a minute?" I said to her. "I'll be right back."

I went outside. Rain and her friends were walking up the block. "Hey, Rain," I shouted.

She turned around. "I've got nothing to say to you."

I walked up to her. "I've got something to say to you. I *know* you put the butter in my ravioli. Everyone knows it. And one day, you'll get what you deserve."

She rolled her eyes and walked away.

I went back inside. "Sorry about that," I said to Julia. "I feel like I cost you a customer, even if it is Rain."

"Don't worry about it," she said. "That chick and the blonde she was with got into a screaming match with someone sitting at the next table last weekend because he was supposedly slurping his coffee and his kid was making car engine sounds." She finished the shortbread cookie. "Anyway, your samples are amazing," she said to me. "And any friend of Ty's has the seal of approval. I'll take a dozen each of the coconut shortbread cookies, the peanut butter chocolate chip cookies, the tropical fruit scones and vanilla chai cupcakes, and a cherry pie, all for Thursday morning."

Shit, yeah!

Over the next three hours we visited five more shops and I had a huge list of orders for the following week. At Cali Bakes, a café, a woman settling her bill overheard the owner having an orgasm over my Chocolate Espresso Raspberry cake and asked if I could do a rush birthday cake with a sand castle on top for her six-year-old daughter's birthday party the next day—it had to be ready at five. She'd pay me two hundred bucks. Hell, yeah, I could.

One other café couldn't take on new vendors, but like the first, the display was full of whole cakes and pies and this time

I believed Ty that business was probably slow. On the way out he assured me that like the birthday cake lady, once people started having my stuff and saw my Skinny Bitch Bakes labels, I'd get calls and emails for private orders, and soon word-of-mouth would win me the shops that had turned me down.

"You're an empire, Clem," Ty said, slinging his arm around me as we headed toward Montana Avenue.

Which made me remember something.

Ty always puts his arm around you when you're out walking, I heard Sara telling me the night we saw Zach and the redhead.

Yeah, but Ty doesn't fuck ex-girlfriends in his bedroom while she's downstairs slaving over a hot stove auditioning her mushroom burgers for him, Eva had added. *The man has shown his true colors. He's a player. A carnivore player.*

And didn't I get burned badly enough by Ben?

Every time I tried to give Zach some credit, I heard Eva setting me straight. Not that Eva could be counted on for anything resembling sound advice.

"Let's celebrate Skinny Bitch taking over the world," Ty said. "I'm off tonight. Got plans with the billionaire?"

I filled Ty in on Zach, and he was somewhere between Sara and Eva. A you-never-know. But didn't you really? Idiots never knew. Rationalizers never knew. People who were smart enough not to get burned *knew.* But, maybe if Zach called again, I'd tell him, quite casually, that I saw him the other night on Ocean Avenue. And see what he said.

"Remember the time Seamus dumped me because he thought I was cheating on him with the guy I hired to surprise paint our bedroom? I'm telling you, Seamus has zero gaydar. That guy was so straight. You really never know, Clem," he said, squeezing my chin and trying to turn the frown upside down.

Okay, fine. You never knew. *Sometimes*.

———————

Sara had called Duncan the night we'd gotten the scoop from his ex-girlfriend to break the news that she'd moved on with an ex. Almost a week later, at our next cooking class on Tuesday night, he was still down in the dumps.

"I still don't get why she just didn't tell me she hated my shirts," he said, slamming down leeks on his chopping board. "I don't have to wear bowling shirts. There are a million shirts I could wear." He unbuttoned his shirt and flung it off, then stomped on it and threw it in our trash can. "Gone. That easy."

"Honey, it's not the shirt," Sara said. "It's bigger than the shirt."

"And fuck her if she doesn't like your style," I added, turning on the burner for the canola oil. Tonight we were making steamed and fried dumplings with a miso-ginger dipping sauce and sesame broccoli. "You're supposed to dress all L.A. or skater or whatever because she doesn't like the geek-nerd look?"

"Yes, actually," Eva said, doing a pretty good job mincing the ginger. "Do what you have to do to keep the person."

Sara made a face. "So he was supposed to wear leather pants or whatever and Dita sunglasses?"

Eva slid her ginger into a bowl. "If he wanted to keep her, yeah."

"You changed your style for your husband?" Sara asked.

"Yeah, I did. Big whoop. He didn't like me in T-shirts and jeans. So I amped it up."

"Well, it didn't—" Sara clamped her mouth shut. "We're talking about Duncan anyway."

"No, it didn't *what*?" Eva asked, staring at Sara. "He cheated on me anyway and hooked up with some skank in his Pilates class, so it didn't matter anyway?"

"Something like that, yeah," Sara said.

Eva looked as though she was about to fling the bowl of ginger at Sara, so I stepped between them. "Okay, moving on, guys. We're cooking here. Duncan, the tofu is mashed enough—good work," I added, even though he'd been taking out his frustration on it. "Sara, the radishes need to be more finely chopped. More chopping, less chatting."

"Yeah, mind your fucking business," Eva said to Sara.

Sara rolled her eyes.

"I'm gonna mind mine," Duncan said. "I'm giving up. Moving on and all that. She doesn't love me, doesn't want me. I'm sick of being pathetic about it."

Eva put her knife down. "I'm not." She looked like she was going to cry. "I miss my husband so much. Why did he have to cheat? I really thought we would grow old and gray together. Two of us, against the world."

"How long were you married?" I asked. I turned to Duncan for a sec. "Let's get the leeks and radishes sautéing."

"Almost five years. You know how long it took me to get married? Forever. I finally find the guy, think he's forever, think I've got everything that I always dreamed of when I was like seventeen and never had a boyfriend because I was chubby and had bad hair. And it felt great. Having a ring on my finger. The word fiancé. Someone chose me, you know? A wedding. A wedding ring. I loved everything about being married."

"So what went wrong? He just suddenly started cheating?"

"Well, I admit I was like twenty-five pounds skinnier when we met. And I dressed how he liked. And pretended to be into the As and trips to Vegas. But then I relaxed a little bit. It was so exhausting pretending to be what he wanted."

"So the real Eva came out and he started cheating?" I asked. That sucked.

Her eyes teared up—unless that was the ginger. "I have to change. I have to get skinny and dress cuter and be interested in buying investment businesses, which I could give two shits about."

"Eva, you don't have to be anyone but you," Duncan said, giving the vegetables a stir. "You're great the way you are."

"Yeah, Eva," Sara said. "Even I like you. And I'm not just saying that because you scare me."

"Same here," I said. "You're great the way you are." I glanced in the sauté pan, then told everyone to combine all the other ingredients in a separate bowl.

"Right, that's why I have men beating down my door," Eva said. "You know how many responses I got to my Match profile? Four. Out of gazillions. And all four only wanted to know what position I like best."

"Eva, they don't represent all men," Duncan said, mixing the sautéed leeks and radishes into the tofu mixture. "Some of us appreciate real women with curves and minds of their own."

Sara shot Duncan a moony smile. "Yeah, Eva. You'll find your guy. Maybe you just have to rethink what you're looking for. Maybe you're looking for guys who remind you of your husband."

Eva brightened. "You might be right. Huh."

It was time to fill the wonton wrappers, so everyone got busy on that. Eva seemed to feel better.

We were working on the sesame sauce for the broccoli when the intercom buzzer rang.

"Yeah?" That was my new way of saying the whole Skinny Bitch spiel.

"It's Zach."

I froze for a second. Zach. Was not expecting him to just show up, though he'd certainly done it before. I jabbed the UNLOCK button and opened the door.

He appeared on the steps. God, he was fucking gorgeous. "I knew I'd find you here for your class. You don't return calls or texts."

Sara, Duncan, and Eva had stopped their chopping and slicing and were staring at me to see what I'd say.

I stepped out into the hall and shut the door. The four-year-old kid from 2C was riding his tricycle up and down the hall. He got perilously close to my foot.

"I was out last Wednesday night on Ocean Avenue." I watched his face for dawning awareness that I was onto him. Nothing. "I saw you with your arm around some chick. A redhead in a shiny weird dress, if you can't remember which of your women I might be referring to. I'm not doing this, Zach. I appreciate that you drove me to the hospital. I appreciate that you paid for my family's hotel rooms. I appreciate a few other things, too. But I'm not doing this."

He crossed his arms over his chest. "Not doing what exactly?"

"Not getting involved with you."

"I see. So you're not getting involved with me because you saw me out on Ocean Avenue Wednesday night with my arm around Avery, who by the way, is my fraternal twin sister."

"Right. Your fraternal twin sister."

He pulled out his iPhone and typed something, then held it out to me. An article in *L.A. Magazine* about Zach and his sister Avery Jeffries who raised a quarter of a million dollars for the renovation at Montague Park. There was a photo, too. Avery Jeffries looked amazingly like the redhead in the weird dress. Fuck.

In a good way, a weight lifted off me, even if I felt like an idiot.

"Oh, hell. Sorry. You guys don't look alike at all. You must hear that a lot."

"Actually, we look a lot alike, except for her red hair. And the weird dresses." He stared at me for a second. "You know, Clementine, maybe I'm the one who's not going to do this.

Get involved with someone who keeps jumping to all kinds of wild conclusions about me. And then doesn't even give me a chance to explain." The kid on the trike chose that moment to ride into Zach's shin, but he shot the kid something of a half smile and then was gone.

Shit.

"Well, he could have mentioned he had a fraternal twin sister," Sara said when I came back inside.

"Not that we were listening," Duncan added.

"I say he's full of shit," Eva said, rinsing the broccoli. "Anyone can pull a fraternal twin sister out of their ass."

I explained about the photographic proof. Sara went to my laptop on the coffee table in the living room, typed something, and read, "Zach Jeffries comes from a large northern California family, including his Pulitzer Prize–winning journalist brother, Gareth, and his fraternal twin sister, socialite philanthropist Avery."

"Whatevs," Eva said. "I still say he's lying about something."

Sara laughed. "He's not evil just because he's rich and hot."

"So I suppose you have to make amends," Duncan said, adding the sesame seeds to the pan of oil on the stove.

"If I'm going there," I pointed out. "Am I going there?"

Sara nodded. "You're already there."

My text: *Sorry. I owe you an apology. Now it's my turn to ask for a do-over.*

His text, which took a good hour: *Dinner at my place tomor-*

row night. See you at 7. P.S. Remind me to tell you I have news to share if I forget while you're groveling.

I woke up at 2 a.m. after having a dream that Zach and I were in bed when three women, all with the same face and long blond hair, barged in and stood there, arms over their chests.

"Who are they?" I dream asked.

"Who's who?" he asked, running his hands up and down my naked body.

"Those women. Right there," I said, pointing. The three of them were just standing there, as though they were waiting for him to be done with me.

"I don't see anyone," he said and then kissed me so hard that everything went black.

Which was when I woke up.

This had to be one of those classic anxiety dreams. He's-cheating-on-you dreams. He'll-never-really-be-yours dreams.

I tried to go back to sleep, but I kept staring at my alarm clock. 2:12. 2:13. 2:14. I finally got up at 2:15. I needed one of my peanut butter chocolate chip cookies and a mug of strong black tea. Or maybe just a shot of Jack Daniel's.

So as not to wake Sara, lightest sleeper on earth, I tiptoed around the partition into the living room and down the hall, but her bedroom door opened and unless Sara had grown six inches, a guy was coming out of her room.

"One more kiss before you go," I heard Sara say in a sexy voice, and the guy was pulled back in.

Okay, who the hell was this?

I stepped back into the bathroom, hoping whoever it was didn't need to pee or something.

A few seconds later, Duncan appeared in the hall, and I stepped farther back into the bathroom.

Duncan? *What?*

Sara, in her silky kimono, flashing serious cleavage, walked him to the front door. They whispered something, then made out for an interminable minute. The second Sara locked the door behind him I blurted out, "Okay, *what?*"

She almost jumped. "Oh, hell. I wasn't sure if I was going to tell you."

I leaned against the kitchen doorway. "Why not?"

"Because I know you'll say he's on the rebound and I should be careful. But I don't want to be careful."

I didn't have Duncan all figured out or anything, but something about him rubbed me the wrong way—and more than that he *was* on the rebound. He was half snob, half jerk. I had a bad feeling about this.

"I get it, so just—"

"Clem, he's over her. He said so in class tonight. And he told me that twice just now."

"He spent the past two weeks moping and trying to get her back. I don't think he's anywhere close to being over her. And I don't want you to get hurt."

"Well, I think he really likes me," she said, and I could tell by the goofy, I'm-in-love smile on her face that they'd definitely had sex.

"Just be careful, okay?"

"This is *exactly* why I didn't tell you. He likes me, I like him. We're both single. Lay off." She stalked off into her bedroom and closed the door.

Shit. Who was I to give advice on relationships, anyway? I went back and forth about Alexander every other day. And Zach was going to kill me. I knew it.

I sat down at the kitchen table and ate my peanut butter chocolate chip cookie, then half a vanilla chai cupcake, and went for the shot of whiskey, after all.

Chapter 11

Because of the shitheads drilling at Zach's restaurant at 7:30 the next morning, I was up early enough to find out that Sara had left way before she had to for work. Which meant she was still mad and sitting in Babe's or Julia's or Cali Bakes to avoid me. I'd knocked on her door last night, but she'd ignored me, and when I opened it anyway and poked my head in, she flew at me to shut it in my face and then locked it.

I honestly wasn't sure if Duncan was a good guy or a total ass. But either way, he was still very obviously in love with the ex. Sara was comfort food right now. That worried me—that he was just rebounding.

I texted her, but she didn't respond. I did forty-five minutes of hot yoga downstairs, came back and took a shower, then spent a half hour deciding on an outfit for the date with Zach.

Tiny dress and heels? New maxidress and flip-flops? Skinny jeans and over-the-knee boots? I couldn't decide and hit the kitchen and baked two dozen scones, three dozen cupcakes, three dozen cookies, and one cherry pie for my clients for tomorrow morning. Still no text or call from Sara. She always texted all day to report on what her asshole boss said or something Dickhead Pete got humiliated in front of everyone for. And it was now almost one o'clock.

I hated when Sara and I were on the outs, which wasn't often. We totally understood each other, trusted each other. If I got all honest with her about something, she usually knew it was because she needed to hear it. Just like I needed to listen when she pulled me back from making a total ass of myself with Zach the night I saw him with his . . . sister. If she was this pissed at me, she either really liked Duncan, which she probably did, or I struck a nerve because something else was bugging her.

I made my deliveries to Julia's and Cali Bakes—no Sara— and then detoured so I could pass my space for Clementine's No Crap Café. Still perfect. Still had to have it. Still didn't have anywhere near the money for it.

I was about to head home when my phone rang—Alexander, saying hi, thanking me again for the cupcakes, telling me how Emil, executive chef at Fresh, had grabbed a knife the wrong way out of the grill chef's hand the other day and was now bandaged up and out of commission again, much to everyone's joy. Alexander reported on his love life, and I reported on mine with the same *so far, so good*. We hung up and I stared in my restaurant space again. Clementine Cooper, owner and executive chef, who didn't grab knives out of her staff's hands like an idiot.

"Hey."

I turned around to find Sara sticking her tongue out at me.

"I'm mad at you, but I miss you," she said. "Being in a fight with you sucks."

Yeah, no kidding. "I know. I've been moping all morning. That's why I came over here, to stare into my new dream spot for my restaurant."

She peered in. "Great location. And with all your new baking stuff, you really might pull it off, Clem. That's awesome." She pushed her sunglasses on top of her head. "And I guess you could be right about Duncan. Forewarned and all that. I really like him, though. You should see his pecs, Clem. He's so hot."

I wouldn't go that far. But Sara was staring dreamily into space, and if she thought so, that was all that mattered.

"So how did you two hook up, anyway?" I asked, noticing all the foot traffic on either side of the storefront for my restaurant—lots of great shops around it.

"Remember after the class ended I promised Eva I'd go for one drink with her even though I thought I'd kill myself if I had to listen to her go on about her asshat husband for another half a second? Well, we got downstairs, and then Duncan asked if he could join us, and Eva said fine, he could give the male point of view, but after like one sip of her drink, Eva got a call from her friend—yes, she actually has one—and ditched us, thank God. So it was just me and Duncan, and we were just hanging out, talking—really talking, though—about everything, and then he just looked at me and told me I had beautiful eyes. And beautiful hair. And he leaned over and kissed me. So I grabbed his face and we were making out and then we went to another bar, and then another, and then we came back to our place since Duncan's roommate's girlfriend sleeps over like every night."

"How'd you leave things?" I asked.

"I don't know. We just left things. He'll call today and we'll hang out. Or something."

Yeah, or something. I had no idea if I was being cynical or if their drunken sex now meant things would be awkward between them—and for the class.

"So why were you coming from this direction, anyway?" I asked. "You didn't have to work today?"

"Took the day off. Because guess who got a second callback for the Attractive Friend commercial?"

"I knew it! So awesome, Sara!"

"I know. I can't believe it. Not the Fat Friend callback. The Attractive Friend callback—and the second one. And I've only lost eleven pounds so far. Let's go celebrate. I'll treat us to a slice of your chocolate raspberry cake at Julia's. I swear I'll only eat a quarter and save the rest for tomorrow and the next day."

"You can eat a whole slice every once in a while," I assured her. "We're celebrating."

"Ooh, you know what?" she said. "I have a better idea. Did

you see a new tat shop opened where the massage place used to be? I keep thinking about getting something on my ankle. Should I? Like the size of yours."

I had a little yin-yang symbol next to my left hip bone near my stomach. "Let's both get one. Right now. I want one for my upper arm."

She grinned and we headed in to Brat Tat. I couldn't decide between a Pisces symbol or a tiny cupcake.

"You have to get the cupcake, Clem," Sara said. "Pink frosting."

I was thinking chocolate frosting but pink frosting would be damned cute. "What are you getting?"

She was flipping through a book and glancing at all the photos on the walls. "Maybe an armband. No, wait, that might not work for some roles. Ooh, that," she said, tapping her finger in the book. It was a tiny Leo symbol, the outline of a lion's head and mane in cool copper lines. "That is me."

Five minutes later, I was gritting my teeth and pretending getting inked didn't hurt like hell so that tattoo virgin Sara wouldn't run out the door. The few minutes of pain would be worth it.

"You said it didn't hurt, liar," Sara growled at me as the tattoo artist—a woman whose arms were her advertisement—got to work near Sara's right hip bone. "Ow. Ow. Ow." Sara forgot her pain the second the woman was done. "I love it!" she screamed. But then the tattoo artist covered it, as she had mine. "I can't wait to get this bandage off. I want to walk around naked to show off my tat."

Since we had to keep them covered for a couple of hours, and I didn't want to go anywhere with the bandage on my arm, we went back home and celebrated Sara's callback and her first tattoo with my German chocolate cake.

In between bites, she checked her phone—at least ten times in an hour.

"I'm sure he'll call, Sara. He's Duncan Ridley, librarian."

"I know. Just can't help it," she said, breaking into the goof smile.

Sara didn't hate my guts. My Skinny Bitch business was taking off. I had a fabulous new tattoo. And a date with Zach. Not bad.

"Damn, you look good," was the first thing Zach said to me.

Yeah, I did. Tiny, tight, sort of shiny very dark purple dress and flip-flops, since Zach said we were eating on the beach.

Carrying a picnic basket, he led the way outside, his beagle, Charlie, scampering after us. Zach spread a blanket halfway to the water, then sat across from me. I couldn't stop staring at his face, even though I tried to look everywhere else: the gorgeous blue ocean, the boats I could see shimmering in the distance. A dog chasing after a Frisbee. Two little kids working on a lopsided sand castle.

"I made your portobello mushroom burgers," he said, handing me one on a plastic plate. "Which also has to do with the good news I've been wanting to tell you. For a week," he added, play kicking my foot.

"Sorry about that," I said. "I do like good news."

He set out plates of pasta salad and a bowl of red grapes. "My chef thumbs-upped your recipes. They'll be on the Silver Steer menu on opening night."

"Excellent," I said. "That is good news."

He poured us glasses of wine, then held up his to clink mine. "Maybe you'll actually eat there now."

"Maybe I will."

"I realized something while you were avoiding me," he said, taking a bite of the burger. "That I missed you. Everything about you."

"Everything?"

He nodded slowly, staring at me. "Except that little cupcake on your arm. Because that wasn't there last time I saw you."

"Just got it today. I have another one. Somewhere you can't see right now."

"Shoulder blade?" he asked, leaning over and past me to look at my back. He slid a finger inside the armhole and peeked inside.

"Not there."

"Tailbone?" he asked, playing with the hem of my dress.

"Nope."

"Mmm, maybe on your neck." He came closer and lifted up my hair in one fist. He kissed my neck, then my lips. "Maybe I'll find out where when we finish eating and go inside."

"Maybe," I said, barely hanging on to my usual composure. I wanted this guy. Right here on the beach.

He stayed next to me, his leg leaning against mine as we ate our burgers and pasta salad and grapes and drank our wine. We smiled as a tiny old man, who Zach told me was a regular on this stretch, jogged so slowly at the water's edge that it was like he wasn't moving at all. Charlie gnawed on a biscuit on the edge of our blanket. The sun was setting, casting a red-pink glow on the horizon. I could stay there all night.

"I brought dessert," I told him, reaching into my bag for my box of chocolate chip cookies.

"Skinny Bitch Bakes," he said, reading the label. "I like saying that."

I handed him a cookie. "I just started a new baking arm of my business. I have clients all over Santa Monica."

"So you weren't kidding about being busy," he said. "Wow, this is good. It reminds me of my grandmother's cookies, and that's the highest compliment I could give."

I smiled and held his hand. "I'll take it."

"I said it before, and I'll say it now, Clementine Cooper. You impress me."

"You're going to give me a bigger head than I already have."

"Oh, I'll knock you down to size if need be."

"No doubt," I said. "And same here."

"Yeah, I know," he said and kissed me again. Looked at me. And then kissed me again, pressing me down on the blanket. "Let's go inside."

Yeah, let's. Fast.

We packed up and headed back, Charlie walking beside me, which according to Zach said lots about my character. Inside, he went into the kitchen and told me to make myself comfortable in his living room. He came back with two glasses of wine, then put on some low music and sat down very close to me.

Within seconds, the wineglasses were on the coffee table, and he was tilting up my face and kissing me. His hands were everywhere—in my hair, on my face, my shoulders, and moving down, trying to slide inside the V of my dress, but that was what I got for going with such a tight dress. I wanted his hands on every inch of me.

He reached behind me and zipped down, way down, when the doorbell rang. Twice.

Oh come on.

He ignored it.

I couldn't.

"Zach. Seriously?"

"There's no one it could possibly be," he said.

Then came banging on the door. And a voice. "Zach, it's me!"

He sat up and zipped my dress back up. Then closed his eyes for a moment. "Give me two seconds."

I was very close to getting up and walking out. If this was what being involved with Zach Jeffries meant, then forget it. How many times was I—

In walked a girl—seriously, a girl—who couldn't be more than eighteen. And a skinny, cute guy behind her, with longish, almost grunge hair and two different Converse sneakers.

"My sister Jolie and her boyfriend, Rufus."

Sister? I thought there was just the redhead. This girl looked nothing like Zach. She looked more like me. Dirty-blond, silky hair in layers to almost her butt. Cat-like green eyes. A pound of gold and silver jewelry everywhere. Great clothes. And skinny like her boyfriend.

"I'm totally cut off," she said. "None of my cards work. 'If you think you're adult enough to blow off college and get married, you're adult enough to pay your own way.' That's what he said."

"Jolie, I'm—"

"Yeah, I know, I can see. You're in the middle of something," she said, looking at me and smiling. She extended her hand. "I'm Zach's half sister. His father's daughter with the second wife. There's a third wife, too, but I think they're almost history. And Dad's lecturing me about marriage? I'm eighteen."

Rufus said nothing; he just sat down and petted the beagle and looked around. Jolie explained all without a breath. Apparently, she'd changed her mind about attending college in the fall and wanted to marry Rufus and become an actress while she was still young and hot and nowhere near twenty-five. So Daddy cut her off and now she and Rufus had nowhere to live.

"Is that supposed to be your engagement ring?" Zach asked, eyeing the stack of silver rings on her ring finger. "Don't you always wear that, just on a different finger?"

Jolie crossed her arms over her chest. "It's not about the ring, Zach. It's symbolic. And who cares? This is about love, not some three carat rock."

He picked up his wine and took a sip. "Jolie, you can go to college and audition for acting jobs—you can even be engaged for a few years, even though you're way too young."

"I don't want to go to college. I want to be an actress. If I'm going to school at all, it's to take acting classes."

"You know how many actresses I've known who've never gotten past an audition?" he asked. "Or a minimum-wage-earning job as an extra?"

"Yeah, how many Zach?"

"A lot. And Clem," he added, turning to me, "isn't your roommate trying to be an actress? Tell Jolie what it's really like."

"Sara could tell you horror stories," I said.

She eyed me. "I don't want to hear horror stories." She walked up to Zach. "Stop telling me I'm going to be a failure before I even try. You're just like Dad."

"Oh God, don't go there."

"Rufus, tell him."

"You kinda sound like him now," was Rufus's contribution. "Just not as loud."

"And Rufus, how exactly do you plan to support yourself?" Zach asked. "Let me guess—you're in a band."

Rufus looked at him in all earnestness. "How'd you know?"

Zach turned toward the sliding glass doors to the deck. He was taking a moment, I saw. He turned around. "You guys can stay here for two weeks, Jolie. Two weeks. You mess up the place or leave the door unlocked or fuck up in any way, and you're out. You have two weeks to finds jobs and get an apartment."

Jolie beamed and threw her arms around Zach, then grabbed Rufus's hands and headed upstairs.

"Do me a huge favor," Zach said to me. "Tomorrow morning, I'll send Jolie over to your place. I want her to see what a real apartment looks like. I want her to hear firsthand from Sara what it's like to audition and never get anywhere. I want her to hear what it's like to have to work some crap office job she hates to pay bills."

"A lot of people have to do that, Zach."

"My entitled sister would last two days as someone's admin, trust me. And she'd mess up every order as a waitress. She's been pampered her whole life. I just want her to go to college in the fall and not marry Doofus."

Despite his being three-quarters right and one-quarter total snob, I couldn't help laughing.

He pulled me into his arms. "We were somewhere good before. I was doing this, I think," he added, trailing kisses down my neck, his hands going everywhere again.

"Zach, do you have an extra iPod dock?" came a shrill eighteen-year-old voice.

"We'll have to make this night up," he said to me. "And soon, because she's going to drive me out of my mind."

We stood there in front of the sliding glass doors, and the kiss he gave me topped every one before it.

"Zaaach?" Jolie called again at the top of her lungs.

"Don't send her over before ten," I said. "We won't be able to deal."

He gave me one last kiss before Jolie came flip-flopping downstairs.

I slipped out the back door and missed him immediately.

Chapter 12

"We're *what?*" Sara asked the next morning when I poured her coffee and made her breakfast to get on her good side. "Did you say we're babysitting Zach's spoiled-rotten teenaged sister?"

Sara was already in a bad mood because guess who hadn't called her yesterday. She'd been expecting flowers, too. A surprise visit just because he had to see her face. But all day: nothing. I went the "it's just one day, and he's probably just letting it all settle in his head, being with someone new, etc., etc." route, but all it got from Sara was a "Yeah, right" face and a shrug.

"Well, his sister's eighteen, so it's not babysitting. We're showing her real life. Can you take her on the open call today for the Hospital Orderly? She'll show up in four-inch Zanottis and deal with the line for twelve seconds before she calls the boyfriend to come get her and leaves. Then she'll go back to Daddy's. And I can actually have sex with Zach."

Sara laughed. "Gotcha. But what if she sticks around and actually does get my part? Is she gorgeous?"

"Yeah, she is, actually. But so is every other chick waiting to hand over her head shot."

"Yeah, I guess. Okay, I'll take her. But you're coming, too."

Shit.

Because I idiotically told Zach that Sara and I would take Jolie along to the open casting call for Hospital Orderlies (and Cafeteria Workers) for *Babe, MD,* the stupidest show on television, the girl showed up in scrubs, a hideous pair of maroon clogs with backs, her hair in a low ponytail, and practicing her deeply caring expressions.

"How's this?" Jolie asked as she walked in my apartment. "Yes, ma'am, I'm wheeling you up to surgery. But we're all pulling for you here at St. Michael's Hospital." She made an earnest face and I laughed, and she bit her lip. "Bad?"

"No, actually," I said, totally honestly. "That was pretty good."

Sara would not be happy.

"Wow, this is your apartment?" she asked, looking all around.

"Yeah, this is it."

"What's that funny sound?" she asked.

"The drilling or the water?"

"The water."

"That's my roommate in the shower. Our shower sucks and comes out in bursts." The second the door buzzer rang, Sara had dashed into the bathroom to avoid dealing with Jolie for as long as possible. Little did she know she was actually doing her share.

"I love it," Jolie said, smiling. "Love it all." She peered her head into the kitchen. She went in the living room and slowly sat down on the red velvet couch that Ty found for me in a B actress's estate sale. "I love it. I love this couch. I love the rug. I love how small and cozy it is. It's your own place, paid for with your own money."

"Yeah, wow," I said.

"No, I'm totally serious. You earn the money to pay the rent. Pay for that lamp to turn on. Pay for cable and whatever else. For food. For that really great shirt you're wearing. That's what I want to do—pay my way."

"If my rich father wanted to pay my way through UCLA when I was eighteen, I'd have gone in a second." Which was actually not true. I was going to cooking school only, and I paid for it myself. I couldn't even imagine my father writing a big check to anyone. First of all, he didn't have the money. And second, my brother and sister and I were given jobs on the farm by age 3. That was how we rolled. And still did.

"Yeah, well, that's not what I want," she said. "I just graduated from high school. I'm eighteen. I'm doing it my way."

This was not going *Zach's* way, but he'd just have to deal. This was her life, anyway. Getting married at eighteen might be beyond dumb, but then again, maybe not. This girl wasn't completely the spoiled airhead princess I'd taken her for yesterday.

"And did you go to a four-year college or cooking school?" she asked, eyeing me.

She had me there. "I went to one of the best vegan culinary schools in the country."

"So why can't I go to a great acting school here in L.A.? Why do I have to take English Lit and Chemistry and four more years of French when I know what I want to do—act?"

Ping. A text from Zach saved me from having to directly answer. I didn't want to get into contradicting Zach when I didn't know anything about this chick. Maybe she'd wanted to quit high school and try out for *American Idol,* too. Who knew the crap she'd pulled before this? Or maybe the girl was smart and knew what she wanted, had a plan, and was going for it. Until I got a better sense of her, I'd keep my mouth shut.

I read Zach's text. *Did she run out screaming when she saw your tiny bathroom?*

Not yet, I typed back.

Work on it, he wrote back.

"Can I see your bedroom?" Jolie asked.

Zach would appreciate this part of the grand tour. There was no way she'd like the lack of door, lack of privacy, lack of real room. "It's right there, behind that glass brick partition."

She got up and peered around the almost-to-the-ceiling

L-shaped "wall" Ty had built me. "So cool. This makes me realize that Rufus and I can look for a studio apartment and do
something like this to make a sleeping nook. Or build a loft."

Sorry, Zach, but it was true. They could.

I was running out of things to show her, so I offered her
coffee and one of my homemade scones.

She paused at the table, her attention on the refrigerator
door. The photo booth strips of Sara and me making funny
faces. A picture of one of my parents' dogs nose to nose with
their giant mutant rabbit who was scared of nothing. A new
hand-scrawled recipe for dairy-free, nut-free, gluten-free
apple-cinnamon muffins. A photo of Sara's niece, age four,
on a scooter. Two open-call notices. The ridiculously expensive cable bill because Sara insisted on HBO and DVR. And a
Skinny Bitch Bakes label plastered right on the door.

"This is what I want," Jolie said as she sat down at the table
and dumped two of Sara's fake sugars and soy milk into her
mug of coffee. "My own fridge. With my own crap on it. My
own place."

"And your own bills," I said. For Zach, and because it was
true. Jolie Jeffries probably had no idea how much an apple
cost. "See that cable bill? Add it to rent, electricity, phone,
cell phone, car payment, gas, groceries. There's not much
left over for great clothes and shoes or going out to eat and
for drinks."

"That does sound like a downside," she said, sipping her
coffee. "But I'd figure something out. Work part-time in a
great boutique or something for the discount." She bit into the

scone. "Holy shit, this is incredible." She took another bite. "Jesus."

I laughed. "I just made those last night. I have to bring two dozen to two of my clients later this morning."

"I'd go wherever these are sold—miles out of my way. That's how amazing they are. Zach said you started your own business baking for coffee shops and cafés in Santa Monica but that you're probably not making enough to even cover your rent."

Oh, yeah? He said that? Because he believed it, or because he was trying to get Jolie to forget the real world for four years and go to college?

"Well, Zach is—" Wrong, I was about to say. But I had a mission here. Still, I had a breaking point, and Zach was coming close. "Zach doesn't know the ins and outs of my business. I'm a personal chef and run a cooking class, too. I work around the clock."

"That is so cool," she said. "Working like crazy twenty-four/seven doing what you love. That's how life is supposed to be."

Yes, it is.

"I've got two very intricate cakes to make this morning, so I'd better hit the oven," I told her, putting on my Get Out of My Kitchen apron and making a low bun of my hair by stabbing one of Sara's chopsticks through it.

"Can I help? I love baking. I suck at it, but I love making brownies and cookies and whatever."

I handed her an apron so she wouldn't mess up her scrubs.

"Oh good, I don't have be Clem's assistant for once," Sara

said, coming into the kitchen twisting her long damp curls into ringlet perfection. "I'm the roommate, Sara."

"The actress!" Jolie said, beaming and grabbing Sara's hand to shake. "I'm so glad to meet you. I can't wait to go to the open call. Just to see what it's all about. And you never know, right?" she added, pointing at her scrubs and hideous clogs.

"You never know" was the phrase of the month, apparently. And so annoyingly true.

An hour later, baking in a small kitchen with a crap oven was "absolutely amazing" and I "made it look so easy and fun that it hardly seemed like work at all, just pure joy." She even called Rufus and told him every detail and how she would love to find a place like mine for the two of them. She added an "I love you too, baby."

Sorry, Zach, but it looked like you were losing this fight.

"There's always hope for the casting call," Sara whispered. "There'll be hundreds there. There's no way she'll hang out for two hours in a cramped room with obnoxious twits waving their head shots around.

I had a feeling she would, though.

The casting call was in Burbank in some decrepit-looking studio without windows. Not a peep of complaint out of Jolie. Everything was "so cool!"

Three quarters of the people there—men, women, all different ages and races and nationalities—were in scrubs. Some even wore hairnets, clearly hoping to show how gorgeous they still were as potential cafeteria workers.

Jolie barely blinked at all her competition. She was just as pretty, if not prettier, than the best-looking women there. There were also lots of "regular"-looking people who, according to Sara, were in high demand for these kinds of walk-on roles. How gorgeous were orderlies and cafeteria workers, after all?

And Jolie had head shots of her own, even if they weren't taken by a professional photographer. Turned out Rufus was decent with a digital camera. And since Jolie was gorgeous, she had good pictures.

Sara and Jolie had numbers forty-four and forty-five. Their group of fifty was the first to be called in—so much for waiting around for hours. I put in my headphones and blasted '70s Bee Gees songs to drown out the annoying conversations going on around me. The most annoying was a stage mother type droning on to her daughter—they looked exactly alike, but twenty-fiveish years apart—to arch her back and show her stuff, even if she had to step slightly off her line, if there was one. "You want to call just a little bit of attention to yourself," the woman said, and number forty-seven nodded, then practiced thrusting out her huge chest.

As "Night Fever" blasted in my ears, I almost burst out laughing as one woman—in a hairnet and purple print scrubs—practiced her smile in her Cover Girl compact mirror. She looked so ridiculous sitting there grinning at herself. Another two women got into an argument, which I could hear over Barry Gibb's falsetto, and actually started pushing each other until one of them stomped over to a chair across the room. A middle-aged woman across from me was staring at me, which was annoying, so I shut my eyes and leaned my head back against the wall.

I felt a tap on my shoulder and opened my eyes.

It was the staring woman. I yanked out my earphones.

"If you fall asleep," she said, "you'll miss your number being called."

"I'm just the moral support."

"That's nice of you," she said. "This is my tenth audition this week. No one ever comes with me. And I never get picked, so I don't even know why I keep trying."

I should stick Jolie next to this woman for five minutes. Maybe she'd depress Jolie right out of the business.

Sara and Jolie's group had been gone about ten minutes when the door opened and they started filing back into the room, most sulking.

Like Sara.

But not Jolie.

"She gets chosen to audition and I don't," Sara said, mock glaring at Jolie as we left the building. "It's because you're eighteen and blond."

"You're what, twenty-five? And you have amazing hair," Jolie said.

"True, but you still stole my audition."

"I read this really interesting book about the acting profession and how you have to have a really thick skin," Jolie said. "But it must always suck not to get a callback."

"It does," Sara said. "It sucks like you would not believe."

Zach would be pleased to hear her say it. Not that it had anything to do with Jolie. Her first time out and wham. A shot.

"Sometimes I think I should just give up," Sara said. "Become a paralegal like my mom thinks I should."

"You can't give up," Jolie said. "Ever. You never know when you'll make it. And then you'll be living your dream."

"Well, I'm not living my dream now," Sara said. "Though I did get a second callback for a commercial I really wanted."

"See?" Jolie said. "Awesome." She glanced at her watch. "I'm supposed to meet Rufus at four, but now I have two hours to kill."

"Let's go to the pier," I told her. "We can get lunch from the trucks and hang out."

"And you can tell us all about Zach," Sara said to Jolie. "We want info."

"No, we don't," I said, elbowing Sara in the ribs.

Sara gave me a shove. "Yeah, we do. And you're giving it for stealing my audition."

"I'll tell you everything," Jolie said. "And there's a lot to tell."

We parked our butts on a bench as far away as we could from the guy strumming his guitar and singing depressing seventies-era songs. It was one of those perfect southern California afternoons—seventy-two degrees and sunny and breezy—and the pier was mobbed. Jolie and I had had to wait fifteen minutes on line at the best Thai truck.

Sara took a huge bite of her veggie burrito. I knew she was dying to ask Jolie for the lowdown on Zach, but while she'd been pumping salsa on her burrito at the truck, I'd sidled up behind her and ordered her not to.

"So give us the lowdown on your brother," Sara said to Jolie, ignoring the glare I shot her.

"Zach is great. He can be annoying, but not as annoying as my father."

"Did you two grow up together?" Sara asked.

"When I was born, Zach was fourteen," she said. "He and his brother and sister totally doted on me, even though they can't stand my mother. I can't either half the time, so I get it."

"So you're all close?" I asked. "That's great."

"I'm the closest to Zach and always have been. Avery's great, too, but she's way too serious for me. If I'd gone to her last night about my dad cutting me off she would have said he was right and told me to grow up. At least Zach tries to understand, you know? And Gareth—my other brother—is cool and all, but he's the opposite of Avery—not a serious bone in his body. Zach is the only one I can really talk to."

"Okay, so be totally honest," Sara said. "Does he have a girlfriend in every major city or what?"

"Don't answer that," I said.

"He should be a total player, but he's really not," Jolie said, forkful of pad thai en route to her mouth. "Gareth isn't, either. You watch your mother get totally betrayed and it has an effect, you know?"

"Gotcha," Sara said. "My father cheated on my mother with

a friend of ours. My brother got married pretty young, like at twenty-two, and he's totally devoted to his wife. I can't imagine him ever cheating."

"I'd think some guys might avoid commitment, though," I said, not really meaning to say it aloud.

"Maybe" Jolie said. "But Zach's always been kind of intense about his girlfriends. He's had years-long relationships. Then again, he's never been engaged, so who knows? Probably because of Vivienne, some French women's magazine editor who managed to break his heart."

Vivienne. I hated her gorgeous French name. "Broke his heart, huh?"

"*Devastated* him. I'd never seen Zach like that before. I think he was planning to propose, too. I don't know what happened, though."

Well, shit.

Jolie eyed me like she realized she'd said too much. She started to say something, but her phone rang. "Hey, Rufus. Omigod, I'm coming right now." She jumped up. "Rufus found us an amazing legal sublet on 9th Street, not too far from Montana. I'm going to see it now." She threw out her containers, then held out her arms. "Thank you guys so much for today. Thanks to you, I have my start in acting—and I didn't even expect it. You guys are the best."

Zach wasn't going to be happy that a) we got his sister an audition and b) that she was probably going to sign a lease on an apartment today. I knew he'd been expecting her to go back home in a couple of weeks, completely battered by the real world. Instead, in one day, she'd accomplished a hell of a lot. Including impressing me. And depressing the fuck out of me.

"I hate that I like her so much," Sara said as we watched her race away to meet Rufus. "She's gorgeous and stole my audition. And maybe talks too much, after all." She peered at me. "You okay?"

"Eh. He got his heart smashed same as I did, same as everyone does." But something told me Zach was even more guarded than I was.

Sara's phone rang, and she dug around in her bag for it. "Please be a callback for one of four casting calls I went on this week." She finally found it and glanced at the number on the screen. "Ooh, it's Duncan—finally. Hi, Duncan. Yeah, that sounds great. Me, too. Okay, bye." She was beaming. "We're having dinner tomorrow night. At Vinettos."

"I love that place," I said.

"I mentioned it was my favorite restaurant the other night. Which meant he was actually listening to me and not just thinking of sex." She pulled me up. "Let's go shopping—I need something amazing for hitting the seventeen-pound mark."

I still wasn't sold on Duncan.

Ping. Text from Zach.

My sister's seen the light, right?

I texted back. *Not quite.*

And I know way more about you than I should, too.

Chapter 13

Once again, way too early in the morning, the drilling from The Silver Fucking Steer woke me up. What was the point in knowing the owner if you couldn't get him to stop the jackhammering before a normal human hour?

I was slogging into the kitchen to make a strong pot of tea when the buzzer rang.

Zach.

Really? I looked like hell. And why was he coming over at eight something in the morning anyway? I went into the bathroom to brush my teeth and check myself out. I didn't look half bad, though my hair was kind of wild, and I didn't have on a stitch of makeup.

I opened the front door and then headed into the kitchen to start the tea.

He knocked then came in. And did not look happy. "Jolie

announced this morning that she's still planning to marry Doo-fus, and if our dad won't pay for it, they'll just get married on the beach and have the reception in the new studio apartment they found yesterday."

"Zach, I—"

"You and Sara did a *great* job yesterday," he interrupted, staring at me like he wanted to throttle me. "Thanks a lot, Clem. She's definitely *not* going to college in the fall—all because she got an audition for a pathetic walk-on role. Not even the part—just an audition."

I'd seen Zach a little pissed before, but he was seriously upset. "Zach, I did everything you asked me to do. Showed her my crummy apartment—and thanks for *that*, by the way. Had her watch me slave over a hot stove for a home business you're sure doesn't even cover my rent. And then we took her on the open call so she'd be turned off to the un-glam side of acting, and *she* gets the callback—not Sara."

He dropped down in a chair. "Do you have coffee? I need coffee."

I made him coffee. Gave him one of my tropical fruit scones to calm him down.

"God, this is good," he said.

I smiled. "Zach, I totally expected Jolie to run back to Daddy Dearest and beg to go to UCLA. But she surprised me on a number of levels."

"She's eighteen. She's impressionable. Everything is 'amazing and cool.' You should have told her how hard it all is, shown her that."

"Zach, my life is fine. Sorry."

He stared at me. "Really. You like living in this dump? You like not being able to get hired in any of the restaurants you used to love eating in? You like having to tack up signs for your 'business' on streetlamps? Come on. And don't tell me you like baking cookies all night."

Okay, whoa. He actually air-quoted the word business.

"First of all, yeah, I do like baking all night. And my Skinny Bitch business is as legitimate as yours—so don't you ever air quote that word around me again. And this place is not a dump." Though it kind of was.

He stalked into the living room and faced the windows, looking out on his own "business" and the made-me-want-to-vomit dead deer sign.

"You have nothing to say?" I asked. Like an apology.

He turned around. "I asked you to help me. And you did the opposite."

"You know, Zach, I realized how messed up it was of you to ask me to show my life and my best friend's life as a way to dissuade your sister from our pathetic existences, but I got it, okay? Being twenty-six and trying to make it in L.A. isn't all fun and games. And she's eighteen and wearing her own cheap rings as her engagement ring. I get it. But you're insulting me and the way I live."

"This isn't about you. It's about my sister."

"No, it's about me. If the way I live is so pathetic, I'm surprised you're even interested in me."

"Clem, I don't have the energy for this, okay? I spent the

past hour telling my sister she'd better not marry that kid and her telling me to mind my own fucking business. And now I've got a code violation in the space for wanting to enlarge the kitchen. So cut me a break."

"You know what? I won't. I don't cut breaks to people who claim to like who I am, to be impressed with who I am, but then show the opposite. And tell your fucking workers to stop drilling before nine a.m. or I'll call the complaint bureau again."

"Go ahead," he said and slammed out.

On Friday night my tiny apartment ended up full of people stuffing their faces with my baking mistakes—oddly shaped cookies and a cake I managed to flatten half of by accident because I was upset about Zach. Like I had time to screw up a gluten-free chocolate cake with lemon vanilla glaze. I had four big orders for Saturday morning and too much on my mind. Like Zach, who, yeah, was worried about his kid half sister screwing up her life, but who'd totally insulted me—and I hadn't heard from him since he huffed out this morning.

And like Sara, who'd texted me an hour ago from the women's restroom at Vinettos to report that Duncan had given her the "It's Not You, It's Me" speech and that he liked her but wasn't ready to commit and wanted to be up front about that, and did that mean she shouldn't sleep with him tonight if she wanted to.

And like my dad, who my mom had said on the phone earlier was bored out of his mind and maybe I could come up to visit this weekend and bring that fun roommate of mine who'd always made my dad laugh.

And then my sister and her fiancé had stopped by on their way to dinner on my block, and then Sara and Duncan stopped up so Sara could get a jacket because she was freezing, supposedly, and then Ty and Seamus stopped up because they were on the way to the movies and smelled something amazing coming from my windows, which couldn't possibly be true. And that was how I ended up having something of an impromptu party.

My sister and her fiancé—who did kind of look like Elmer Fudd—were sitting on the red velvet couch, each having a slice of my half-flattened chocolate cake.

"So you going home this weekend to cheer up Dad?" Elizabeth asked. "I can't because Doug and I have long-standing plans with my future in-laws to see a show."

"This cake is fantastic, Clementine," her fiancé said. I'd almost expected him to say "This wake ih wantastic, Wemenwine."

"Thanks, Doug. There are lots of mistake cookies, too, if you have room after that. And I'm thinking about it," I told my sister. "I can make my deliveries early since everything opens at the crack of dawn, and I don't have any personal chef clients this weekend." I was about to ask Sara if she wanted to go with me when I got a brainstorm. The ole two birdies with one stone idea. I'd make my dad happy—and Sara.

"Hey, Sara and Duncan, what do you think of holding our

next cooking class tomorrow at my parents' farm up in Bluff Valley? We can cook from what we harvest."

"Dad would love that," Elizabeth said. "He'll take over the class."

"*I* love it," Sara said. As I knew she would. A chance to get Duncan to herself for the day.

"Um, not overnight, though, right?" Duncan asked, glancing at Sara and then at me. Uneasily.

"Just for the day," I said. "Though there's room if anyone wants to stay the night."

"Eva on the farm," Sara said. "Are we ready for that? Is anyone ready for that?"

"I haven't asked her yet, but I'm sure she'll be into it."

Two minutes later I got the news that Eva would be very into it.

———————

The road trip was on. Eva had some monstrous SUV, so she offered to pick everyone up and do the driving. The thought of being in a car with Eva for three hours there and three hours back at first had Sara insisting we should drive up ourselves, but then she realized that one car meant that if everyone wanted to stay the night, Duncan would have to also.

When Eva pulled up at nine thirty, Duncan was in the passenger seat.

"Duncan, come sit in the back with me so Clem can give Eva directions," Sara said.

"Oh, that's all right," Eva said. "I have GPS."

"Bitch," Sara muttered, and I couldn't help laughing.

We spent the next three hours listening to Eva talk about her husband who'd dumped the "skank" and was working over-time to prove he'd be faithful from now on.

"So he's moving back in to your place?" Duncan asked. "That's great. At least someone's love life is—" He clammed up fast, as though remembering that the recipient of his It's Not You, It's Me crap was sitting in the backseat.

And squeezing the banana she'd been eating. *Letting it go,* she mouthed to me. *Letting. It. Go.*

Eva reapplied her gooey tinted lip balm, her red lips flash-ing at me in the rearview mirror. "He still thinks we should live separately, though, not rush back into anything because he'd hate to hurt me again. Isn't that sweet?"

"I guess," Sara said. "It just all sounds so complicated, you know?"

"Love is complicated," Eva said. "Anyone who says it's sup-posed to be easy is an idiot."

"Guess that means I'm no idiot," Sara whispered to me. "If I don't survive the day, bury me in your parents' backyard."

"What?" Eva asked, peering at us in the rearview mirror.

"Nothing," Sara said. "Just singing to the radio."

I stared out the window at the trees and the wide-open spaces that meant we were nearing Bluff Valley. Was love—if that's what this thing between me and Zach was heading for—supposed to be *this* complicated? So complicated that every other day you thought it was over?

"Holy shit, it's a real farm," Eva said as she pulled up the long dirt drive to the white house surrounded by gray wood fencing, weathered red barns, and acres of land. "Look at all those rows of corn. Is that a tractor?"

"Forget the tractor," Sara said. "Check out that mutant bunny!"

"That's Trevor," I said. "Get too close and he'll attack."

Duncan eyed the super-sized rabbit, whose long ears dragged on the ground. "Really?"

"Just messing with you," I said. "But see that little sheep?" I pointed where a family of sheep were grazing in one of the penned-in fields. "Get too close to her and her dad—the big one—will charge you like a bull."

"Ravaged by petting zoo animals," Eva said. "Charming."

My parents, their dogs beside them, came out to meet us. My dad, in his wheelchair, looked good—still frail, but he had great color in his cheeks, and he was happy, I could see. In his element. A captive audience to lecture about farm life and growing crops and cooking from the land. His favorite subjects.

After twenty minutes in the living room—with introductions and iced tea and Eva thrilled to see from family photos dotting the room that I really did have Bellatrix Lestrange hair and zero curves as a gangly fourteen-year-old—my mother handed everyone a basket.

"To the fields," my father said. "We're making Harvest Pizza today."

Harvest Pizza meant anything that was ready to be pulled up or plucked went on top of the vegan mozzarella cheese.

Luckily, I remembered to tell everyone to wear their crappiest shoes.

Eva wore bright red Hunter rain boots. "The air is amazing up here. I'm gonna tell Derek that we should plan a weekend at a B&B up here in farm country. Just us and nature."

"It does wonders for the head," my father said, wheeling beside us on the wood planks my mother had built for him. He stopped alongside a tangle of eggplant dangling amid white and purple flowers and gave a mini lecture about how eggplant was a fruit, not a vegetable, and classified as a berry. Duncan was actually taking notes in his Moleskine notebook, thrilling my father to no end.

"A berry!" Duncan said. "I had no clue."

"Do I want a boyfriend who'd geek out over eggplant anyway?" Sara whispered. "I hate that I do," she added, making a face.

Duncan had already moved along to the zucchini, full of questions for my father. I was hoping that the more nerd notes Duncan took, the more relieved Sara would be that he Just Wasn't That Into Her. But I caught her watching him constantly, laughing at the not-all-that-funny jokes he made. She had it bad for the guy.

Once our baskets were full of eggplant and zucchini and mushrooms and onions and spinach, we headed back to the kitchen. I let my dad run the class, which seemed to make him very happy. I went into the living room and stared out the window. Trevor was sleeping in his pen, his giant ears lying against the ground.

"What's the matter, Clementine?" my mom asked, putting her arm around me.

I leaned my head against her shoulder for a second. "Nothing. Just some stupid guy trouble."

"That good-looking one who paid for our rooms at the Mayfair?"

"Yeah, that one."

"He has instant points in my book," my mom said.

"I know. Mine, too. But he gets them taken away a lot."

She smiled. "Most people do."

I wondered what he was doing right now. Yelling at Jolie, probably. Telling Rufus to get a job. Offering him a job and getting turned down. Telling Jolie that proved his point that they were too immature for marriage.

Thinking about the French heartbreaker, Vivienne.

"I hope things work out the way you want," my mother said. She kissed the top of my head. "Your dad's really happy you came up and brought your class. He's in his element."

We listened to my father explaining how not to over-knead the dough for the pizza crust, which was made from organic whole wheat flour and water. Eva was asking if she could throw hers up in the air like they did in pizza joints in movies. My dad said sure, and a second later, everyone was laughing.

"Ah, the joy of risk," my dad said. "You try to catch it, and it sometimes ends up on your head or the floor. No worries. Just make a new one."

I headed back in the kitchen, almost surprised to see how much Sara, Eva, and Duncan had learned from my classes. They knew how to slice zucchini. How to properly peel an onion. How to mince garlic. How to make an incredible tomato sauce from scratch. After brushing the round dough with olive oil and layering on shredded vegan mozzarella, they topped the pizzas with the sliced vegetables.

Duncan slid each gorgeous, colorful pizza into the oven. "So we're heading back tonight, right?" He glanced at me, then at his watch.

"Or we could all stay overnight," Sara said, looking around at everyone. Her gaze stopped on Duncan and she smiled. "How often do any of us get to spend a night in the country?"

Okay, I had no idea what was going to happen between these two. But I realized that Sara had the confidence to go for what she wanted. The old Sara would have let it go. But here she was, giving it her all. She deserved applause.

"The roosters wake up at four thirty in the morning," my dad said. "But you're all welcome to stay."

"I need to get back, actually," Duncan said. "I, uh, have early plans tomorrow morning."

"Doing what?" Eva asked.

Sara was staring at him. Very unhappily.

"Uh, I'm running a 5K in Palisades Park."

"I didn't know you were into running," Sara said. Clearly not believing a word.

"Yeah, well, I am," he said, taking a sip of the home-brewed beer my father handed to everyone.

Shit.

"Omigod, is something going on between you two?" Eva asked, staring from Duncan to Sara. "There is!"

"Or was," Sara muttered. "Whatever."

"Sara, I told you—I was honest about everything yesterday," Duncan said.

"I said, whatever, Duncan. No big deal. If you want to go, we'll go."

"I said I *need* to go."

The oven timer dinged. Saved by Harvest Pizza. My father ignored the tension in the room and assigned Duncan the job of removing the pizzas and placing them on the table. The pizzas looked and smelled great. My dad sliced them up and told everyone to dig in.

"We're not having class on Tuesday, right?" Duncan asked me, slice of pizza halfway to his mouth. "This is in lieu, right?"

"*Right,*" Sara snapped. She walked out of the room, and I followed her into the hall. "He sucks. I lost seventeen pounds for this? To be treated the same fucking way? I thought things would be different."

"Dating sucks no matter what you look like. Zach hates me because we managed to charm his sister with our twentysomething-girlsish lives."

"He's mad at you? Really?"

"Yeah, he's furious. Jolie really plans to get married, too."

"That's not your fault, Clem."

"I know. But his plan backfired and he's all upset."

"So I could lose fifteen more pounds and look like you and I'll still be standing in a hallway pissed at my boyfriend?"

I smiled. "Yeah."

"I'm eating an entire pizza myself," she said and led the way back into the kitchen.

As Eva continued to comment on every photo of me and on how different Elizabeth looked from me and Kale—style-wise—Duncan kept asking my father question after question about farm life. At first I thought Duncan was trying to keep the convo from steering back to his love life, but I could tell he was totally into every detail my father was saying about leeks. He even had the little Moleskine notebook out again. My dad was in the middle of telling the story of the freak storm of '98 when my phone rang. Zach.

About damned time I thought, surprised at how much I wanted him to call. How much I wanted to hear his voice. Hear him say he was sorry, that everything had come out all wrong—even if it really hadn't.

I stepped out the back door in front of the rabbit's pen. "Hey."

"Hey. Look, I'm stuck up at my dad's ranch dealing with Jolie's mess, but I wanted to say I'm sorry. I was an asshole. I just really care about Jolie and I got freaked out. I didn't mean to take it out on you."

"I'm up in Bluff Valley," I said.

"Seriously?"

"Yeah. Today's field-trip day for my cooking class. We just made pizza with veggies we harvested ourselves."

"Tell me you're free tonight. I need you to be free tonight."

"If you can drive me home tomorrow. The class needs to go back tonight, and we came in one car."

"I'll pick you up at eight," he said. "I can't wait to see you."

"Me, too," I whispered, caught off guard.

As usual when it came to Zach.

"Maybe I'll finally get to see that hidden tattoo," he said.

"Maybe you will."

———————

"EVA!" Sara shouted from the front passenger seat of Eva's car. "Where the hell is she already?"

Eva had been in the car, about to drive off after hugs and food baskets from my parents, but then she'd called her husband to make plans for when she got back to Santa Monica and ended up getting out of the car to talk in private.

Which left Sara alone with Duncan, who sat in the backseat, flipping through his little notebook.

"She's been gone for like fifteen minutes," Duncan said. "I have to get back."

"You're an ass, Duncan Ridley. I just want you to know that," Sara said, turning around.

"Sara, I like you. I really do. But I'm just not ready to get involved with anyone."

"Well, you could have said that before we had sex."

Duncan threw up his hands and flung himself back in his seat.

This was my cue to go look for Eva so they could talk privately.

I walked around the side of the house and found Eva kicking rocks. She was crying, blackish-brown mascara streaks down her face.

"You okay?" I asked.

She whirled around and dabbed at her eyes. "He's such an asshole!"

There was a lot of that going around. "Your husband?"

"All I said was that I'd had an amazing day at my cooking teacher's farm and when I got back tonight, why didn't I come over and we'd plan a weekend to a B&B up here. He said he had plans tonight. So I said how about tomorrow, and he has plans tomorrow, too. So I said I thought we were getting back together, and he's like, we are, but I don't want to rush things. And then it turned into this huge stupid argument and he hung up on me."

"Maybe it's good that he wants to take it slow," I said, having no idea what else to say.

"You really think so?" she asked.

"Well, you know him better than anyone," I said. "What do you think?"

"EVA!" came Sara's very loud shout. "Come on, already!"

Eva ignored Sara. "I just don't know. I wish I knew if I could trust him. I want to."

"You just have to go with your gut. The gut knows everything."

She nodded and blew her nose and stared out at the distant evergreens. I was hoping Sara would come drag her away when Eva finally let out a deep breath. "I think you're right about that. Thanks, Clem." We started walking back to the car.

Sara rolled her window back down. "Finally."

At her car door, Eva pulled me into a hug. "You're a really nice person," she said. "I mean, underneath it all."

I laughed, and she got in and buckled up.

"Yeah, she's so nice that she's trapping me in this car alone with you two," Sara muttered.

"We can hear you," Duncan said.

And then, finally, Eva drove off.

Twenty minutes later, the black Mercedes pulled up in the same spot.

Chapter 14

The entrance to the Silver Creek Ranch was a ridiculously ornate bronze-colored gate that swung open on both sides, a huge black swirly letter J on the left. About a half hour away from my parents' farm, the Jeffries's family ranch was more like a palatial estate. No mutant rabbits or pet sheep wandered around. And I couldn't hear a sound—if there were cattle and horses, they were in soundproof barns. The grounds were manicured to look perfectly wild and natural, yet neat. Yeah. As expected.

Zach drove us up the winding dirt road and passed a huge, sprawling white house with wraparound porches, balconies on the upper levels, and more flowers than at the botanical gardens. I could see smaller cottage-like homes in the distance, and, finally, a few miles down, Zach pulled up in front of a gorgeous stone house. Behind it was a red barn and open fields.

"So I take it this is the Jeffries family compound," I said.

He nodded like it was perfectly normal to basically have your own town for your relatives and staff. "We all have our own houses up here. Close enough that it's family property, but far enough away so we don't kill each other. The main operation is another few miles down the road."

Ah. That explained the lack of mooing. I got out of the car and sucked in an amazing breath of clean, fresh air, something that always caught me by surprise, even though I'd grown up in farm country. Side effect of life in the city. Zach took my hand and led me inside. Except for the gross leather couches, the house was *Architectural Digest* ready. In the large living room a huge stone fireplace took up an entire wall. Windows, another. The other two walls were bookcases and art. Not a dead-deer head anywhere.

He didn't stop in the living room as I thought he might. Or the kitchen. He led me to the back deck, where a bottle of champagne and two glasses were waiting for us on a table between two cushioned chaise lounges under a canopy of leaves from a huge, old oak tree. The sun had set but it wasn't quite dark, and out here with all the quiet it was like Zach and I were the only two people on earth.

Before I could say a word, he pulled me against him and kissed me hard, then looked at me, holding my face in both his hands before kissing me again, harder, deeper.

"I'm crazy about you," he said. "You know that, right?"

Me, too, but I wasn't crazy about *that*. "Maybe."

He stood so close to me, his arms around my neck. "I'm

sorry about this morning. Nothing came out like I meant it to or wanted it to."

"But it did come out," I said. "I *do* live in that dump. I *do* tack Skinny Bitch signs on lampposts. I *am* saving every buck to have the start-up costs for the new space I found for my restaurant. That's my life. Your life is a family compound. And an amazing beach house and who knows what else. You own multimillion-dollar businesses and properties. You're opening a steakhouse. I'm a *vegan*. Me and you? We're not supposed to work."

"Maybe not. But I'm going to try, Clem." He trailed kisses along my collarbone. "You?"

I looked at him, into those blue eyes, and knew two things. 1) He'd had me at "hey" on the phone earlier and 2) I was already trying and didn't think I could stop anyway.

"You in?" he asked, tugging me closer against him.

"Not if you're sleeping with half of L.A."

He froze for a second. "I'm not. But I can't make you any promises, either, Clem. I'll be very honest with you—I thought I was going to marry someone, and she eloped with someone else. Blindsided me. I don't know if I'll ever be able to—" He stopped talking and stepped back.

"Trust anyone again?"

"Something like that." He pulled me back against him. "I just know there's something between us."

"Me, too."

He kissed me again and pulled my shirt over my head and dropped it on one of the chaises. I might own crappy shoes for visits to my parents' farm, but when it came to bras and underwear, there was only sexy, black, and lacy. He stepped back and looked me up and down. Down and up. "Damn, Clementine."

He took off his T-shirt and was as amazing as I expected.

Next went my jeans. Then his.

And under the moonlight just beginning to filter through the leaves of that old oak tree, Zach easily found my other tattoo.

Sometime during the past couple of hours, we'd moved to his bed, which was huge and so comfortable I never wanted to get out. We lay naked on our backs on the cool white sheets, my head in the crook of one of his arms, his other arm slung across my chest. I almost couldn't believe I was really here, that any of this was real, so how did this feel so right?

He pulled me tighter against him. "I knew despite all those differences you keep bringing up that we'd be very, very, very compatible in the sack."

"You were right, too."

"I usually am."

I turned over and bit him on the shoulder for that.

He pulled me on top of him. "Not letting you go."

"Fine with me."

"I keep forgetting to tell you because I'm either mad at you or you're mad at me—I mentioned to a few friends of

mine who own restaurants that a top vegan chef is design-
ing a couple of vegan dishes for The Silver Steer, and they
all want you. Everybody needs to up the model/celeb factor,
and vegan offerings will bring them in, even if they're not
vegans. Figure on charging twelve, maybe fifteen hundred
for the menu."

I sat up, a chill going down my spine. Why did this sound
so slick to me?

"And you're not thanking me," he said.

"I just want to make sure *I'm* the reason for the jobs—not
because of favors millionaires owe each other. 'Could you give
the chick I'm sleeping with a break?' That makes me sick."

"Jesus, Clem. How is this different than what Ty did for
you with Skinny Bitch Bakes?"

It was. Somehow.

"I'll tell them you're not interested," he said, his hands
behind his head instead of all over me.

"I want to do it, Zach. I just want to make sure I'm getting
the gigs because of my menus and my food. That's all."

"I'll tell them yes, then. I'll have my assistant email you
their contact info. You'll have those start-up costs a lot sooner
than you expected—because of your talent, not me. Tell me
about the new space."

I flopped onto my back and put his arm across my chest
again. "It's perfect. Just the right size. It's not as cool-looking
as the space for The Silver Steer—on the corner with those
amazing windows and the arched door—but it's a great little
spot. Lots of foot traffic."

"So I really did steal that space from you? I remember you said that the first time I saw you—when you barged in and pushed past Clipboard."

I remembered that, too. How he'd leaned back in his chair to see who was arguing with Lady Clipboard. How immediately attracted I was. Now here I was in bed with him.

"It's not like I had the money to lease the place, so technically you didn't steal it. But for the past couple of years, I've walked past that location every day thinking it's where I'd open my own restaurant."

"Clementine's No Crap Café."

"It's the perfect location. And right across the street from my apartment. I love that red door. And the curved stone entrance. The way the light hits the big windows in the morning. Alice—she owns the hot yoga place downstairs—told me the tree in front of the place is over two hundred years old. A steakhouse in that perfect space? Makes me shudder."

"I thought *I* made you shudder."

I smiled at him.

"I'm glad you found another location you like. And that I can help you out in some way. Once word gets around that you're consulting on menu planning, you'll get calls from all over L.A. Beyond, too."

"Did I say thanks? I meant to."

He pulled me back on top of him. "Don't give anyone else my mushroom burger or blackened tofu," he said, trailing kisses along my collarbone and neck. "They're mine. *You're* mine."

I never really knew it was possible to feel happy and kind of freaked out at the same time.

He ran his fingers through my hair. "This is when you're supposed to say 'ditto.'"

"I like 'ditto.' But I got seriously burned the last time I *did* ditto on that. I'm in, like I said, but this is still . . ."

"Still what?

"Insane."

He laughed. "Insane, but good insane. So I eat meat, wear leather jackets, like how chemicals do a good job. I have ex-girlfriends. A commitment issue. I'm rich. I put a 3D deer sign, as you called it, outside your window. I stole your space for your restaurant. I waste fuel emissions. I can sometimes be an asshole. Anything else?"

"Ha. I think you covered just about everything. Now you can start on me."

"I've got nothing."

"Come on. I'm a preachy vegan. There's lots to start with there alone."

"I like that you're a preachy vegan. And you're actually not preachy at all, now that I think about it. I like you as is, Clementine Cooper."

"Ditto," I said and pulled the covers over our heads.

———

Zach drove me back to my parents' house the next morning so I could say good-bye before we hit the road again. How weird was it to watch him shake hands with my dad and get hugged and thanked by my mom for what he did for us when Dad had been in the hospital?

I'd only *just* slept with the guy and there were parents involved.

They loaded him up with all kinds of fruit and vegetables from their fields and the Irish soda bread my mother had made that morning, then I once again found myself in the passenger seat of his sleek black Mercedes for the long drive back to Santa Monica.

"What's this?" he asked, picking up a small, oval-shaped fruit from the goodie bag my dad had packed us. "Some kind of orange?"

"It's a kumquat."

"At least I know my raspberries," he said, grabbing a bunch.

"Actually, those are salmonberries."

"I knew I was smart to hire you for The Silver Steer," he said. "Salmonberries. Never heard of them."

My ringing phone interrupted me from saying something sarcastic about a restaurant owner not knowing anything about food. I glanced at the display screen. Gerry from Cali Bakes. I owed him two dozen scones and two dozen mixed cookies on Friday. Bet he was calling to double the order.

"Hey, Gerry."

"Clementine, I'm sorry to have to say this, but I need to cancel my order for Friday. I'm afraid the scones I ordered Saturday haven't sold. And I only sold one slice of the chocolate pudding pie. And it's not just your stuff. I'm having to cancel orders from other vendors, too. Competition is crazy in Santa Monica."

Well, shit. "Will you check out my website—I added five new amazing things. Rosewater cheesecake cookies and—"

"I wish I could, Clem," he interrupted. "I love your stuff. But I'll have to pass."

Ty had told me to expect calls like this and not to take it personally, that it was a reflection of a particular café's business and not me or Skinny Bitch Bakes. But I still would have liked my cupcakes and cookies and scones to edge out other vendors because mine completely killed.

"Well, thanks for trying me out. I appreciate that, Gerry." We hung up and I leaned back in my seat.

"What's up?" Zach asked.

"I just lost a client. A good one, too—Cali Bakes. My stuff didn't sell."

"Sorry to hear that. And surprised. I've had your cookies and my sister didn't shut up about that scone she had at your place. You're an amazing baker."

The praise did make me feel better. "It's just one client, right? No big deal."

He nodded. "Exactly. And it says more about the place, or the economy, than your pies and cookies, Clem. They're probably just not moving a lot of baked goods. You lost one client, but you're about to take on three more and branch out in a whole new way."

He filled me in on the restaurants that wanted me to design vegan menus—the two four-star steakhouses that needed to get more models and starlets in, and an Asian Fusion place that did have vegan stuff on the menu but no one was ordering any of it. I'd make good money, and he had no doubt there'd be more restaurants down the line.

Thousand here, thousand there. Couple hundred here, couple hundred there. In a few weeks I'd announce a new cooking class, maybe two. That little spot up Montana would definitely be mine soon enough. Cali Bakes or not.

"In fact, I wish I had one of your scones instead of this weird-looking fruit," he said, one hand on the wheel, the other picking up a couple of salmonberries as he turned on to the freeway.

"So you said you were trying to ref between your father and Jolie yesterday?" I asked. "Success?"

"Took me a couple of hours of arguing with him, but I won. Well, Jolie won."

"He's re-funding her life?"

"Just her education—if she chooses an acting school that Meryl Streep or Robert DeNiro attended. And her apartment, since he decided it's like a dorm while she's studying her craft."

"That's cool. What's your father like?"

"Loud, stubborn, intimidates everyone. You have to know how to work him, and Jolie usually does, but sometimes her pride gets in her way and she tells him to butt out. He's crazy about Jolie, but his third wife got burned on the casting couch, so he was mostly just nervous for her."

"What's the third wife like?" I asked.

"About to be divorced."

"For number four?"

"Yup. One of his lawyers, too. And she's his age. Shocking. That had better be some prenup."

"My parents have been married for thirty years. Equally shocking."

He glanced at me. "You just have to get married for the right reasons. At the right time. Then you end up growing old together, picking kumquats and salmonberries."

"Yeah, but half the people in the world don't do that. Something bad happens. Like the husband wants someone else."

"Or the wife."

Weirder than watching Zach Jeffries shake my dad's hand and hug my mom was sitting in his black Mercedes talking about people's marriages.

"Well, at least your trip up here ended with good news for Jolie," I said. "I like that girl."

"Me, too. And it ended with good news for me."

I shot him a smile.

It didn't end with good news for Sara, who called to report that she and Duncan had gotten into a huge argument on the way back with Eva trying to referee. Sara had made Eva stop the car miles from our apartment because she was so pissed, then was even more pissed at having to walk all the way home.

"I am over that dickhead!" she shouted so loud into the phone that even Zach heard her.

"I want you to know right now that I'm not a dickhead," Zach whispered. "Never was, never will be."

"We'll see," I whispered back, shooting him another smile.

Chapter 15

"How is he in bed?" Sara asked the minute she walked in the door on Sunday afternoon. "I want details."

I'd been trying not to think about Zach so I could concentrate on my work. I let my pencil drop down on my pad. For the past hour I'd been sitting at the kitchen table with very strong black tea, making lists of vegan dinners and sides that sounded four-star-restaurant worthy. Nothing too ordinary, nothing too Cherry Seitan Napoleon. Something in between. I'd emailed back and forth with two of the three restaurant owners so far. I had a couple of weeks to come up with five entrees and three sides, different ones for both restaurants, and the third owner would probably get back to me tomorrow and want the same. But now instead of pasta and eggplant and interesting things to do with beans,

I had Zach on the brain. I could feel the stupid moony smile coming.

"That smile tells me everything I need to know."

"Does it tell you how complicated everything is, too? Just when I think everything's great, everything sucks."

"Yeah, I know that feeling."

"You okay about Duncan?" I asked. "Will the class be too awkward for you?"

"Who?" she asked. "Awkward used to be my middle name. I can handle Duncan Ridley, librarian. Can anyone handle Zach Jeffries, though? That is the question."

"Me and Dead Deer Sign Jeffries. Am I really doing this?"

"Yeah, you are. And I kind of love it. He's the opposite of you. Of course, it's not easy."

"I know. Nothing about us makes sense."

"So he's amazing in bed?" she asked again with an evil smile, but my phone rang before I could tell her to get out. I'd forgotten to set the timer on my vanilla chai cupcakes and was too distracted as it was. "Probably your boyfriend," she sing-songed and darted out.

It wasn't Zach. It was Alexander, with another nonpaying job for me. He was teaching a class on healthy eating at the after-school program Jesse went to on Thursday and did I want to be his copilot? Paid in karma, he said with that hopeful British accent of his.

I could always use some good karma.

Monday night: Three dozen red roses arrived from Zach.

Followed by nothing. For two days.

Wednesday night: *Friday night, come over at 7. I miss the hell out of you. Z*

On the way to the kiddie center on Thursday I got a call from Java Joe's, which happened to be steps away from Zach's beach house and a place I never went because Emil, asshole owner of Fresh, hung out there and knew the manager. Java Joe's was one of the most popular coffee bars in Santa Monica, packed all day long. And this would be the third new baking client this week. I knew the first two were probably word-of-mouth referrals from Ty and Julia, but no way would Ty even bother trying to get me into Java Joe's.

I called Zach. "Guess who just got into Java Joe's? They never take anyone new. Joe said he tasted my Chocolate Espresso Raspberry cake at his biggest competition—Julia's— to see what the fuss was all about and bought her out of it. Tomorrow night, let's celebrate this up-yours-Emil coup."

"Oh, we will. And you're welcome. Sometimes money really does talk, Clem. So I'm thinking Napa tomorrow night. I want to show you a spot—"

I stopped in the middle of the sidewalk on Wilshire Boulevard and a man walking two French poodles almost slammed into me. "Wait, what? You paid Java Joe's to order from me?"

"I just said I'd cover what didn't sell. To just give you a try."

Hear someone letting out a low growl of frustration on Wilshire? It's me. "I don't need that kind of help, Zach. We already went over this." Though, granted, we were naked in bed at the time, so maybe he had my body instead of my business on the brain. "That's not how I do things. That's not how I want to run my business."

"Clem, it *is* business. And I only did it because I know the second he puts your stuff out for sale, he'll sell out. You're that good."

Okay, he didn't get it. And he thought he was helping. But. Still. What part of I'm-not-a-mooching-gold-digging-ass-kisser didn't he understand? "Zach, I appreciate that you think so. I really do. But I don't need you to cover my ass. Ever."

"Jesus, Clem. I'm just trying to help. Calling a friend. It's done all the time. Give and take."

"So that's how I got O'Hara's and Bakery 310 to order from me? You got me in those two places the same way? This is bullshit. I told you I didn't want my success to be based on favors my rich boyfriend pulls for me."

"Clem, calm down. And yeah, I'm going to say this: Grow up. Just say thank you and let's move on."

Asshole. "Excuse me? Thank you? Move on?"

"I think you're on repeat, Clem. Come on, just—"

"I have to go." *Click.*

This kind of mover and shaker kiss-ass favor-trading bullshit made me kind of sick. It just seemed so . . . fake—and condescending.

My brother once paid a guy on the lacrosse team at his high school a hundred bucks to ask Kale's good friend, a girl with zero sex appeal whose name I forget, to the senior prom. The girl was crazy about the guy and spent a fortune on a dress and had her hair and makeup and nails done at a spa, and when it came out on the way to the prom that the date had been bought, the girl flipped out, but went because she wanted to, then punched Kale in the stomach and never spoke to him again. Which was what I would have done, too.

I had to plaster something of a smile on my face because I'd reached the Welcome Youth Center. Three kids dribbling basketballs almost knocked me over at the door. Was I in the mood to be here in the slightest? No.

Alexander had told me to meet him upstairs in a room marked "Kitchen." I found him standing in the large room surrounded by kids—eleven- and twelve-year-olds from the looks of them—all with white chef hats on. I had a feeling he'd bought the hats.

Alexander introduced me as a famous chef and told the kids we were going to make the best burritos they'd ever had. Which was how I ended up talking fractions and measuring cups and beans and spices with half the kids at one long table. They weren't allowed to use knives, so Alexander had pre-chopped the veggies. Each kid got a tortilla and spooned in the good stuff; trying to properly fold the burrito at the ends had them either giggling or telling dirty jokes about butts.

The kids liked Alexander, clearly. They liked his accent. That he called the boys "blokes." They liked how he spoke to them—kindly, even if one kid flung a tortilla at another kid and a fight broke out, which he cleared up fast. And Jesse worshipped him.

One annoying girl who never stopped whining made a fist and slammed it down on the burrito the girl next to her had just painstakingly folded.

"Oh, shit, come on," I said.

"She said the S-word!" a boy yelled.

Hysterical laughter from every kid in the room.

Alexander was trying not to smile at me. I mouthed a "sorry" at him. Clearly, I wasn't cut out for Cooking 101 with tweens.

"Are you Alexander's girlfriend?" a kid asked, drawing out the word girlfriend and shaking his skinny hips. Fifteen pairs of eyes stared at me. Two girls made kissing noises.

"Chef Clementine is a very good friend of mine," Alexander said, smiling at me.

Someone took a bite of his Healthful Eating Burrito, declared it "actually good," and the kids shut up long enough to eat every bite.

Alexander insisted on buying me a drink for my time and trouble. Over margaritas at Fontana's, he told me about his now *ex*-girlfriend, the one I'd met over the Dr. Who cupcakes, who'd turned out to be a jealous freak who he'd caught following him one night when he'd said he'd had to visit his sick grandmother. I told him about the four-star restaurants hiring me to design vegan menus for them, that I was baking all over town, which he knew because he'd ordered a slice of my German chocolate cake the other day at Julia's. We had so much to say to each other, got each other's references, knew all the same people. I could sit here at this wobbly round table and talk to Alexander all day.

We were on our second margaritas when he leaned over so fast and kissed me, full on the lips.

Unexpected.

"I couldn't help it, sorry," he said. "I know you're seeing someone."

Someone I wanted to punch.

This kiss wasn't quite the blah one like before. Maybe because I *was* seeing someone. Or maybe because there was something between Alexander and me, something . . . easy. When nothing about being with Zach was easy.

But I realized something while I was sitting there at the bar in Fontana's, sipping a margarita across from Alexander, my perfect match. I had it bad for Zach Jeffries. He infuriated me. He was the antithesis of me. But he challenged me. Made me think. And he was so damned complicated. An ass one minute, but incredibly great the next.

And had I actually referred to him as my *boyfriend*—to him—without even realizing it?

I needed a plan. Something to show Zach Jeffries once and for all that I didn't need his help, that I'd take over this town on my own. And as Alexander chatted up the bartender—who wanted to know the British version of his favorite curse words, and then wrote them all down on a napkin and taped it to the wall—a lightbulb blinked on.

It took me until midnight, but I emailed every major and minor newspaper, television station, radio station, and cooking website a one-page press announcement about Skinny Bitch. My background. Skinny Bitch Cooks. Skinny Bitch Bakes. Skinny Bitch Cooking Classes. Skinny Bitch at Your Service. Skinny Bitch Vegan Menus—and how hot restaurants had hired me to design vegan offerings for them. If I wanted to take over L.A., everyone had to know about Skinny Bitch—from me.

The next morning, I went to Chill to help Ty bake twelve hundred fancy cookies for a wedding reception being held there that night. As we mixed batters and took tray after tray from the ovens, I filled him in on Alexander. On Zach. On my press announcement—that so far had been completely ignored. Then again, I'd emailed it at one a.m. It wasn't even nine in the morning yet.

"I know who Alexander Orr is," Ty said. "British, tall, great ass, right?"

"Decent ass," I said, dropping down on a chair for a break. "But he's so . . . *sweet.*"

"Sweet is good, Clem. Like this blackberry granita I'm testing here tomorrow night." He took a container out of the freezer and then handed me a tiny bowl of the semi-frozen slushy not–ice cream. Which was damned good.

"What am I supposed to do about Zach?" I asked.

"Exactly what you're doing. Calling him on his crap when he needs it. Same thing he's doing with you."

"So you think I'm wrong to be pissed at him about what he did with Java Joe's?"

"That's who he is, Clem. He's a fucking billionaire. Covering a few hundred bucks of your cookies that might not sell? It's like the pennies some people throw out because they're pennies. He thought he was doing you a favor because you lost Cali Bakes."

"I know, but—"

"You're teaching him how to be with you, Clem. And he's teaching you how to be with him. You're gonna bump heads sometimes. You'll get pissed at him. He'll get pissed at you. You'll have amazing make-up sex."

Ty went into the pantry to get more flour. I ate up the granita and thought about what he had said. And about that make-up sex.

My phone rang. Unfamiliar number.

"Clementine Cooper?" a woman asked.

"Yeah, that's me."

"I'm Stephanie Stemmel, a reporter with the *Los Angeles Times*. I'd like to talk to you about your press announcement about Skinny Bitch. Can we arrange an interview—a photo shoot, too, of you cooking? Maybe we'll shoot some video, also, for the online interactive feature. Sound good?"

Hell, yeah!

When we hung up—with plans made for the reporter to stop by my cooking class on Tuesday for the interview and photo shoot—Ty was staring at me.

"Who was that?" he asked.

"Skinny Bitch is going to be in the *L.A. Times*," I said. "The *L.A. Times*. Interview. Pictures. A video interactive thing of me teaching my class."

"Shove it in the hot billionaire's face!"

"Oh, I will." Said billionaire would be very happy for me, though. I had no doubt.

———————

So maybe you were right was the text from Zach after word spread about my press announcement. *No wonder I like you so much.*

Damned straight. No Sugar Daddy was going to save my ass. Ever.

By the time Friday night rolled around, I texted Zach to say I was coming over, if he still wanted me to.

You know I do was his response.

He had this way of making a smile spread inside me, even when I was pissed at him.

I put on skinny jeans and a cute yellow peasant shirt that showed off my tiny cupcake tattoo, dabbed my favorite perfume in my cleavage and behind my ears, then packed up a box of Zach's favorite scones, and headed over to the beach.

It was another gorgeous night in California. Warm and breezy and the streets were mobbed with people out on a Friday night. By the time I got down to Ocean Avenue, I was dying to see Zach: his gorgeous face, his amazing body. I'd missed him like crazy and it had only been two nights since I'd seen him.

"I want to kill you *and* I owe you," I said when he opened the door, Charlie the beagle at his knee. "If you hadn't been selling me up and down the street, I never would have gotten pissed enough at you to send out my press announcement."

He took the bakery box, set it behind him on the console table, then pulled me into a hug.

I wrapped my arms around his neck. "Why do I think this is how it's always going to be?"

"Maybe we'll mellow out as we get to know each other better. But I have a feeling neither of us will make this easy on the other. Ever. I can take it. I think you're worth it."

He made that smile spread inside me again. "I think you're worth it, too. And by the way, I do like favors—and appreciate them. Just don't *buy* me favors."

"Noted," he said. "My father would call it cutting off your nose to spite your face. But you impress me once again, Clem. I've dated women who would have given me a long list of other vendors to call on their behalf."

I was about to say something about his blowhard father, but then remembered a) I shouldn't and b) his father had done okay by Jolie, after all. "I operate on my own behalf just fine. The *L.A. Times* is going to do a photo shoot of my cooking class on Tuesday night. That's huge for Skinny Bitch."

He handed me a glass of champagne and clinked it with his. Then we spent the next four hours in his bed, leaving only to get the scones and the rest of the champagne from the kitchen. There was a surprise downpour, a hard rain hitting the windows while we explored every inch of each other. Zach ordered in Japanese and we ate while watching movies—*When Harry Met Sally,* which he'd somehow managed never to have seen before, and *Casablanca*—with Charlie lying next to me, his paw on my stomach.

On Saturday we flew up to Napa in his private plane—which I could get easily used to—and stayed in an amazing hotel with pre-warmed hand towels. We drank the best wine I'd ever had. We had the most amazing sex I'd ever had. We had an hour-long couples massage that was almost better than the amazing sex. We ate good food, talked and talked and talked. And Zach told me stories about his stepmothers that made me laugh my ass off—and be very grateful my parents *were* still married after thirty years.

And in between wine tastings and tours of the winery and all that hot sex, I got to know Zach Jeffries better and better. He was everything I thought he'd be and nothing like that at all. Everything about him was a contradiction.

We flew back Sunday morning because I had a day of baking ahead of me, menus to create, and a personal chef client who wanted me to introduce her to juicing, which seemed like a no-brainer, but hey, I'd take her two hundred bucks.

He drove me home and kissed me like he'd never see me again, which actually managed to freak me out for a second until I remembered that that was just how Zach kissed.

Chapter 16

Tuesday was not only the final cooking class—which Duncan might or might not show up for—and my interview with the *L.A. Times* reporter, but it was Sara's twenty-sixth birthday. Sara said she wanted a makeover for finally being as old as we were and for hitting the twenty-pound mark on the Skinny Bitch plan, and yeah, because she was kind of bummed about Duncan. Ty and I were all over it.

We were also throwing her a party at our apartment after the cooking class. I needed a night of doing nothing but sitting on my ass and talking to people I liked. For the past couple of days, I'd been busting it on baking and coming up with menus for the restaurants. I had close to thirty original recipes that I'd worked on over the past three or four years, thanks to my father for telling me to keep my recipes handwritten on white paper, my scrawls and additions and deletions for me to clearly see as I changed them. I'd spent the past couple of days shuffling the pages around, coming up with entrees and sides, adding new ingredients, deleting others. On Sunday night, after I taught a woman with a serious Texas drawl how to juice all her favorites, I'd come home and made a lasagna and then one of my favorite pastas: organic brown rice fettuccini with porcini mushrooms in a wine sauce. The fettuccini was perfection, but the lasagna was missing something. Monday, I'd worked on the lasagna all day, but it was still meh. I'd gone over the recipe with my dad on the phone, and he suggested adding a layer of avocado or pesto. Didn't I say the man was brilliant?

Tonight, when everyone was gone, I'd get back to work on it. And tomorrow morning I'd work on my blackened pad thai for Asia Asia.

But right now, I had a birthday party to make happen. Ty and I had spent two hours in boutiques looking for the perfect outfit as a gift to Sara from me, while Ty's sister Val, a famed hairstylist who specialized in curly hair, went at Sara with her scissors, Ty's present. Apparently you were supposed to individually snip each curl in the center of the S to stop frizz. When we'd left, Sara had been in a swivel chair in front of Ty's huge hall mirror for an hour, and only one side of her hair had been "carved."

When we got back to Ty's with a dress I knew Sara would love—short, shimmery, and blousy and tight at the same time—and a cool, long necklace, Sara was smiling and shaking her hair around. It was still long, but fell in perfect, shiny, shampoo-commercial ringlets.

I made her close her eyes while I got her into the dress and her strappy four-inch sandals and clasped the necklace. We sat her back in the chair by the mirror, but swiveled her around so her transformation would be a surprise. I did her makeup, vamping her up a bit.

Swivel time.

"I. Look. Amazing!" she screamed, staring at herself, then going into Ty's bedroom to look in the floor-to-ceiling mirror. "Where'd this dress come from?"

"I got it for you. For your birthday. And for kicking ass on the diet."

"I love it!" she screamed again. "Are those my legs?" she asked, sticking out her gams in the hot four-inch-high plat-forms. "Where'd my fat calves go?"

"You look gorgeous, Sara," Ty said, giving her a hug.

"Suck it, Duncan," she said, making kissy faces at herself in the mirror.

Everyone brought a birthday present to that night's final class. Including Duncan, who'd surprised me—and Sara—by actu-ally showing.

"Wow," he said, eyeing Sara up and down. "You look great."

"I know," Sara said, beaming. "Clem and her friend Ty glammed me up for my birthday."

"Well, they did an amazing job," he said. "I barely recognize you."

"Meaning I looked like shit before?" she asked.

"Meaning you look great. That's it. Jesus. Here," he said, handing her the wrapped rectangle with a red bow on it.

His gift was a biography of Hillary Clinton and a Barnes & Noble bookmark. Sara thanked him, then rolled her eyes and put on the funky earrings Eva had bought her.

"You really do look incredible," Eva said, spinning Sara around for the up and down assessment. "I can't believe it's you."

"I don't look *that* different," Sara said. "Okay, I do. Clem's makeup skills, Ty's sister's hair chops, and a great dress. And twenty pounds gone. But I'm still the same Sara I was last week."

Duncan said something under his breath.

"What was that?" Sara asked.

"I said I can't stay—I have, um, plans I can't change," Duncan said, smiling awkwardly at me. Then glancing at Sara. "But I wanted to say thanks to Clem for the great class. I learned a lot. And it was great meeting you, Eva. You're really funny."

"Yeah, I'm a shitload of laughs," Eva said, grabbing him into a hug. She was in a very good mood and wearing her wedding ring again, so maybe things had worked out with her husband. She wore a low-cut black dress with thigh-high boots, and her usual bobbed hair had a more stylish edge.

"Can you stay long enough for the *L.A. Times* reporter to come and go?" I asked Duncan. "Since you're here anyway. Then she won't think I suck enough that a student dropped out."

"Wait, what?" Eva said. "Why does the *L.A. Times* care about our class?"

I explained about Zach's press release and the menus I was working on for the restaurants and my Skinny Bitch Bakes business taking off.

"Wow, Clem," Duncan said. "Skinny Bitch is going to be famous. We'll say we knew you when. I'll definitely stick around—until the reporter leaves," he added, glancing at Sara.

"Can I bash him over the head with the book he gave me?" Sara whispered as I set two butternut squashes on the counter. "Oh wait, it's not even a hardcover. Just a cheapo paperback."

"So what are we making?" Eva asked. "It'd better be something amazing for the *L.A. Times*."

"It is," I assured her. And a little bit of a fuck-you to Rain Welch and Emil Jones, too. My Butternut Squash Ravioli in Garlic and Sage Sauce. The very dish that had stolen my five seconds of fame in *L.A. Magazine* when Rain screwed me. And the very dish that I'd now show everyone was the best they'd ever had.

———

Stephanie Stemmel of the *L.A. Times* looked no older than Jolie Jeffries, but she wore a wedding ring, so I figured she wasn't a teenager. Then again, Jolie Jeffries would be rocking a wedding ring any time now, so who knew? Stephanie showed up with a very tall cameraman and a hunk of Portuguese bread just as I was showing everyone how to roll out the dough for the wonton wrappers. She made several raviolis herself, then helped cut up vegetables for the salad.

Stephanie had managed to interview me while we were cooking, so it really just seemed like talking. Eva made her laugh. Duncan had tried to flirt, which led Sara to fling a slice of onion at his back while he was sautéing garlic—and it had stuck there, too.

The camera guy, who told us to ignore him and act like he wasn't there at all, took photos and shot some footage of the cooking class: chopping, sautéing, blending. I made a point of talking up how I made my garlic sage sauce—I wasn't going to say a word about the incident that had gotten me fired at Fresh; my sister told me not to, but since the reporter asked, I told her exactly what I thought had happened without naming names. I grabbed my packet of recipes from the mail sorter holder on the counter and showed her the pages for my ravioli. Not a drop of butter. She even had the camera guy take some video of me flipping through the paper-clipped stack as though I was choosing what to have the class make. Then she interviewed me on how I chose the recipes for the vegan menus for the restaurants that were hiring me as a menu consultant.

The ravioli was done, so we plated it, dressed the salad, and sat down to eat.

"This is fantastic," Stephanie Stemmel said, digging her fork into another ravioli. "Incredible. And I'm no vegan."

Her camera guy took some photos and video of the reporter having an orgasm over her little plate, which I truly appreciated.

"Hey, Duncan," Sara said. "I sure hope your ex-girlfriend doesn't read the *L.A. Times*. She'll see the pics of us and know you sent us into Ocean 88 to spy out why she dumped you."

He looked kind of nervous for a second, but then shrugged. "Whatever. It's not like I have a chance with *her* anyway."

Sara rolled her eyes.

As the reporter and the camera guy were leaving, Duncan grabbed his messenger bag, wished Sara a happy birthday, and booked out of our apartment, the onion slice still stuck to his back.

I saw Sara's face fall. No matter what she said about not caring or being over him, she wasn't. "Forget him," I told her. "He geeks out over eggplant. He wears bad shirts. And he's a clichéd jerk who has sex with women and *then* decides he's not interested. A jerk who smells like onions, too."

"This," she said, sweeping her hand up and down her body, "was supposed to be my in to whatever guy I wanted. It just sucks that it doesn't matter what I look like. It means the problem is *me*."

"Sara, it's not you. Duncan's just not your guy. That's all it means."

"He's too much of a priss for you anyway," Eva said, pulling out a compact and glossing up her lips. "Wait till you meet my husband—now *that* is a man. A man's man."

Sara burst out laughing and got a glare from Eva.

"I can't *wait*," Sara whispered to me.

The doorbell rang. Maybe it was the man's man.

But it was Duncan.

"Um, Sara, can I talk to you for a sec?" he asked.

She raised her eyebrow at me and walked over to the door. I pretended to be busy cleaning up the counter.

"Wow, Sara, you really do look amazing," he said, his gaze traveling up and down her body. "And I just wanted to say that after the party, if you want to stop by . . ."

"I doubt the party will wind down till after one," she said. "Maybe even two."

"That's fine. I've got plans tonight, but I should be home by one. Come by."

Ew. This had booty call stamped all over it.

She was smiling at him. Shit. "Duncan, do you know what a Skinny Bitch is?" she asked.

"A vegan, I guess. Why?"

"Actually," Sara said, "being a Skinny Bitch is about cutting the crap out of your life. So buh-bye." She closed the door in his face, then turned to a very proud me. "Let's get this party started!"

———————

The buzzer buzzed a half hour later, and Sara perked up even more. Party time. Zach was away on business in San Francisco—something about meetings; he would have come otherwise. The first to arrive was Alexander with a bowl of salsa and a tray of mini veggie empanadas he'd made. Then Ty and Seamus showed up. Sara's friend Trish from work and her best friends from high school. An obnoxious couple that Sara had met last week in hot yoga who kept interrupting everyone to tell their own boring stories. Sara's sister who lived in Malibu brought her boyfriend. The cute new guy on the floor above us in 3C stopped by with a bottle of wine and flirted with Sara, which made her very happy, but he left after a half hour. Jolie and Rufus came by with a coffee-table book called *Actors Through the Decades* with black-and-white shots of stars from the silent screen to a steamy one of Ryan Gosling. "This is so regifted," Sara whispered. She got a ton of presents, everything from gift certificates to bracelets and a tiny red iPod from her sister.

Sara and I were hoping Eva's husband would show up so we could get a glimpse of the man's man—what a husband of Eva's would look like, we had no possible clue—but he never did.

Finally, at close to two-thirty in the morning, the apartment cleared out and Sara had crashed. I was totally awake, though, and still had all this energy, so I figured I'd try an avocado paste as a layer for the lasagna. I made some black tea and went to get my packet of recipes from the mail sorter on the kitchen counter. But it wasn't there. Just a cable bill and two casting-call notices.

Maybe Sara had moved it so it wouldn't get splattered with the salsa that Alexander had brought. I looked all over the kitchen. Not there. The living room, under the magazines on the coffee table. Under the huge *Actors* coffee-table book. Under couch cushions. Under the couch. Found an old remote control and three bucks, but no recipes.

I looked in my room. Under my pillow. Had I totally forgotten putting the recipes away somewhere? Yeah, I'd had a couple of glasses of wine, but I wasn't blitzed or anything.

I tore the place apart and finally, by the front door, I noticed the big green-and-white-striped paper clip that I'd used to keep the pages together.

As though someone had taken the too-thick packet and the paper clip had popped off as they were leaving.

Okay, did someone take my recipes? What the fuck for?

I opened the door into the dimly lit hallway. Just to the left of the stairwell was a piece of paper lying faceup. I went over to get it. My scratched-over recipe for Hungarian Mushroom Soup.

Okay. This made zero sense. Someone stole my recipes. Seriously?

As I stood there in the middle of the hallway trying to figure out what could have happened, a drunken couple started coming up the stairs, so I went back inside my apartment.

All that work—gone. And I had my first demonstration for Stark 22 in three days.

Chapter 17

"Who would steal your recipes?" Sara asked the next morning as I sat at the kitchen table, rewriting as much as I could remember of five recipes I needed to get straight for Stark 22. She handed me a mug of coffee, which I rarely drank but needed this morning. And lots of it.

"No one. It makes no sense that anyone would take them. Why would they?"

She sat down and dunked soy milk in her coffee. "Maybe someone's taking them as a surprise, like to transcribe for you or something."

"Who'd do that?"

"I would. But I didn't."

"This party was more your friends. And the only other person who'd take them for that kind of weird do-gooder act would be Ty, and he'd know I'd freak out if they were just suddenly gone. Someone took them. Or I accidentally threw them out when I was cleaning up after class."

Except I knew I didn't. When I scrubbed down the sticky counter, I remember glancing at the packet in the mail sorter and thinking I'd work on the avocado paste for the lasagna after the party. I hadn't touched it.

The buzzer rang. Then again. And again. And again.

"Okay, Jesus," I said, going over to the intercom.

"Maybe it's your recipes, saying they want back where they belong," Sara said, then disappeared into the bathroom.

I pressed TALK. "Yeah?"

A wail came out of the tinny intercom. Then another. "Clementine? It's Jolie." Another wail.

"I'll let you handle this one," Sara said from the bathroom, the sound of the shower turning on.

I pressed UNLOCK and opened the door. I wouldn't even have to ask her what was wrong. My money was on Rufus cheating. Or saying maybe they shouldn't get married so fast.

Her head appeared on the stairs, followed by her skinny body. She was wearing dark gray yoga pants and at least four long, tight, ribbed tank tops with her usual pound of jewelry. Her light blond hair was in a loose ponytail with strands sticking to her wet face.

"Why are guys such assholes? Whyyyyyy?" She covered her face with her hands and slid down the back of the door onto her butt.

I called that one. "You and Rufus got into a fight?" I pulled out a chair for her. "Come sit."

She dragged herself over and dropped down on the chair. "There's a new background vocalist in his band. A gorgeous girl named Bebe. I showed up at rehearsal last night, and he could barely take his eyes off her. He hung on her every word. And every suggestion she made for how to play the song, he took."

I poured her a cup of the coffee Sara always forgot to shut off. "Maybe it just seemed like that."

"He was totally flirting. And she touched him at every chance she got. 'How about aiming the bass like *this* when you hit that chord, Rufus?'" she mimicked. "While finding every excuse to put her hands on him. He was loving it."

"It's just the new chick syndrome. She'll get attention for, like, five minutes, then become one of the guys. You're worrying for nothing." Not that I was so sure.

"She's too gorgeous for that. She's prettier than *I* am. Sexier, anyway. Huge boobs. He's probably with her right now."

"How long have you and Rufus been together?" I asked.

She sipped the coffee, then asked for milk and Equal. She'd have to settle for soy milk and the real thing, since I dumped Sara's toxic fake sugar long ago. "Since sophomore year. Almost three and a half years."

"So you know him pretty well, right? Do you trust him?"

"I guess. But this isn't high school anymore where there were, like, two other girls he might have been interested in. There are girls *everywhere* here. One more gorgeous than the next. I hate it."

"So Rufus is only with you because you're gorgeous?" I asked.

"No, he really loves me."

"Why?"

"He thinks I'm really smart. And I'm the only person who gets his weird sense of humor. He thinks it's really cool that I turned down my father's credit cards to make it as an actress. He respects me."

"So big boobs and a gorgeous face wouldn't be enough to make him cheat probably."

"Yeah, I guess not. He hates phonies. And stupid girls. And snots. And Bebe is totally phony. She was kissing up to their manager, this short, bald dude who discovered Fierce and Brothers Beck. She's as fake as her chest."

"So you have nothing to worry about, do you?" I asked, glancing at the recipe I'd written up for the lasagna. *Go have make-up sex with your boyfriend so I can get to work,* I sent Jolie telepathically.

"You're totally right," she said, her face lighting up. "I really, really, really love him."

"And from what I saw, he really loves you. But you guys *are* eighteen. You're gonna meet a ton of different people. Have wild experiences. That's what you're supposed to do at eighteen."

She sat back, crossing her arms over her chest. "So now you're saying it's okay if he cheats on me?"

"No, I'm saying that maybe you guys shouldn't be talking about marriage right now. If you stay together, great. If you do both end up meeting other people, that's okay, too. You're supposed to do all this now so that by the time you do get married, you've been through enough shit to know who you want, what you want."

"I just want Rufus."

"So tell him his flirting with that girl made you feel like shit. Just tell him outright. Don't get all passive aggressive and give him the silent treatment and act like a bitch. Just tell him what's up. See what he says."

She nodded and took a sip of her coffee. "What's all that stuff?" she asked, upping her chin at the counter where I'd set out everything that went into making lasagna.

"Want to help me make the best lasagna you ever tasted?"

"Not really," she said. "I want to go talk to Rufus. I actually did give him the silent treatment all night and acted like a bitch this morning."

I smiled. "Go."

"We had a good time at the party last night," she said. "Your friend Ty is really great."

"Yeah, he is," I said, giving her a vanilla chai cupcake for the road.

She squeezed me into a hug, then raced down the steps, which made me wonder if I'd get a call from Zach in a couple of hours about how I should have advised her to dump the boyfriend.

"God, Clem," Sara said from the bathroom. "Did you just counsel a Confused Young Person? Impressive." The blow-dryer started up, then Sara came into the kitchen. "My hair looks nothing like Ty's sister made it look yesterday."

"Still looks great, though," I told her.

She promised she'd help me look for my recipes when she got home from work, just in case someone had drunkenly mistaken them for a bunch of napkins or something and they were in the garbage or behind a table. Which they weren't. I'd looked everywhere.

When Sara left, I checked my calendar. I'd cleared today to work on the final recipes, so at least I didn't have to bake anything or deal with any personal chef clients. For the next half hour, I re-created the lasagna recipe on paper, using Sara's copy of the recipe I'd handed out the first night of class, which was more Desdemona's than mine. I'd changed it around over the past couple of years, making it mine, but now I couldn't remember the exact amounts, which sucked. At least I had the cooking class copy, or I would have forgotten the sea salt, which I was out of. I was also running low on tomatoes, so I headed to my favorite farmers' market by the Santa Monica Pier.

I detoured past my new dream space for Clementine's No Crap Café. Which made my blood boil. All my years of work on those recipes—and just like that, gone. The menus I created for the restaurants had to be the *best*—and original. Not trumped-up copies from restaurants I'd worked in.

And five recipes were due to be demonstrated for the owner and chef of Stark 22 on Friday. Two days.

Because I had no time to stand there and whine about it, I hit up the farmers' market, stuffing my bag with tomatoes and sea salt and olive oil, and then couldn't resist the chocolate bark table. I bought a piece and then stopped at a juice booth—and did a double take.

Because there was no fucking way I was seeing what I was seeing.

Alexander. And Rain Welch. All over each other on a bench across from the market.

My Alexander. And Rain Welch, who'd gotten me fired from Fresh and then tried to screw me out of an account with Julia's for Skinny Bitch Bakes. They were both sitting, and she was leaning back against him, her head tilted back for a kiss. Then she practically straddled him and they were making out.

Alexander and Rain?

The thought slammed into me that Alexander had been at my party last night. The party where my recipes had been until someone there had taken them.

And now here he was getting a lap dance from Rain.

She must have talked him into screwing me over somehow. Alexander knew that the *L.A. Times* reporter would be coming to the class; I'd told him when I called to invite him to Sara's party. Maybe Rain had told him all kinds of lies about me and now he thought I was the asshole, so he'd stolen the recipes as payback or something. Or just to ensure a good lay that night.

Maybe he *had* been sent by Emil to check up on me that first night he'd showed up in my apartment clutching a cooking class flyer, all apologetic about getting a great gig at my expense. To find out what my plans were, where I was working. To report back so Emil could get his revenge somehow. Or maybe he and Rain had always been seeing each other, and he'd been doing her dirty work that night. I tried to remember the times I'd mentioned her, if Alexander had said anything about her, but I couldn't. I was pretty sure he'd said everyone knew she'd sabotaged me. But maybe he was bullshitting.

And like anyone really brought their ill grand*mum* soup.

But then I thought about him placing a chef's hat on Jesse's head and showing a shy girl how to fold a burrito. Giving Jesse a standing ovation and wolf-whistling at his school concert. Standing in his kitchen in his sort-of tux, thanking me for being such a cool friend and helping him with the Dr. Who cupcakes.

Kissing me at Fontana's.

No way would Alexander screw me like that. He wouldn't. But I wouldn't have believed he'd hook up with Rain either. And there he was, all over her.

By the end of the day, I had a whole wheat lasagna noodle on my foot, my orgasmic red sauce on the ends of my hair, and vegan mozzarella under my nails. And I smelled like vegan ground "beef." But I'd re-created the lasagna recipe to my very high standards and then made Ty taste it.

"Incredible," he said, standing next to me by the oven, where I'd barely been able to wait for the lasagna to cool enough not to burn his lips. He forked another bite. "Perfect."

Relief. If it was good enough for Ty and me, it was done.

On to fettuccini. Stark 22 wanted at least two pasta dishes. And my fettuccini with porcini mushrooms was one of my own favorites. I was deciding between whole wheat or brown rice for the pasta when Ty grabbed my long yellow pad from me. "This can wait a half hour. Go talk to Alexander—not to accuse him, just to bring up seeing him with Rain."

"What am I supposed to say, exactly?"

"Whatever comes out of your mouth will work," he said, handing me my phone.

I called Alexander and said I wanted to talk to him about something and when could we meet up.

Now was no good because he was on his way to work. After work was no good because he was meeting Jesse. Later tonight was no good because he had plans.

Yeah, no doubt with Rain. He was clearly trying to avoid me.

"Tomorrow sometime? It's kind of important."

Now, Ty mouthed at me.

"Scratch tomorrow. I really need to talk to you *now*."

"You could meet me on 14th and walk me to work," he said.

Yeah, so he and Rain could ambush me and stuff me in the freezer, never to be found again. You never knew, right?

He was standing on the corner in front of the used bookstore and tapping on his phone when I arrived. He wore a gray T-shirt, low-slung jeans, and a messenger bag probably stuffed with my recipes across his torso.

"So what's up?" he asked as we started walking.

Dammit. This was not the face, the expression of the guilty. He looked all fresh-scrubbed as usual, his dark brown eyes as sweet and warm and open as always.

But now he was shooting me these weird glances. Like he knew I knew. Like he *was* guilty and maybe felt bad about it.

"Anything you want to say to me?" I asked.

He stared at me for a second like he had no clue what I was talking about. "Ah. I know what this is about."

Yeah. Big surprise.

"It's about that kiss. At Fontana's."

"Actually, no," I said. "It's not about that at all." Was he stalling or what? "Okay, fine. I'll just say it like it happened."

"Please do, Clem, because I have no clue what you're talking about."

Right. Just like you thought Rain was a bitch a couple of months ago who got what she deserved.

"Last night, right before people started showing up for Sara's party, I had a thick packet on my kitchen counter of the recipes I was developing for the restaurants. After the party, the recipes were gone."

"Gone?" he repeated.

"Gone. I found one of the recipes in the hallway. Which makes me think someone took them and dropped one on the way out."

"Why would someone steal your recipes, though, Clem?"

"Maybe because someone's suddenly seeing someone who hates my guts? And she talked him into it?"

"Like who?"

"I saw you practically fucking Rain Welch on a bench at the pier this morning, Alexander."

He stopped in the middle of the street. "Wait," he said, staring at me. "You're saying you think I stole your recipes? Me. You're saying that."

He sounded so . . . hurt that for a second I doubted it all over again.

"I just know what I saw. You and Rain. She got me fired from Fresh, remember? Where you now work. And you two are suddenly together."

"Right. So because I was making out with Rain, I stole your recipes. What exactly did I do with them, anyway? I'm curious. Give them to Rain with my mwa-ha-ha evil laugh? And what would she do with them?"

"She'd have them. So I wouldn't. So I wouldn't have my original recipes that I've worked on my entire life. She'd pass them off as hers."

"I see." He didn't sound hurt anymore. Just pissed. "I'm going to say this once, Clem. I didn't take your recipes."

"Then why—"

"I don't need to explain who I'm dating to you," he interrupted. "I know you and Rain have your issues. I know what you said she did to you at Fresh. I know what she said she didn't do. But the fact that you actually think *I'd* do something so bloody awful to you?" He shook his head. "Have a nice life."

He crossed the street and kept walking.

So did he or didn't he? Was he just covering his ass? And Rain's?

Either he hadn't taken my recipes or he was a really good actor. But who else could have taken them?

I went through every person who'd walked through the door the night of Sara's party. There was no reason for anyone to have taken my recipes. First of all, no one but Ty and I were even vegans.

Someone who was jealous? Someone who hated me? No one at that party hated me. I didn't think so anyway.

But someone had stolen the recipes. Paper clip by the door. Soup recipe found on the stairwell. Someone had stolen them.

I headed toward the farmers' market where I'd seen Alexander and Rain. I had porcini mushrooms to buy. And fettuccini to perfect.

Three hours later, I not only had the recipe down—and copied—but an exquisite plate of brown rice fettuccini with porcini mushrooms and an amazing creamy garlic sauce.

Except instead of feeling relieved and happy, I felt like shit.

According to Zach, whose chest I lay against in the Jacuzzi tub in his bathroom, a great guy could be driven to shitty acts by a manipulative woman, so Alexander *could* be guilty. But as Zach made squiggles on my stomach with hot bubbly soap, he said to go with my gut instinct, which was . . . wobbling. It wasn't like I knew Alexander *that* well, but I knew him well enough that *asshole* and *prick* weren't on the list of words that described him.

And he was a do-gooder. He spent hours as a Big Brother to a twelve-year-old who hadn't seen his father in years. He volunteered at the youth center. He brought his grandmother soup when she was sick. Would that guy turn around and steal years' worth of my original recipes because the woman he was seeing wanted me brought down?

"I once did some stupid crap for a woman I was infatuated with," Zach said, wrapping his arms around me. "I wised up after a while, but in the middle of it, I would have done anything. It's like your brain is gone when you're that infatuated."

Alexander probably was that infatuated. Rain had always had guys after her at Fresh. She wasn't even beautiful, but she had something. Ty couldn't stand her and thought what she had was the I'm-a-bad-girl-but-so-vulnerable-help-me bullshit down pat. I could see Alexander falling for it. She had that same look as the jealous one he'd dumped.

"If you don't get the recipes back, you'll just re-create them," he said.

"It's not that easy. It took me three years to get my lasagna perfect. If I hadn't had the copy of the recipe from my cooking class, I would have had to guesstimate everything instead of the additions and deletions I've made over the past couple of years. You know how intricate my pad thai is? I definitely need my recipe to make that for Asia Asia."

"I'm not saying it's going to be simple. I'm saying I have faith in you."

"Oh." I turned over and kissed him.

The doorbell rang. And rang and rang.

"Has to be Jolie," he said. "We're not home."

The front door opened. "Zach?" Jolie yelled.

"Why did I give her a key?" he asked.

So much for our delicious bath. I could have stayed in there for another hour at least.

"Gimme a second," he called downstairs, holding a towel but not giving it to me.

"Do you want your sister to see me naked?"

"*I* want to see you naked," he said. He pulled me against him and kissed me, then sighed and wrapped the towel around me.

When we went downstairs after getting dressed, Jolie and Rufus were lip-locked by the door to the deck.

"Oh hi, Clementine," Jolie said. "I'm glad you're here. You can both hear our amazing news!" She held up her hand and waved it around. The little diamond twinkled in the dimly lit room. "We're officially engaged!"

I glanced at Zach. He was sort of shaking his head. Jolie was frowning. Rufus just looked like he wanted to get the hell out of here.

Zach was glaring at Jolie. "Am I supposed to say congratulations? You graduated from high school all of two weeks ago."

"Yeah, you *are* supposed to," Jolie said. "I'm engaged. It doesn't matter how old I am. It matters how we feel about each other." She turned to me and grabbed my hands. "Clementine, you totally have to be in the bridal party. If it wasn't for you and everything you said the other day, this wouldn't have happened at all." She squeezed me into a hug.

Zach stared at me. "Wait a minute. You talked her *into* getting married?"

"It wasn't like that," I said. "I wasn't talking about getting married. I was talking—"

"You're not getting married," Zach interrupted, shooting daggers at Jolie and Rufus. "Unless you want to make a huge mistake."

"Yeah, it's a huge mistake that we love each other," she said. "That we're committed to each other so much that we want to get married. Big mistake."

"Jolie, you're *eighteen*."

"So fucking what. Whatever. Come on, Rufus. Let's go celebrate with people who'll actually be happy for us."

She stalked out, Rufus behind her. I could only assume the guy had working vocal cords, since he was in a band, but I'd never actually heard him utter more than five words.

"So this was you again?" he said to me. "You've got to be kidding me."

"Zach, she came over sobbing the other day because Rufus was flirting with some girl in the band. I just asked her questions to help her see whether or not she could trust him, and she could, so she left all happy. That was it."

He paced for a few moments and shook his head again. "Well, she trusts him so much she's marrying him. There's no way she'll ask him to sign a prenup."

"Wait, that's why you're so against this?"

He let out a breath. "If you had any idea how much our family is worth, you'd get it."

"And if your family had no money?"

"I'd still think she was a moron for getting married at eigh-teen. No one knows who they are at eighteen. I was backpack-ing through Italy and Switzerland at eighteen, crushed over a girl whose last name I can't even remember."

"Well, Jolie seems pretty smart to me," I said.

He stared at me like I'd sprouted another head. "Smart? She's a princess. Please."

How did I keep getting dragged into the Jeffries' family reality show drama? "She doesn't seem like a princess to me."

"You've known her for what—a week? Don't give me advice when you don't know what you're talking about."

"Excuse me? I don't know what I'm talking about? I don't have an opinion?"

"Not when it comes to Jolie. She's a fucking kid, Clem. And you've already—" He let out a breath and stalked over to the kitchen and poured himself a glass of wine.

"I've already what? Screwed things up? Been a bad influ-ence?"

"Something like that. Yeah."

Asshole. ASSHOLE. "Well, I'll tell you what. Since we're through, you can tell your sister to go to your next girlfriend for advice."

I grabbed my bag and pulled open the door, startled to find Jolie marching up the walkway, Rufus with his hands stuffed in his pockets behind her.

"And another thing, Zach," she shouted past me at him. "Just because Vivienne didn't want to marry you doesn't mean you can't be happy for anyone else who *does* want to get married!" Then she huffed off.

Whoa. I turned around and Zach looked half pissed as hell and half . . . very, very sad.

"You were leaving, Clem," he said through gritted teeth. "So do it."

Good, he was back to being an ass. I slammed the door on the way out.

Chapter 18

My so-called love life, stolen recipes, and British chefs who hated my guts would have to wait because the *Los Angeles Times* article on me and Skinny Bitch came out the next morning. Front page of the Food section.

Front page.

Because she was great, Sara had bought ten copies of the paper on her way back from sunrise yoga even though she was only in the photos—and in the fifteen-second video of the class—in the online edition. In the newspaper, there was a big-ass photo of me spooning the butternut squash into a wonton wrapper. Caption: *Chef Clementine Cooper of Skinny Bitch is in high demand in L.A.*

My phone started ringing at 7:30 a.m. and didn't stop. Including calls from every restaurant that had slammed the door in my face after Emil had fired me from Fresh. Ha! Suddenly they all wanted me. I told them I'd get back to them, which I wouldn't. I took way too many baking orders from coffee shops and cafés and boutiques all over L.A. and even had to waitlist some that I'd never heard of. The personal assistants of twelve celebs—ranging from A list to *who?*—called to book my personal chef services. Eleven more restaurants wanted me as a menu consultant. I now charged two thousand bucks for the service. Yeah, I did.

By the end of the day, I also had seven speaking gigs. Me, at a podium, talking. For thousands of dollars.

Between what I had saved up now and what I'd have in a couple of months, that space on Montana was mine.

L.A. *Times*, bank statements, and a business plan (which Elizabeth Cooper, Esquire, helped me write Thursday night) in hand, I walked into my bank on Friday and met with the same suit who practically laughed in my face the last time I sat in this ugly blue chair across from her.

I just about had the money to lease the little space for six months, but I needed capital for buying everything I'd need for my restaurant. Like tables. Pot and pans. Dishes. Booze. Paint for the walls. At least two waiters. Boring crap like insurance, according to my sister. And my sign. Not sparing any expense there.

"Let me look over everything, and you'll hear from us within a week, Ms. Cooper," she said, shaking my hand.

Last time there was no handshake.

Friday afternoon, I walked into Stark 22 with my ingredients and pans, shook hands with the owner, a tall, burly guy named Eric Arley, and shot the shit for a few minutes about the *Times* article and veganism and the restaurant business. He complimented my baking skills and told me he'd had a Skinny Bitch Bakes muffin just that morning. He already had a top pastry chef, otherwise, he said, he might try to get me to bake for him.

He was smarmy and kept checking me out, but not in a sickening way. Once he led the way into the kitchen and introduced me to his chef, he and his slightly overpowering cologne finally disappeared.

"I get why he's interested in hiring you," the chef said, his white jacket already stained even though it was only two thirty. "I could make vegan whatever, but I'd forget not to use real milk and then I'd get in trouble like you did at Fresh."

"God, does everyone know that story?" I asked, setting out my ingredients. This was a place where there really were dead cow carcasses and bloody axes in the back room. I didn't think the two worlds mixed.

"Yeah, but everyone knows Rain Welch sabotaged you and Emil. She admitted it to a chef friend of mine that she was dating, but then she cheated on him, and he told a bunch of people what she'd said. It's been a couple of months, so she obviously figured enough time has gone by to fess up. She was pissed that you got her promotion and thought it meant you were sleeping with Emil."

"Ew," I said. "Never in a million years."

He laughed.

Even if smarmy Eric Arley didn't want my lasagna and fettuccini and the other dishes I was making for him today, coming here and working my ass off on these five recipes was worth it for that bit of news.

But two hours later, I had a check for two thousand dollars for creating a kick-ass vegan menu for Stark 22.

1:14 a.m. Friday night text from Zach: *I miss you.*

Me: *You piss me off.*

Him: *Ditto. Will you ever cut me a break?*

Me: *Nope.*

Him: *Don't know about this, Clem. I miss you, but I don't know.*

Me: *Ditto.*

On Saturday night, to celebrate the *Times* article, getting Stark 22, and the ten recipes I'd rewritten and tested since Tuesday night, Ty, Seamus, and Sara were taking me out to Georgina's, one of my favorite restaurants, even if Georgina wouldn't hire me after I got fired from Fresh. In her defense, she had a great staff already and no need for another head chef or sous chef.

"Hey, look, Clem. Prime already has your menu advertised," Seamus said, stopping in front of the steakhouse just two doors down from Georgina's. A blackboard hanging in the window read: ENJOY OUR NEW VEGAN DISHES! MEDITERRANEAN LASAGNA, CAJUN-SPICED JAMBALAYA, AND SWEET POTATO AND SPINACH EMPANADAS. SUPERMODELS WELCOME! "That last line is stupid, but now I'm in the mood for jambalaya. Maybe we should just go here for dinner."

"I can smell the dead cows from here," Ty said, stepping back.

I walked over and stared at the blackboard. "What the hell? Not only is Prime *not* one of the restaurants that asked me to come up with a menu for them, but these three dishes were in that packet of stolen recipes. I even gave them those exact working names."

Sara pulled open the door. "Let's go confront the manager or whoever and make them take down the sign and take the dishes off the menu."

"Wait," Seamus said. "It's not like you can prove these are your recipes. Lasagna, jambalaya, and empanadas aren't exactly uncommon."

"And they'll say they saw the *Times* article, thought a vegan menu was a great idea, and instituted one of their own," Ty said. "Let's find out who owns the place first. A hundred bucks says it's a relative of Rain's."

I pulled out my phone and called Zach. "Do you know who owns Prime, the steakhouse on Wilshire?"

"Hello to you, too," he said.

"Do you know?"

He sighed. "Dan Gloves. I don't know him personally, though. Why?"

"Because three of my stolen recipes are featured in his window as their new vegan menu. And this is not one of the restaurants that hired me."

"That's really weird. Dan is known as being an okay guy. Hold up a second and let me see if he has partners." He came back on a minute later. "One partner. A guy named Derek Ackerman. He only has a twenty percent stake in the place. I don't know him at all."

Derek Ackerman. Why did that name sound familiar?

"Okay, thanks. I'll sic my sister on him. The lawyer in the family."

"We should talk, Clem. I hate when we're not in sync. Tomorrow night?"

I hate when we're not in sync, too. "Tomorrow night." We hung up, the name Derek Ackerman echoing in my head. "Why does the name Derek Ackerman sound familiar?" I asked Sara, Ty, and Seamus. Where had I heard that name before?

They all shrugged.

"Wait, yeah," Sara said. "I feel like I know it, too. The Derek part. Like I heard it somewhere recently."

"I know. Me, too," I said. "I can't remember where, though."

I took a picture of Prime's window, making sure I got the name and the blackboard in the shot, then did a Google search for Derek Ackerman. Balding dude in his late thirties, maybe early forties. Kind of *Jersey Shore*–looking, but with wire-rimmed glasses. There were countless hits, one after another, about some self-published book series he wrote called *Invest with Nothing!*

Yeah, by stealing people's stuff.

I typed in "Rain Welch" and "Derek Ackerman" to see if there was a joint hit. Nothing.

"Alexander Orr" and "Derek Ackerman."

Still nothing.

Who was this asshole?

Between Ty's hilarious story about the sauté chef at Chill and Sara telling us about a coworker who'd managed to get herself fired on her first day, I finally got my mind off of Prime and the fact that people were eating my Cajun Jambalaya, one of the recipes it would take me days to re-create. We sat at a round table at Georgina's, which was packed—just the way my restaurant would be. I dug into my vegetable curry, studying what the place was doing right. Good music, not too loud. Good waitstaff, without smug asshole expressions on their faces as though they were too model-actor-singer to explain a dish. Perfect lighting. And excellent food.

"Hey, look, that waitress has Eva's new haircut," Sara said. "I can't believe I'm saying this, but I actually want something Eva has. Think my hair would do that?"

"You'd have to straighten it every day," Ty said. "My sister would kill you, too. She said you have the perfect curly hair."

I glanced over, and yup, the woman had an ear-length pointy bob with blunt bangs, except hers was white-blond instead of Eva's dark red—

Eva.

Now I knew why the name Derek sounded so familiar.

Eva's husband's name was Derek.

And her last name was Ackerman.

"I'm Eva Ackerman. Eva. Just Eva. Not Eve. Not Evie . . ."

Okay, this had to be a coincidence. Had. To. Be. Eva was a royal bitch, but she was my royal bitch. I would even call her a friend.

"Sara, do you remember what Eva's husband's name is?" I asked.

"She just always calls him her husband. Oh wait, I think it's Darren or Dylan or something like that."

Yeah. Maybe it was Dylan or Darren. Dylan Ackerman. Darren Ackerman. I really didn't want it to be Derek Ackerman.

I pulled out my phone and typed into the search bar "Eva Ackerman" and "Derek Ackerman."

Well, shit.

Wedding announcement in the *Modesto Bee* five years ago.

Investor Derek Ackerman and sales consultant Eva Brine were married last night at St. Michael's . . .

There was a bad photo of the two of them, Eva with the same red bob and Ackerman looking even more *Jersey Shore* than he had in his head shot.

"Turns out Eva's husband's name is Derek," I said, holding up my phone. "Derek Ackerman, to be exact."

"Eva's husband owns that restaurant that stole your reci-pes?" Sara asked, looking confused. "That's weird."

"Or not."

I saw the lightbulb blink on over Sara's head. She grabbed my phone. "Eva stole your recipes and gave them to her hus-band to use at Prime? What?"

"And I accused Alexander." Shit. Shit, shit, shit. My appe-tite was totally gone. "I've got to go see Alexander."

"Go," Ty said. "I'll get your curry boxed up for you."

"Wait," Sara said as I got up. "What about Eva?"

"She's next," I said. "But first I have to fix things with Alex-ander."

Like that would happen so easily.

I doubted Alexander would be home at 8:40 on a Saturday night; he was probably working, but I walked to his house any-way. I wanted to talk to him in person. If he wasn't home, maybe I'd leave a note in his mailbox saying that I was sorry, that I was wrong, that I'd totally get it if he never spoke to me again, but I really, really wanted him to. I'd write a whole thing about how I jumped to conclusions, like Zach was always accusing me of, and that I should have known Alexander would never do that to me, that he wasn't capable in the first place.

I walked up the three porch steps and rang the bell. The house was dark. No answer. I dropped down on the second step and stared up at the almost twilight sky. Shit, shit, shit.

It took a lot to shock me. A lot. And Eva Ackerman had pulled it off.

Of all the people to screw me over. Eva.

I thought of the way she'd hugged me by her car at my parents' house, her way of thanking me for talking to her about her husband when she'd been so upset.

I wish I knew if I could trust him, she'd said. *I want to.*

You just have to go with your gut, I'd told her. *The gut knows everything.*

So the gut didn't know everything, after all. That sucked, too.

I was so relieved that Alexander hadn't stolen my recipes that I just wanted everything to go back to the way it was before. I hadn't known how important a friend he'd become until the friendship had gotten squashed.

Fucking Eva.

I waited on the steps for twenty minutes, watching people jog by and walk their dogs, before I realized that if Alexander did come home, Rain might be with him. I was not dealing with her. I got up and started heading down the steps when Alexander turned the corner, his dogs beside him. He stopped when he saw me.

"I owe you a huge apology," I said. "I'm an idiot."

"Yeah, you are," he said coming toward me. He looked as pissed off at me as he did the day I'd confronted him.

Lizzie ran up to me and I rubbed her head. "I screwed up. I know you didn't take my recipes. I knew it even when I was confronting you, but I was freaked out when I saw you with

Rain, and it seemed so wrong to me to see you two together that anything seemed possible, you know?"

"Actually, no. I don't know. I thought we were better friends than that. But we're clearly not friends at all."

And with that, Alexander walked up the steps to his house and shut the door behind him.

Chapter 19

As I walked home from the crap encounter with Alexander, I tried to remember what had been going on with Eva at Sara's birthday party. She'd been expecting her husband to show up, and he hadn't. Once, when she'd been in the kitchen, grossly double-dipping tortilla chips into a little cup of salsa, the buzzer had rung, and she'd jumped, almost spilling the salsa on me. She'd rushed to the intercom, and when it turned out to be a coworker of Sara's, Eva had flung the chip in the sink and stalked off with her phone in hand. I'd taken it as the usual crazy bullshit of Eva's "they are; they aren't" status update. She'd probably called her husband and asked where the hell he was and if he was coming to the party like she'd told everyone he was. Between that call and my missing recipes was her motive. To suck up to him? To win him back? To prove her undying love?

I punched her number in my phone. Fuming.

No answer. But it rang a bunch of times before going to voice mail, which meant she was ignoring it. After the beep, I left a message. "Eva, it's Clementine. I passed Prime tonight, which your husband co-owns, I just found out, and three of my recipes are hanging on a blackboard in the window. I'm doubting this is a coincidence." *Click.*

By the time I got home twenty minutes later, she called back.

"Clementine, that's crazy. I would never. Never."

"Really. So it's a coincidence."

"It absolutely has to be," she said. "What was on the menu? Veggie burgers? That's on *every* menu."

"Actually, my jambalaya, my empanadas, and my lasagna."

"*Your* lasagna? Clem, come on. You think you're the one chef who ever came up with Mediterranean Lasagna?" She snorted.

There was dead silence for a moment, so she clearly knew she'd outed herself. Lasagna? Yeah. On every menu. Mediterranean Lasagna? No.

"Well, if you're saying I stole your recipes and gave them to my husband to use at Prime, you're wrong. Because I didn't. Yeah, I saw the recipes at the cooking class when you were showing them to the reporter. And yeah, my husband has a stake in Prime. But I'd never betray you like that, Clem. I swear."

Right.

"So someone else stole my recipes."

"Or you misplaced them. The thing with Prime is total coincidence. Okay, yeah, I mentioned to Derek that you were creating vegan menus for some restaurants. And yeah, he thought that was a great idea. So he obviously mentioned it to his chef, and his chef made up some dishes. I'm sure once he saw the *L.A Times* article he wanted to make sure he had something going for the weekend crowd."

"You're a liar, Eva," I said. "I thought we were friends." And then I hung up on her.

———

Sara and I were watching *Top Chef* when the buzzer rang.

Eva.

When I opened the door, she started crying.

"It was all for nothing, too," she said, blackish-brown mascara streaks running down her face. "He's back with the skank."

"Are we supposed to feel bad for you?" Sara asked. "Because I don't. You, Clem?"

"Not in the slightest."

"Clem, just let me try to explain, okay?" Eva said.

"What's to explain? You betrayed me to suck up to your husband. Do I have that right?"

More tears. "I just felt so desperate. He's been stringing me along for sex. And when I told him about the menus you're creating for restaurants, it was the first time in a long time that he actually listened to me. He paid attention to me, you know?"

"You know who else paid attention to you, Eva? Clemen-tine," Sara said. "When you were crying your eyes out over that douche at Clem's parents' farm, who went to go to talk to you? Clem. Who calmed you down? Clem. Who gave you good advice? Clem. And you fucked her over. I can't believe it."

"I didn't mean to, I swear," Eva said, looking from Sara to me. "When I told him about the vegan menus, he thought it was such a great idea and was asking me all kinds of questions about what we covered in class and if I'd saved any of the recipes, which I didn't. So then he got all pissed at me for not keeping them and what was the point of telling him about the vegan menus if I couldn't help him out. The main owner of Prime can't stand him and was trying to buy him out. I thought if I could help him, he'd be so grateful and—" She started crying again.

"Jesus, Eva," Sara said. "This isn't any kind of excuse."

"I'm just trying to explain. No excuse, okay?" She reached into her bag and pulled out a gross wadded-up tissue and dabbed at her nose. "He's just been so hot and cold and leaving me totally hanging. So when he didn't come to the party, I just got so upset, and then I saw the pack of recipes in the kitchen and I thought if I gave them to him, he'd be so grateful and would want me back."

"So now he has my recipes and he's back with the Pilates chick instead," I said.

She nodded and blew her nose again.

"You also screwed up Clem's friendship with someone else," Sara said. "She accused someone else of taking the recipes."

Actually, that one's on me, I thought but didn't say.

"I'm really sorry, Clementine. Really, really sorry. If I could make it up to you somehow, I would. I feel like such an ass."

Sara rolled her eyes and handed Eva a clean tissue. "We're missing who's gonna get cut from *Top Chef*, so . . ."

Eva eyed me. "I am really sorry, Clem." Then she ran down the stairs.

———

My sister talked a mile a minute about lawsuits and intellectual property to the point that my brain was going to explode. I'd called her after Eva left and filled her in on everything. Elizabeth said I had to do something to legally document how my recipes had ended up at Prime so that a) the asshole couldn't sell them as Skinny Bitch recipes in his possession and b) so I wouldn't get sued for selling my own recipes that he had on his menu.

"Any way you cut it," Elizabeth said, "Eva will have to be deposed. Will she tell the truth?"

"Not sure," I said. "She seems to feel guilty enough. But get her husband in possible deep shit? I don't know."

"Don't worry about it. I'll get on it. Wow, Clem. Recipe theft. I guess this means you've really arrived."

Whoo-hoo.

———

I had the weirdest dreams that night. Eva trying to stab me with a fork. Alexander saying "I thought we were friends." And

Zach throwing hundred-dollar bills at me. I woke up Sunday morning feeling like total crap. But I had to get the hell out of bed. I had a zillion orders to fulfill by seven thirty. Because people—including me—liked to hang in coffee shops with the *Times* and pastries, Sundays were my busiest days.

Which meant I was too busy to think about any of it—Eva backstabbing me, Alexander hating me, Zach being . . . Zach. I got out of bed and took a long, hot shower, flung my hair into a bun, and hit the kitchen, turning on ABBA as loud as I could for five thirty in the morning, which meant I could barely hear "Fernando" and "Dancing Queen."

And then, as always, it happened. The feel of flour, the scent of vanilla, the taste of chocolate on my fingers—it all combined to take me away, make me forget everything. Baking for me was as good as meditating or doing hot yoga. And in a couple of hours I had six dozen cupcakes—cherry almond, chocolate raspberry, and vanilla chai—four dozen tropical fruit scones, and seven dozen cookies. I'd make my deliveries, then come back and test my blackened seitan fajitas; I had a cooking demonstration and tasting for the chef at Surf in the afternoon.

I left Sara a scone and even made her a pot of coffee, then went to make my deliveries. The manager at Runyon's flirted with me, as always, and the grumpy owner of Delia's barely cracked a smile, also as always. I had no idea what she was always so grumpy about, considering she owned an always-packed coffee shop. She hadn't even smiled as she was telling me my gluten-free cookies were the best she ever had.

Deliveries made, I headed in the direction of my space for

Clementine's No Crap Café. I was so close to making it mine. The bank should be calling me in a few days to tell me I got the loan, and then I could rip down the FOR LEASE sign. I couldn't wait to do that. I couldn't wait to stand in front of that storefront and know the place was mine. Open the door with my key instead of pressing my face against the glass and imagining what I'd do if it were mine.

It *would* be mine.

Maybe I'll finally call the Realtor listing the space and make an appointment to tour it, I thought as I approached the door, getting out my phone to key in the Realtor's number.

Except there was a new sign up on my space.

LAST CHANCE FOR BIDS FRIDAY, AUGUST 15TH!

Friday, August 15th, was seven days away. The loan would come through, and I'd make the deadline. I punched in the Realtor's number and told her I was interested in the space.

"Well, the owner of the building has two offers and will be making final decisions on the 15th. What's your intended use of the space?"

"A vegan restaurant. Ten, maybe twelve tables. A few tables out back."

"Well, you'd be up against a bar, a knitting store, and a coffee shop. Once you see the space, if you're sold on it you'll need to make an offer by the 15th."

I was sold on it and made an appointment to see it the next morning.

I already knew it was perfect. All I needed was that loan from Ms. Pritchard to come through.

———————

That night I went to Zach's. All I wanted was a strong drink, some good food that didn't involve me going near an oven, and hours of amazing, mind-blowing, forget-everything sex. But when I saw Zach, I was reminded of what Jolie had said about the French heartbreaker. What Zach had said about not being able to trust anyone. Maybe he was pining away for her.

"You don't look like someone who's the new It Girl," Zach said.

He handed me a glass of white wine and I took a sip. Then I updated him on everything: about the recipes, about Alexander, about Eva, about finding a new space and the deadline. "And something else has been on my mind. What Jolie said . . ."

He glanced away. "Not talking about Jolie. Talking about Jolie gets me into trouble."

"Okay, let's talk about you then. And Vivienne."

"So if the loan doesn't come through," he said, totally ignoring what had just come out of my mouth, "you'll just save up and find another space." He put his arm around me as he sat down next to me on a love seat.

I inched away from him. "Why *wouldn't* it come through?"

"You said you don't have a lot in the bank. And you don't own any property. You're a tough sell."

"That doesn't mean I won't get the loan. All the publicity from the *Times* article, all my new business, all the business I have lined up. I can't lose this new space. If I can't have the one some steakhouse with a huge dead deer sign went into on my corner, I want this new one."

"I want to show you something," he said, taking my hand and leading me out the door, Charlie trailing on his leash behind him. "As a just in case—just in case the loan doesn't come through—I want you to see there are a lot of other spaces that could work. I looked at everything when I was scouting for a location for The Silver Steer."

For the next two hours, as Charlie scampered along happily sniffing at everything, Zach took me on a walking tour of my own city, explaining restaurants and location and space to me in ways I'd never thought of before. I'd been inside restaurants for years, obviously, and deep in the kitchen, starting from nothing on prep and vegetables. But I had no idea how many hoops I'd have to jump through to open my own place. There were so many boring legal issues that he talked so much about that he started to sound like my sister. I'd long forgotten about Vivienne and how he dodged the question. Wasn't my business anyway. Sort of. I'd bring it back up when and if the time was right.

We passed by Prime and I noticed the blackboard that had listed my vegan dishes now noted the specials, all involving dead animals. Either Eva let her husband know he'd better take it down or my sister had gotten her claws in Ackerman.

We ended up in front of The Silver Steer with its gorgeous arched stone entryway and red door. "Bastard," I said, punching him in the arm. "This place is gorgeous. Nothing can top it."

"I thought that about a spot I lost out on," he said. "Then I found this place. You'll make your new place gorgeous, whether it's the one you're vying for or another one."

We kept walking, taking turns with Charlie's leash, Zach telling me how each restaurant we passed was doing. The last two we walked by would last another six weeks tops, but three more were doing amazing business. He talked about word-of-mouth and publicity and great food and, of course, location. He showed me a space on Third Street but it would need a lot of work. And a place near his on the beach that I'd never be able to afford.

We stopped in front of my dream space on Montana. "I was trying to show you that this isn't the only option, but I ended up bumming you out, didn't I?" he asked.

"I've just got this place all set up in my mind, what kind of tables and where they'll go, how the staff will dress."

"You're on your way, Clem," he said, pulling me close.

"Get a room," a familiar voice said and laughed.

I turned around to find Jolie and Rufus walking toward us, holding hands.

"Zach, don't speak," she said. "I apologize for being an ass the last time I saw you. But every time you open your mouth, you say something that pisses me off. So I'm going to talk to Clementine instead. I read the piece on you in the *Times*. How awesome is that?"

I smiled. "Hey, Rufus," I said. If the guy *could* speak, he didn't now. He just nodded at me.

"So, did Zach tell you that Rufus and I are getting married on the beach in September?"

"Can I bring a date?" I asked, linking arms with Zach.

"She's not getting married," Zach said. "She's eighteen. How is Rufus going to say 'I do' when he doesn't even talk? Clearly, he only sings."

"I talk," Rufus said, and we all turned to stare at him. The guy was drop-dead model beautiful and seemingly vacant, but Jolie was no idiot. If she loved the guy, there had to be more to him.

"We're on our way to a dinner party in our honor," Jolie said. "Some people are actually excited for us."

I watched them head down Montana. "Maybe there is more to Rufus than it seems. Jolie's a smart girl."

"No, there's less," Zach said as we headed back toward the beach. "And she's not smart. Smart people don't get married at eighteen. Smart people make their singing fiancés sign prenups so that millions in family trusts are protected. Smart people don't throw their future away on some stupid one-in-a-million dream. You think she'll make it as an actress? Please. She's just another pretty girl in a town full of them."

Way to be supportive. "Zach, it's her mistake to make."

"No, it's all of ours. Everything she does affects me. Cleaning up her mess, handling it with my father—"

"Jesus, Zach, so *don't*. Let her make her mistakes. I'm trying to imagine if my father told me not to go to culinary school, that chefs were a dime a dozen or whatever that cliché is. That I should study teaching or something."

"Clem, how much money do you have in the bank? Five thousand bucks? Yeah, you're the It Girl right now. You'll rake it in for the next six months. But five more vegan chefs will come along on your publicity trail and you'll be just another vegan chef. Someone else will have a better gimmick. And the money will dry up. Then what? This is why you're a tough sell for the loan. Get it?"

I stared at him. "Did you say *gimmick*? Being a vegan chef is a *gimmick*?"

"Clem, don't pick at what I'm saying. I'm not sugarcoating the real world and finance and how things work."

"So you're an expert and everyone else is an idiot."

"Did I say that? I'm just realistic."

"You sound more like someone who doesn't think I'm going to make it."

He sighed. "I'm just saying that—"

"Yeah, I know what you're saying. And here's what I'm saying: Bye."

I turned and walked away fast, my heart beating like crazy. Why did every beautiful night with Zach always seem to end like this?

Chapter 20

I was perfecting my Cha-Cha Chili for an audition at the very popular, very expensive Lola's Bar & Grill when Sara came home.

"God, what's smells so amazing?" She came over and poked her face in the pan. "Mmm, what's that?"

"It's going to be my kick-ass chili," I said, adding a pinch of cayenne pepper. "The beans are cooking after soaking overnight, so I'm working on the onions and spices, sautéing in coconut oil. Wanna cut up some bell peppers for me?"

Sara bit her lip and eyed me, which was Sara speak for "I have something to tell you but I'm scared to."

Shit. Something was up. She'd hooked up with Duncan again? Lost the part of Attractive Friend? No way. Had to be something else.

She grabbed the green and red peppers and a knife—the

right one, I was pleased to see as her teacher—and got to chopping.

"Everything okay?" I asked.

"Yup. You?"

If I talked, she'd talk. "Everything's up in the air. Including Zach. And if I don't get that loan, I'll lose that great spot on Montana near the tattoo place."

She added the diced peppers into the pan, and then I got her on the tomatoes. "What's up with Zach?"

"He morphed into asshole businessman." I stirred the veggies and told her what he'd said about the publicity starting a trail of wannabes, how I'd lose my supposed It Girl status in a month.

"No one wants a wannabe. Everyone wants the real thing. The original. That's you."

"But what Eva said, about restaurants getting the idea to create vegan menus from the *Times* article, that could happen. Is happening. It's not like they have to hire me for that. They can type 'vegan recipes' into Google and—bam—get ten decent ones on the spot."

"Yeah, but you're Clementine Cooper, famed vegan chef." She sniffed the pan. "I want to devour this."

"You will, promise." I wanted to keep her talking, to find out what was wrong, but I also had a zillion cookies to bake. And a birthday cake. And a personal chef client at two o'clock. A married couple who wanted to know more about "this vegan thing."

She bit her lip again. "I have really good news," she said, a huge grin on her face. "I got called back for an audition—and not a commercial."

So why did she look so nervous? "Awesome! For what?"

"A real role. A recurring character. A snarky nurse who makes under-the-breath comments at the nurses' station. It's for a pilot for an hour-long hospital show. They loved me!"

"No one can play snarky better than you. So great, Sara."

"And there's one more thing you might want to know. But I'm scared to tell you what."

That kind of scared me in itself. Sara wasn't scared of anything. "Why?"

"Because . . . it's white, rectangular, and has the return address of your bank on it." She took the envelope out of her bag. "I know how much you want this, Clem." She handed it to me.

Not very weighty. Good sign? Bad sign?

"So you don't think I'm getting the loan either?" I asked.

"Of course, I think you're getting it. But if you don't, it'll suck."

I stared at the envelope. Tried to read through it. Tapped it against the counter.

"Okay, open it," Sara said. "You got the loan. I know it."

I slid open the envelope and pulled out the piece of paper.

"It starts with 'Congratulations, you have been approved!'" Shit, yeah!

"Celebrating all around," Sara said. "Afternoon mimosas." She grabbed the bottle of champagne left over from her party and the OJ.

"Oh," I said, scanning the rest of the letter. Forget about mimosas.

"What?" she asked.

"This says I've been approved for a loan of *fifteen hundred* bucks. What am I supposed to do with fifteen hundred dollars?" I grabbed my cell phone and called the loan officer, Ms. Pritchard.

"Fifteen hundred dollars will cover *paint*," I told Ms. Pritchard. "I need to buy tables and chairs. Equipment. Dishes. Good pans. *Insurance*." I needed ten times the amount she'd given me.

"I'm sorry, Ms. Cooper, but your current net worth simply isn't enough to justify a larger loan. Perhaps six months from now, when your net worth is significantly higher per your business plan, we can revisit."

Shit.

I couldn't get a decent loan, but at least my phone never stopped ringing. While I was elbows-deep in batter and frosting, I received constant orders for Skinny Bitch Bakes. Three more personal chef clients, including a "celeb"—who'd actually introduced herself that way—wanting to learn more about becoming vegan. One speaking gig. Maybe I could make another ten, twenty grand in a week so I'd have enough in my account to make the landlord of the Montana space pick me over the bar or knitting or coffee places.

Right.

I almost let the last call go to voice mail so that I could get the cupcakes in the oven before the batter got all cementy, but I grabbed it at the last minute.

And good thing, too.

It was a producer for *Eat Me,* an obnoxious cooking show on cable, hosted by a gross slob of a "chef" named Joe "Steak" Johannsen. I was being invited to appear on *Eat Me*'s live cook-off Thursday night. Apparently, the chef booked for this week had canceled and left them hanging, and the producer had me on her radar from seeing the *Times* article. Johannsen did special live cook-off episodes to prove that no one made better Man Food than he did. He wanted to prove to America that he, Joe "Steak" Johannsen, could make a better Eggplant Parmesan than "that Skinny Bitch, vegan chef Clementine Coooper."

"He wanted me to be sure to mention that he's not even sure you could *lift* an eggplant," the producer said. "'No meat makes Clementine a wimpy girl,' he said."

"Wait, what?" I asked. What the hell?

"You know Joe 'Steak' Johannsen!" she said, as if I did. "He's raring to go on this challenge. No matter who wins the cook-off, the charity of his choice gets $25,000. You win, you get the $25,000."

Was I interested, she wanted to know.

Fuck, yeah.

For the next ten minutes she gave me the lowdown and said she'd email all kinds of forms I had to print out and sign and send back. The deal was this: I would randomly select ten names from the audience and the producer would select nine names. Those nineteen would vote on which Eggplant Parmesan they thought was better.

If I could make twenty slobs who ate nothing but red meat think my Eggplant Parmesan was better than Johannsen's, the money was mine. All the money I'd need to get Clementine's No Crap Café on its way next week.

Ha. I'd been making Eggplant Parmesan since I was eight. I'd perfected my vegan cheese. No one made better tomato sauce than I did. And I knew how to select the best eggplant for the job. How to infuse it with flavor that would blow Joe's cheese-slathered, overcooked slab away.

"You can bring an assistant to help you," the producer went on. "Only one person, eighteen or older. Oh, and make sure your assistant is kind of mouthy."

"Mouthy?" I repeated.

"Have you ever seen the show?"

"Um, no."

"Watch one today," she said. "You can see full episodes online. Make sure you can handle it. Then call me back no later than 1 p.m."

Handle it? What was to handle? I could take on some gross slob any day.

Mouthy. Sara was mouthy. And she'd been my assistant during the entire cooking class and knew her way around chopping and slicing and watching timers. But she wasn't trained, not like, say, Alexander was. Then again, Alexander wasn't talking to me. And no one would call him mouthy. But I needed a trained chef to assist me. Someone who wouldn't miss a step, a beat, mistake oregano for dried thyme. I needed Alexander. I could teach him how to be "mouthy." I could load him up with all kinds of American expressions that he wouldn't know were snarky.

I grabbed my phone and punched in his number. Come on, answer. I let it ring and ring and ring, which meant he saw it was me and was letting it go to voice mail. For like the tenth time.

"Sara, come watch *Eat Me* with me," I called out. I told her about the call. "The producer wants me to make sure I can handle it."

"Ha."

"I know."

"Okay, making popcorn," she said, then came in a few minutes later with a big bowl and sat down next to me. "And handle what? Carrying all the money out the door at the end?"

Two seconds later, we both understood what the producer had meant. Neither of us had ever actually seen the show; we just knew Johannsen's schtick from his commercials and what we read about him online. He was always trending on Twitter for some very un-PC thing he said or did.

From the moment Joe "Steak" Johannsen appeared on-screen, he was as obnoxious as we'd heard he could be. He made dirty jokes about spaghetti. He made fun of his female challenger's body, which was on the ample side. And not ten minutes into the challenge for Spaghetti Carbonara, Johannsen had reduced the challenger to tears because her pasta maker had gotten jammed. He slapped a hand against his forehead and laughed for a good minute, then shouted, "Damn fool can't even work the pasta maker!"

The audience went wild, jumping to their feet and chanting "Damn fool!" at the poor woman who flung down her sheet of pasta and continued crying.

"Awwww, she's crying!" Johannsen shouted. "Poor baby!"

"Poor baby!" the audience chanted.

The challenger's assistant, a skinny guy in kitchen whites, walked over to Johannsen and decked him.

"Oh!" the audience shouted. "Pow!"

"I've been bitch-slapped by slices of bacon tougher than you," Johannsen shouted, laughing in the guy's face.

The audience went wild, standing up and clapping and cheering. I pointed the remote at the TV and clicked OFF. I'd seen way too much as it was.

"Sara, how'd you like to tell Johannsen to suck it on national TV? I need a mouthy assistant."

"Oh my God," she shouted. "I am so going to be on TV and we are so going to kick this ass's ass!"

I did what I always did when faced with cooking challenges. I drove up to Bluff Valley on Wednesday and made my Eggplant Parmesan—which I'd been working on for the past two days—for my dad. He shook his head at the first attempt. The sauce wasn't right.

The second try got the nod.

Now that I could actually relax, I went outside and walked around the fields, trying to get Zach off my mind. But the fence where I'd carved "Justin Cole sucks" in seventh grade because he'd asked me to some dorky dance and then took another girl at the last second reminded me of how Zach Jeffries sucked, too. And the spot on the big rock that overlooked the bluffs, where my high school boyfriend had said, "Clementine, despite everything, I kind of love you," and I'd said it right back, reminded me of Zach even more.

I used to be able to come up here and forget everything, because being up at the farm reminded me only of my family. But now being here made me think of Zach and that amazing night we'd had at his ranch house. The incredible sex. The way he looked at me. Everything between us.

I was supposed to be mad at him. But all I did was miss him.

Text from me to Zach that night: *Wanna come see me beat Joe Asshole Johannsen in a cook-off on Thursday night?*

Zach: *You know I do.*

Me: *I'll drop off a ticket in your mailbox.*

Zach: *Better yet, knock.*

I did knock.

He opened the door, pulled me inside, and we did very little talking for an hour.

"I've missed you," he said as we lay in his bed facing each other. His hands were in my hair.

"Me, too."

"We're not going to agree with each other on every little thing. I think we know this already."

"Every big thing, either."

"That, too," he said. "But no matter what, I think you're amazing, Clem. Everything about you. And what Jolie said about that ex of mine. It's long over and has nothing to do with why I don't want Jolie to get married. And it has nothing to do with us. What's past is *long* past."

"Stop making me like you," I said. "Sometimes I wish you were a total asshole, not just partial, so I could—"

I shut up fast. There was no way I'd say what was just about to come out of my mouth.

Jesus.

"So you could what?" he asked.

I tried to kiss my way out of it, but he pinned me down, his dark blue eyes intense on mine.

"So you could not fall in love with me?"

"I didn't say that."

He laughed. "Yeah, I know." He stared at me for a second, then trailed a finger down the side of my face. "But you were about to. Don't deny it, Cooper."

"I will deny it," I said, smiling at him.

"Well, know this, then. No matter what comes out of my mouth when we're arguing, I have nothing but respect for you—everything you're doing, trying to do. Everything."

I wasn't going to tell him all I qualified for was a pathetic fifteen hundred bucks business loan. Zach didn't seem like the "*See?*" type, but still. And I didn't need a loan anymore. My Eggplant Parmesan was all the net worth I needed.

"It's the same for me," I said. "I hate when we're fighting. Everything feels off."

"I know. And plus, I need a date for my sister's wedding."

I grinned at him. He might have the asshole businessman in him, but he wasn't a total loss. "She set a date?"

"Labor Day weekend. If you don't hate my guts by then."

Before I could say anything he pulled me on top of him and gave me one of those kisses that made it so hard to hate him for longer than a half hour.

Chapter 21

On Thursday, Sara and I drove to Studio City and finally found *Eat Me*'s soundstage inside a huge building. The set was wild. State-of-the-art double kitchens with maybe ten feet between them, no barrier or partition, so that Johannsen had full view of the challenger to heckle. The kitchen was built on long stainless steel counters that stretched across the length of the stage: six-burner stove top, oven, sink, garbage hole. Behind the counter was another stretch of table with pots and pans, dishes, utensils, and silverware.

The producer had us arrive three hours before the show was set to begin. A guy with a clipboard had met us at the door and had tried to take our bags of ingredients and my cases with my trusty sauté pans. Yeah, *no*. I didn't trust Joe Asshole Johannsen for a second. My ingredients and my pans were not leaving my sight. We carried them in ourselves and put them on the counter in front of us.

The audience seats were empty, which was probably why Joe Johannsen was nowhere to be seen. No audience, no need to appear. The producer talked our ears off for the next fifteen minutes, explaining timing and that I should keep an eye on the big blinking red digital clock on the wall. Sara would be my time watcher and let me know how much time I had left every fifteen minutes. I'd have ten minutes to prep, twenty minutes to cook, five minutes to plate twenty servings, and then the remaining time would be watching the tasters try both versions and record their favorites. The last five minutes of the show would be declaring the winner.

"You've seen the show, so you know what to expect," she said. "If you let the heckling get to you—from Joe and the audience—he'll win. And that's no fun. Give it back to him."

"Oh, we will," Sara said.

Then it was off to hair and makeup. Sara and I sat in huge swivel chairs in front of a wall of mirrors. It took more than an hour for our makeup artists to make us look completely natural.

By the time we got back to the stage, the audience began filing in, a bunch of staffers directing them to their seats and explaining cue cards and instructions. I heard one woman tell the audience to scream and shout whatever they wanted, to have fun with Joe and his challenger, not to hold back. But no cursing was allowed; anyone who cursed would be escorted out.

One guy raised his hand and asked if "damn" was a curse. No, it was not, a producer assured him.

There were about two hundred people in the audience, their attention taken at the moment by staffers. The first row of the audience was only ten feet or so away from the long kitchen counter, which faced the audience. I looked around for Zach and spotted him in the third row. He winked at me, and I shot him a smile. I'd been given ten tickets to give away (but those names were disqualified from being taste testers). Ty and Seamus were a few rows behind Zach, and they gave me a wave. Julia from the coffee lounge, who'd become a friend, my sister—who'd let me know yesterday that Eva was cooperating on the Prime issue—and her fiancé rounded out the rest.

"Ten minutes to showtime," the producer told Sara and me. "Why don't you get in position and begin setting up? You can't actually start prepping, but you can put your ingredients and cookware on the counter."

Johannsen had yet to make an appearance. All the more to rile up the crowd when he did walk on, I figured. Sara and I put all my stuff on the counter. I was ready.

"And five. Four. Three. Two. And live," called the producer.

The clapping and cheering and "Eat me!" chanting started up immediately. While I started slicing the eggplant, Johannsen appeared and called out, "My challenger calls herself Skinny Bitch! And she doesn't eat or wear or use anything that comes from an animal. I think she could rename herself Stupid Bitch!"

The audience hooted and clapped. "Stupid Bitch!" they chanted.

What a moron. I totally ignored him.

Sara focused on measuring out the dry ingredients, then shouted at Johanssen, "I've already renamed you Knuckle Dragger. Totally fits the Neanderthal over there, right?" she said to the audience. They clapped and cheered and wolf whistled. "I got this," she whispered to me. "No problem."

I heard everything from "Go, Clementine!"—at least twice from Ty's booming voice—to "You suck, Johannsen." Which elicited a "Suck this" from my challenger across the stage. I glanced over and he was holding an eggplant up to his crotch.

Classy.

As I sliced and cut the eggplant into square pieces, Sara had my spices in their measuring cups and spoons ready to go as I asked for them. I got on the tomato sauce and Sara kept her eye on the amazing bread I'd baked myself that morning as it toasted in the oven.

"Too many ingredients over there!" Johannsen shouted, jabbing his finger at me. "What do I always say is the key to good cooking, folks?"

A producer held up a giant cue card. "Kiss! Kiss!" the audience chanted back.

"That's right!" he shouted. "K. I. S. S. Keep it simple, stupid!"

The audience cheered.

"Eggplant," he shouted. "Marinara sauce—made from tomatoes and some garlic and salt. Bread crumbs. Good mozzarella cheese. Done! She's got all of Whole Foods over there!"

I rolled my eyes and focused on my cheese sauce.

"Gross—tofu!" Johannsen shouted, sticking his finger down his throat.

"*You're* gross," Sara shouted back.

He laughed. "How gross am I?" he chanted to the audience.

"So gross!" they shouted back.

This was a cooking show? Seriously? I was getting more and more embarrassed to be there at all, but for $25,000 I needed by the 15th? I'd suck it up.

"Let me tell you something, folks," Johannsen said, slapping mozzarella cheese on his slabs of bread crumb–coated, marinara-soaked eggplant. "That crap she's putting on her eggplant? Not cheese!"

"Not cheese!" the audience chanted back.

Someone shouted, "Go, Crunchy Vegan. All the way back to the farm!"

"Crunch this," Sara shouted at the guy, which elicited claps and cheers and boos.

"I like this chick," Johanssen shouted at the audience, jabbing a thumb Sara's way. "Too bad she's gonna lose!"

More clapping. More cheering.

The more this crap went on, the more grateful I was that Alexander hated my guts and wouldn't answer his phone. He would not have survived five minutes up here. Sara perfectly walked the line between focusing on assisting me, watching the time, and shouting back at Johannsen and the audience. Oscar-worthy performance.

"Fifteen minutes," Sara and Johannsen's assistant called at the same time. I carefully laid each square of eggplant in the four sauté pans.

"Aww, how cute!" Johannsen shouted. "She's so dainty with her planty-loo!" He practically threw his slabs of eggplant in his pans, sauce splattering.

"Aww!" the audience shouted.

"Five minutes!" Sara and the other assistant shouted.

We plated the Eggplant Parmesan, which looked and smelled amazing. I glanced over at the mess Johannsen was serving up.

That money was mine.

The nineteen taste testers were seated at a long table onstage, in front of the kitchens. Each had two plates in front of them— the one that was clearly Johannsen's, with its thick oozing mozzarella cheese and pile of sauce, and mine, which looked a thousand times more delicious than Johannsen's.

They cut bites. They chewed. They took more bites.

Finally, Johannsen took the mike. "Okay, taste testers. Whose Eggplant Parmesan did you like better? Mine or the Skinny Bitch's? No matter who wins, $25,000 goes to the American Heart Association. But if Blondie here wins, she also gets twenty-five thousand big ones. So who's it gonna be?"

One by one, he went down the table of taste testers. They shouted out "Johannsen" or "the Skinny Bitch." I had seven votes so far. Johannsen had eight.

"Four more votes!" Johannsen said.

"The Skinny Bitch!" shouted the next taster, flashing me a thumbs-up.

"Johannsen!" said the next guy.

Shit. He had nine votes. I had eight.

Unless the next two voted for me, I'd lose.

"Okay, taste tester number eighteen," Johannsen said. "Who's it gonna be. Me, right?"

"No! The Skinny Bitch," the guy shouted. "Hers is fantastic. And I love cheese!"

Shit, yeah. I was so close. So close. I shut my eyes for a second, willing the next guy to say "Skinny Bitch."

"Taste tester nineteen!" Johannsen boomed. "The vote is tied. Who's it gonna be? Drumroll, please."

Indeed, there was a drumroll.

"Your vote is . . ." Johannsen shouted.

"I vote for . . ." the guy said, drawing it out, per the cue card that said to. "Oh, man, I can't believe it, but the Skinny Bitch's rocks. Sorry, Joe!"

"You won!" Sara screamed. She jumped up and down. "Clem won!"

Johannsen faux stabbed himself in the heart. "And the winner of the Eggplant Parmesan cook-off is . . . shockingly enough, Clementine Cooper!"

The audience leapt to their feet, cheering and chanting, "Skinny Bitch! Skinny Bitch!"

I did it. And I wasn't talking about beating the gross slob, though I did do that. I won the money. Clementine's No Crap Café was *mine*.

Text from Zach later that night: *Can't wait to celebrate your win. I would have liked your Eggplant Parmesan better, too.*

Me: *You hate tofu.*

Him: *But I love YOU.*

I went completely still for a second. But instead of texting something back, or calling him, I just stared at that text for the longest time. So long that the next thing I knew, birds were chirping like crazy and the sun was shining.

I love you, too, I was thinking.

So why couldn't I say it?

Chapter 22

I took another look at the text that had turned me into a zombie and tried to get all therapisty on myself to figure out what exactly I was thinking, feeling, but got nowhere and started on my orders for today. Three hours later, vintage Bee Gees cranking, I was covered in whole wheat pastry flour and unsweetened applesauce and had three dozen vanilla chai cupcakes, three loaves of Irish soda bread, four dozen glazed cinnamon rolls, and a carrot cake with cream cheese frosting, a favorite of Sara's, to celebrate her audition.

When the clock struck nine, I called the real estate agent and made an appointment to fill out an application to rent the space on Montana. I'd never been so excited to deal with stacks of paperwork in my life.

Zach called just as I was ready to head out. "No response," he said.

I wasn't proud of how I'd left him hanging. But if I was going to tell Zach Jeffries I loved him, it sure as shit wouldn't be via text.

It wasn't about to come out of my mouth, either. Not yet, anyway.

"I have a response," I said. "I'm just—"

"Not saying it."

"Yeah."

"Meet me at your place. I have something to show you."

"And I have something to tell you. Guess who just put in an application to rent that little place on Montana for Clementine's No Crap Café?"

Dead silence. "That's a little far up, though, isn't it?"

At least he was consistent. "Yeah, for your crowd, maybe, Zach. People who have to use Laundromats and take mass transit pass it every day."

"Meet me in front of The Silver Steer at five o'clock."

"Why?"

"Told you. It's a surprise."

I hated surprises.

———

My hand was happily numb from filling out that enormous application. But when I handed it over, I felt like I did when I won that sparkly blue ribbon at eleven. When I graduated from the Vegan Culinary Institute. When I got my first job. My first promotion. When I beat that slob Johannsen.

My own place. It was so close to happening. The real estate agent swore me to secrecy but said I had a ninety-nine percent chance of winning out over the other three applicants: a bar—too noisy too late; a coffee bar—which would compete with the landlord's cousin's place up the street; and a knitting shop, which he was afraid would go out of business and leave him hanging to go through this whole process again. She couldn't promise anything and said fourteen times I shouldn't pin my hopes on it because you never knew.

No kidding.

Still, it was so close I could taste the Cha-Cha Chili. My Double-Dip Fondue. The Spicy Sushi Rolls.

I could see Zach's Mercedes parked in front of The Silver Steer halfway up the block. He was leaning on the other side of it. At just the sight of him, it hit me: *I fucking love you, too.*

It was there, loud as Jesse's tuba concert, clanging away, but it felt stuffed down, like it was smushed inside the tuba and stuck there.

The Silver Steer. Somehow, the place didn't stab me in the gut like it did every time I looked out the window or passed it on the street. The space was still drop-dead gorgeous with its perfect corner location and the stone archway and red door. The apartment building next to it, which I looked out at all day long while I cooked and baked, was the same as usual. From here, I could even see the woman who sometimes walked around naked in her bedroom on the second floor, though she was dressed now and watering her plants. The elderly couple who sat at their round kitchen table by the window every morning having coffee were sitting there having dinner. The fattest cat I'd ever seen was at the usual second-floor window, staring out. But now that I almost had my own little place, Zach's restaurant didn't make me want to scream. I glanced up at the sign, expecting to barely be bothered.

But the sign was gone.

And underneath where it used to be stood Zach, watching me.

"The deed deer head is gone," I said. "You took down the sign because it makes me sick?" He really *did* love me.

"Actually, that's not why I took it down. The city wouldn't let me enlarge the kitchen out the back, so I can't make this space work for The Silver Steer. It's just too small. But I own the building as an investment and this space is mine to do with what I want. And I want to lease it to you."

I stared at him. "What?"

"Clementine's No Crap Café will open right here." He handed me a sheaf of papers. "Your lease."

In some kind of daze, I scanned the document. My name. The space, leased to me for one year. A monthly amount I could now handle—for about four months, tops, anyway. It had to be a big loss to him. And he was clearly planning on financing me once my money ran out.

"And this, too," he said, handing me a check.

It was blank, signed by him. In the memo space, it said: *reasonable*.

"For renovations and equipment, whatever you need. The

twenty-five thousand you won from *Eat Me* is nice, but won't get you very far."

I just stood there, kind of stunned. I stared at the lease, at the check, at the curved stone entranceway that I loved so much.

"Interesting," he said. "Not exactly the response I expected. Twice now."

"Zach, this is incredible of you. But I can't accept this." I held out the lease.

He mock rolled his eyes and wouldn't take it. "Yes, you can."

"It's seriously generous of you, Zach. Too generous. But this isn't how I do things. I don't have things bought for me. I thought I made that clear."

"Crystal," he said. "But I'm trying to show you that I *do* believe in you."

I took his hand and held on to it. "And I appreciate that. But I'll make it on my own. I don't need the Jeffries' millions to fairy godmother me my restaurant. I want this space. Yes. But *I* can't afford it. I can afford the space I put an application in for."

He stared at me. "Clem, I know you're stubborn. I *know* it. But you're doing it again. Cutting off your nose to spite your face. That other place is a starter joint. *This* is a restaurant."

"I love that 'starter joint.' If I get to this place one day, Zach, it'll be because I earned it myself."

"Maybe you're just scared to get what you really want," he said, crossing his arms over his chest. "In fact, I'd say that's exactly what's holding you back from a *couple* of things."

"I'm not scared of anything."

"You're scared shitless of me. And you're scared shitless of your dream coming true. I know this because I'm handing you both and you're saying no."

I was making my dream come true. Why didn't he get that?

"Well then, you don't know me as well as you think you do," I said and felt something squeeze in the center of my chest.

"Maybe I don't," he said and walked away.

"What's the point in having a zillionaire boyfriend if you can't capitalize on the big bucks?" Ty asked the next morning as he walked me part of the way to my personal chef client, a mom who was paying me double for an emergency rush session on how to make kid-friendly meals for her five-year-old, newly diagnosed with a dairy allergy.

"So I should just let him be my sugar daddy? That's gross."

"I'm kidding. Of course, you shouldn't. But cut the guy a break. Like I said, he's a zillionaire. They throw money around. And I talked to him myself for a while after the Johannsen show. He seems totally sincere to me. Not what I expected at all, actually. And damn, he's good-looking."

"I know what you mean. On all counts. But still, Ty. Come on. How are we going to have a relationship?"

He kissed the top of my head. "You'll figure it out."

We got to the corner of Third, so Ty went left to Chill, and I went right and then down near the beach to a gorgeous condo with a doorman.

The client, a woman named Tara who looked kind of *Real Housewife*-ish with a ton of makeup and gobs of long, highlighted hair and a cool shirt I wanted, air-kissed me, then led me upstairs to the main floor of the duplex. A baby grand piano had its own room.

Tara introduced me to five-year-old Caroline who grabbed my hand and yanked me to see her bedroom, Princess Central. I'd never seen so much pink and taffeta. Or wanted to.

Once we were in the kitchen, Tara told me all about Caroline's digestive issues in great detail, which almost made me barf all over Tara's marble counters.

"No ring?" she asked me, eyeing my left hand. "Surprised. You're very attractive. And thin. My husband is a plastic surgeon if you want some advice on your eyes or a boob job."

Please. "My eyes? I'm twenty-six."

"I'm twenty-seven and got my eyes done for the first time at twenty-five. If you do little things gradually, no one will realize you've had work done at all. That's the secret. I just gave you my husband's twenty-five-hundred-dollar consultation for free."

She was twenty-seven? Whoa. She looked ten years older. "Are you an actress?" I asked, figuring she was in the business if she'd shot her face full of crap already.

"I could have been, but then Caroline came along and honestly, being married to one of the premier plastic surgeons in L.A. is a job itself."

I liked money but did not want to be this woman. Not that I *would* be this woman even if I did let Zach hand me gifts like major real estate on prime Santa Monica corner locations. But the more she talked, the more I knew I couldn't, wouldn't take Zach's offer. First of all, it wasn't even an offer; he'd just done it, Zach style—created a lease and filled in the details. Wrote me a check. It wasn't my style. Never would be.

For an hour and a half, I showed Tara how to make all Caroline's cheese-focused favorites, from mac and cheese to grilled cheese to pizza, using my favorite vegan cheeses that she could find in most grocery stores. When I left, I was seven hundred and fifty dollars richer for my time. Not bad.

I was back on the street, about to call Sara to see if she wanted to meet for a drink or go to a movie, when I heard someone call out, "Clem! Clementine!"

I stopped and glanced around. Across the street, Jolie Jeffries was waving at me and trying to cross in the middle of the street without getting killed.

"Hey," she said. "I have to show you my dress! I just bought it two seconds ago. Right around the corner. Pleeeease! I'm dying to show someone and you're right here. Pleeease."

I smiled at her. "Lead the way."

She led the way to a shop I never even noticed before. How, I had no idea, since it was huge. Weddings by Araminta. I'd heard of Araminta—she was always on TV, making some celeb or royal's gown, and she had a shop in New York City, too.

Inside was very lush and pale and satiny. Jolie spoke to the receptionist who disappeared and returned with a dress that was in a plastic bag with huge tags on it and all kinds of writing. She hung it on a high hook, and Jolie lifted the plastic.

"Isn't it gorgeous?" she asked, staring at it all moony-eyed.

"It really is," I said. And it was. I wasn't into wedding dresses, but this one was more like vintage meets 1940s movie star. "It'll look amazing on you."

I couldn't help but notice the price tag. A small fortune.

"Zach has really gotten your father to accept your plans, I see," I said.

"My father told me I'm an idiot to get married so young and will regret it and that he's not paying one penny to see me ruin my life."

"So you're spending a few months' rent on a wedding dress?"

"Zach's taking care of it," she said. "The whole wedding, even though he also thinks it's a huge mistake. It'll be just family and good friends, on the beach, dinner out somewhere amazing afterward. Nothing big. But Zach's paying for everything—the dress, photographer, dinner, even Rufus's tux."

Huh. It had to kill him to pay for the wedding he didn't want to happen. "Well, he may have his opinion, but I guess he really wants you to be happy."

"He might think it's dumb for me to get married at eighteen, but he *knows* me. I've had two boyfriends in my life. The first I dated from age twelve to fourteen. The other from fifteen to now. Rufus is it for me and I think Zach knows that. He believes it, even if he says it's a mistake."

"I get that. He's a realist and an idealist at the same time." Maybe the best kind of balance there was.

And maybe I knew Zach better than I thought I did.

Jolie nodded. "Luckily for me, financing happiness is his thing. He loves money but he gives away a ton of it. He has all kinds of scholarships set up for inner-city high school students and families living in shelters, stuff like that. My dad hates how generous Zach is."

I laughed. "He is pretty generous."

"Yeah, so much so that I finally told him that, *of course,* Rufus will sign a prenup. I love the guy, but I'm not an idiot— no matter what my family thinks of my getting married at eighteen. I just wanted to make Zach sweat a little."

I know exactly what you mean.

She glanced at her watch. "I'd better go. Rufus's parents are flying in to try to talk us out of the wedding. If my father couldn't hack it, no one can."

"Ha. Have fun."

She stuck out her tongue and rolled her eyes, then stared at her beautiful dress before the clerk covered it back up and took it away.

"Tell Zach I said thank you again," she said as we headed outside. "He really is a great guy," she added before rushing off.

What he mostly was: *complicated.*

Now what?

Chapter 23

On Saturday morning I made my crack-of-dawn deliveries for Skinny Bitch Bakes, then did sunrise yoga and went for a long walk on the beach. I recognized the yellow Lab coming toward me before I realized Ben Frasier was two feet away from me.

"Hey, Clem," he said, throwing a ball for the dog to chase. "Never thought I'd see you out and about before noon."

He was the same gorgeous Ben, tall and tanned with all that sun-streaked dirty blond hair. But something was different: me. There wasn't a clench. Or a pang. Not a single memory flitted through my mind. I was standing inches away from the guy I'd thought was un-toppable, and I didn't feel a thing.

"A *lot* has changed," I said, amazed at how true it was. The Lab came bounding up, ball in mouth, and I couldn't even remember his name. I gave the dog a rub on the chin and noticed his tags. Gus—that's right. I smiled and told Ben Frasier I had to go, to have a great day, as though he were any old someone I used to know.

Damn, that felt good.

On the way back, I thought I saw Alexander walking his dogs up ahead, but when I got closer I saw it was a much older guy with one little and one big dog, just like Brit and Lizzie. I'd given up on trying to make Alexander stop hating me. But when I got home and checked my email, the usual twenty-plus for all things Skinny Bitch, one request jumped out at me as a way to do a final *something*, a "gesture," as Alexander would call it, and then let it go once and for all.

I had an email from the principal of Taft Middle School. He'd read the article about me in the *Times* and was inviting me to hold a special assembly for the students and teachers on whole foods and making good choices about healthful eating. The PTA would pay me an honorarium, not that I'd take it. I'd pull a Zach Jeffries and tell the school to keep it, replace a dinged-up trumpet or something.

Taft Middle School was where Jesse, the kid Alexander mentored, went. Where Alexander spent most of his time at events and classroom celebrations and bad concerts. I'd gotten a lot of these types of invitations when the *Times* article came out, and I'd declined each one, since there was no way I could give up so much time during the day anymore. But this felt like somehow doing Alexander a favor, even if he wouldn't know about it.

I'd do it and move on.

Text from Zach: *Whatever's going on or not going on between us, the lease and check stand. You don't even know if you're going to get that other space. If you want to wait and then decide, fine. Z*

I texted back: *My answer is still no, whether I get it or not. Not sure what that means for us. C*

It was Your World Day with my sister for our monthly lunch, which meant I was sitting in the small, beige cafeteria at her law firm on Tuesday afternoon, eating lukewarm grapes and bruised melon. She showed me the sworn statements from Eva's husband, stating that Prime would not use or capitalize on the stolen recipes in any manner and that I was to be financially compensated for all orders of my dishes on the two nights my stuff had been on the menu. That was thanks to Eva's help and documented proof—apparently she often recorded her phone conversations with her husband so she could throw his words back in his face any time she needed to.

"That woman cries a lot," Elizabeth said, taking off her suit jacket, which was beige like the walls. "She had mascara streaks down her face every time she came here."

"I don't know if she feels guilty about stabbing me in the back or if she's just upset about her marriage. I couldn't really get a handle on her. I hate that."

"I know. She reminds me of Carrie Winn from high school—remember her? Best friend one day, user the next. I had to completely cut her off. Some people are just toxic, even if a quarter of the time they mean well."

"Who knows what freaks I'll have in my next class. I've already gotten ten emails from people who want in if I run another class." At first Sara told me there was no way she'd take the class again, even though she was continuing on with the Skinny Bitch diet. But then she said she might sign on as my assistant if there was a cute guy or two, even if the last cute guy she'd met in my cooking class turned out to be an ass.

Elizabeth grabbed one of my grapes. "I know you hate when I get all proud of you, but suck it up, Clem. I'm proud of you. You got fired and look what you did—started your own business. First as a personal chef, then adding cooking classes, then Skinny Bitch Bakes, then creating vegan menus for my favorite restaurants. You're so in demand you've got top restaurants stealing from you. And you beat that creep Johannsen."

Once again, I had to face facts that my uptight lawyer sister, in her beige suit and boring shoes, absolutely rocked. "And Friday I find out if I'm opening my restaurant on Montana."

"I'll be your first customer," she said.

I was trying to remember not to let out any fucks or shits or even damns during my presentation at Taft Middle School on

Wednesday when I saw Alexander walk into the cafeteria and lean against the back wall.

Shit, yeah!

I almost said that aloud.

He nodded at me, then sat down. A good sign.

At first I thought I'd run out of stuff to say to the tough crowd of bored-looking tweens, but they were all staring at me as though they were actually interested, not shooting spitballs or pulling bra straps. I talked about growing up on a farm, how we made dinner with what we'd harvested, and how most of the foods kids loved to stuff their faces with came right out of the ground or off trees, how they were all about whole foods, and didn't have to come from boxes or a freezer.

"Not pizza," a boy called out.

"Actually, yes, pizza," I said, explaining where wheat for the dough came from. Where tomatoes for the sauce came from. Where cheese—whether dairy or soy—came from. Where all the good toppings came from.

During the rest of the Q&A, the tweens stood up and asked lots of good questions, like whether it was true if you could drop dead if you didn't wash an apple before eating it. I kept my rant on pesticides and other shitty chemicals to under thirty seconds. But I could have gone on forever.

Then it was time to make the huge vats of chili that would be served for lunch that day.

"I'm Chef Cooper's assistant for the morning," Alexander said, standing up and walking over to the table. He smiled at me and put on an apron. "Jesse showed me the flyer that went home to parents about your presentation and special lunch," he whispered. "Pretty cool, Clem. Even if it's more for me than them," he added, nodding at the crowd.

I shot him a smile.

"Who can tell me what this is?" he asked the audience, holding up a head of garlic.

The day got much better from there. Even more so when he told me that Rain was now dating the executive chef at White Blossom, where she'd managed to get hired as sous chef.

"Yeah, I wonder how she got that job," I said. "She won't last long."

"No doubt. Why didn't you tell me she was a lying bitch?" he asked, that dimple of his flashing at me. "She told me she did slip the butter in your ravioli the night O. Ellery Rice was there. I couldn't believe that I was not only shagging a woman who'd actually do that to a fellow chef, but someone who was *bragging* to me about it. I told her it was over between us, and she threw a fit and announced she was going to dump me for her boss anyway. I wouldn't be surprised if I find chicken bones in the French onion soup I'm making for Paris bistro week."

Awesome.

When I got home, all I wanted to do was take a long, hot shower and wash the smell of cafeteria off me, but Eva was waiting for me in front of my building, sucking on the straw of her Starbucks iced coffee and holding a manila envelope. I almost didn't recognize her because her hair was dark brown instead of the usual red.

"My natural color," she said, playing with the pointy ends. "It was Derek who thought I should go red, but I never liked it."

I didn't care anymore about Eva's hair or what her asshole husband liked or didn't like. And if she said one more word about him, I was leaving. I'd give her two seconds to get on with it.

She eyed me and chewed her lip for a second, then thrust out the manila envelope. "I was going to leave this in your mailbox, but I decided to give it to you in person."

"What is it?"

"You'll see."

I flipped open the little silver tab. Inside were two copies of my recipes and the original hand-scrawled set bound inside a black-and-white fabric book.

"I know there's nothing I can say, Clementine. I know sorry won't cut it. But I am sorry. I was desperate and acted like a king shit. I'm not even going to ask you to forgive me because I wouldn't forgive someone who pulled something like that on me. I just want you to know that I really am sorry."

"Well, at least you tried to make things right," I said. "If it wasn't for your proof, my sister probably wouldn't have been able to force Prime's hand."

She gave me something of a smile. "Least I could do and all that jazz. So, um, I'm sure you probably don't give a rat's ass, but I wanted you to know I'm really done with him. Moving on for good."

"Actually, I'm glad to hear it."

She bit her lip again, told me she was sorry again, and then started to get teary and hurried away.

———————

When I unlocked the door to the apartment, Sara jumped off the couch and said, "*Finally*."

"Finally, what?"

She looked kind of nervous. "Finally, you're home. I have interesting news. Very interesting news." She gave me a quick glance, then went into the kitchen and poured herself a glass of the iced tea I'd made this morning. She poured me a glass, too.

This didn't sound good. "Are you gonna tell me or what?"

"Guess who got offered the permanent role of snarky assistant on a cooking show?" she asked, barely able to contain her huge grin.

"A cooking show? Like an assistant to the chef? That's amazing. So they saw you on *Eat Me* and saw how great you are?"

"Yup. And the job is mine. No audition. No callback. Mine."

I squeezed her into a hug. "What's the show?"

She took a sip of her drink. "Um, this is the interesting part.

It's as Joe Asshole Johanssen's assistant on *Eat Me*'s weekly live cook-offs."

I was so surprised I almost spit my mouthful of iced tea all over her. "You're kidding."

"Not even a little bit! Get this, Clem—I'm supposed to be snarky only to *him,* not the challengers—that's his job. I'm supposed to tell him to suck it, shove it, whatever I want, and actually boost up the challengers when he tries to knock them down. In fact, the snarkier I am to him, the better."

That was kind of hilarious, actually. "That's awesome, Sara."

"You don't think I should tell him to shove it?" she asked. "As in, the job?"

"Do you want the job?"

The grin was back. "More than anything. Who knows what this will lead to! Does that make me a bigger asshole than he is?"

"Not in the slightest," I assured her. "Just promise me you'll give it to him good."

"Oh, I will," she said, clinking her glass of iced tea with mine. "So weird how life works. The craziest stuff can come from where you least expect it, you know?"

Oh, yeah, I knew.

I stood in front of the window in my bedroom, staring out at the space formerly known as The Silver Steer. Sara and I had gone out to celebrate her new gig, and now it was after one in the morning, the moonlight and streetlamps lighting up the arched stone entryway and the red door as they always did, making it too easy to stand here and imagine the place as mine like I'd been doing all these years. But I couldn't even envision my sign—Clementine's No Crap Café etched into copper—on that space anymore.

Maybe you're just scared to get what you want, I heard Zach say. *In fact, I'd say that's exactly what's holding you back from a couple of things.*

I'm not scared of anything.

You're scared shitless of me. And you're scared shitless of your dream coming true. I know this because I'm handing you both and you're saying no.

I remembered how something squeezed inside my chest when he said that.

Like the truth. Half of it, anyway.

I *was* scared of him. In the best way. But if he wanted me, he'd have to take me as I was.

───────────

On Friday afternoon, I did what I always did when I was freaking out. I cooked. My cell phone was next to the package of vegan cream cheese on my kitchen counter. It had rung at least twenty times in the past hour. But it was never the real estate agent.

If she didn't call me soon I'd go out of my mind.

I was whisking vegan cheddar, jack, Parmesan, and the cream cheese into squash and soy milk for my amazing Macaroni and Four Cheeses when the phone rang.

I grabbed it. "Clementine Cooper speaking."

It *was* the real estate agent. I held my breath.

This is it. Say yes.

"Clementine Cooper, I fully expect dessert on the house when I stop by your new restaurant on Montana Avenue."

I screamed. I barely know what I said back. Promised her free food for the rest of her life, I was pretty sure.

Clementine's No Crap Café. Reality.

———————

Text to Zach: *Talk Friday tonight?*

Zach: *Come by at seven.*

———————

When Zach opened the door to his house, I handed him his lease. Charlie stared up at me and then waddled over to his dog bed.

"I got the space on Montana. Clementine's No Crap Café is a go. My way."

"You want to know what I think about all this?"

"Yeah, I do."

He took my hand. "That you're not the least bit interested in my money."

"I could give a shit about your money," I said. "Actually, I like you less for it."

He laughed. "You can take me out to dinner then. To celebrate."

"I'd rather make you dinner. Here."

He pulled me close to him and kissed me.

"Oh, and by the way, Zach? I love you, too."

Shit, yeah, I said it.

Epilogue

O. ELLERY RICE

Los Angeles Times **Restaurant Critic**

It takes a confident chef to put the word "crap" in the name of her restaurant, and let me tell you, twenty-six-year-old Clementine Cooper, owner and executive chef of Clementine's No Crap Café, has good reason for that confidence. Her terrific new vegan restaurant opened last night on Montana Avenue in Santa Monica with a line wrapped around the block.

From the moment you step inside the gleaming ten-table eatery with its Cali-meets-Moroccan décor, you feel instantly healthier. Raised on an organic farm in northern California, Clementine believes in offering delicious food in its natural form, and with a range of cuisines, this fabulous eatery has something for everyone.

From her famed Butternut Squash Ravioli in Garlic and Sage Sauce to melt-on-the-tongue Curried Chickpea Cakes, Clementine's entrees are healthy and incredibly satisfying. Offerings include Spicy Vegetable Curry, Asian Macaroni and Cheese, Crepes with Raspberry Sauce, Caramelized Eggplant with Red Miso, Lentil Tacos, and some fantastic soups and salads, from the incredible Red Potato Black Olive Salad, to the blissful Kale and White Bean Soup.

A former sous chef at Fresh and several top vegan restaurants, Clementine Cooper has brought to Santa Monica a vegan restaurant so good that it's easy to see why the competition has always run scared from her. Famous for her Skinny Bitch empire, Clementine sat down with me over dessert—a slice of her incredible German Chocolate Cake—and explained that being a Skinny Bitch has always meant cutting the crap out of your life. Clementine's No Crap Café will give you a great way to do just that.

Acknowledgments

Laura Dail, a million thanks for so many things. To Karen Kosztolnyik, I am grateful for your enthusiasm and your belief in me. Heather Hunt, you handle so many details that make everything run so smoothly, and I truly appreciate it. To Louise Burke, Jennifer Bergstrom, Liz Psaltis, Natalie Ebel, Ellen Chan, and Stephanie De Luca at Gallery Books, thank you so much for your help in getting this book made, I am forever grateful. Melissa Senate, you are truly magical. Thank you does not suffice, but still, thank you!

A special shout out to San Diego's La Jolla Beach and Tennis Club; it was there that I got the inspiration to do this novel.

To Keesha Whitehurst Fredricksen and Joylene Loucks, I am the luckiest girl in the world for getting the most amazing BFFs.

And finally, thanks to Stephane and Jack for loving and supporting me, no matter what I decide to do.